EVELYN MONTGOMERY

Indecision

Evelyn Montgomery

First published by Evelyn Montgomery 2018

Copyright © 2018 by Evelyn Montgomery

All rights reserved. No part of this publication may be reproduced, stored or transmitted in any form or by any means, electronic, mechanical, photocopying, recording, scanning, or otherwise without written permission from the publisher. It is illegal to copy this book, post it to a website, or distribute it by any other means without permission.

This novel is entirely a work of fiction. The names, characters and incidents portrayed in it are the work of the author's imagination. Any resemblance to actual persons, living or dead, events or localities is entirely coincidental.

Evelyn Montgomery asserts the moral right to be identified as the author of this work.

Evelyn Montgomery has no responsibility for the persistence or accuracy of URLs for external or third-party Internet Websites referred to in this publication and does not guarantee that any content on such Websites is, or will remain, accurate or appropriate.

Designations used by companies to distinguish their products are often claimed as trademarks. All brand names and product names used in this book and on its cover are trade names, service marks, trademarks and registered trademarks of their respective owners. The publishers and the book are not associated with any product or vendor mentioned in this book. None of the companies referenced within the book have endorsed the book.

Second edition

ISBN: 9780692153468

*This book was professionally typeset on Reedsy.
Find out more at reedsy.com*

To all the girls in the world with a pen and a piece of paper dreaming and wondering "what if."
You can!
I believe in you!

Contents

Prologue	1
Chapter 1	5
Chapter 2	16
Chapter 3	24
Chapter 4	29
Chapter 5	36
Chapter 6	45
Chapter 7	53
Chapter 8	65
Chapter 9	78
Chapter 10	85
Chapter 11	96
Chapter 12	103
Chapter 13	112
Chapter 14	119
Chapter 15	133
Chapter 16	137
Chapter 17	145
Chapter 18	150
Chapter 19	162
Chapter 20	168
Chapter 21	175
Chapter 22	183
Chapter 23	187

Chapter 24	194
Chapter 25	201
Chapter 26	209
Chapter 27	217
Chapter 28	227
Chapter 29	233
Devotion	245
Keep in touch	253
Want More?	254
Like what you read?	261

Prologue

Evelyn

May

As my feet hit the concrete outside, I immediately slip and fall flat on my butt. Damn high heels and pencil skirt. Feet flying, arms flailing, my fall is nothing close to graceful. It's inevitable that the bruise will appear on my backside instantly. I look down at my feet and rotate my right ankle, making sure it still moves.

Grimacing slightly, I look up at the sky. My mind instantly clouds with what just happened and what seems to be happening now. Rain? How did I miss that? It never rains in California; they've actually made songs about it.

And Noah? He can kiss my ass—which is now soaking wet and turning a lovely shade of black and blue. Damn rain ... Damn men.

This is absolutely the last thing I need. What I need is to somehow get to my car and drive. Drive away from here as fast as I can and try to forget everything, including Noah and the terrible mistake he turned out to be. I knew the minute that tempting distraction walked into my life he'd be all kinds of wrong. I should have listened to myself.

He turned out to be a terrible mistake and the one man, I know without a doubt no matter how hard I try, I won't ever get over. As the realization hits me, my tears begin to fall and so does more rain.

Picking my clumsy self up off the sidewalk, I laugh at how stupid I must look. Looking from side to side, I run across the parking, cringing at the idea of anyone seeing my fall, especially Noah. Why the hell did I park so far away when I got here?

This is not what I need right now. What I need right now is a drink. A stiff drink. A very stiff drink followed by several more until my brain goes numb and prevents me from feeling anything.

I also need Gwen, my best friend and sister through everything. She is without a doubt the voice I need and want to hear. She's known for giving me a swift kick in the ass to get my head and heart straight, and she sure as hell always delivers! Getting in my car, I peel out of the parking lot of Gatsby's, hydroplaning and skidding everywhere.

"Damn rain," I say, cursing the sky.

I run over the curb but keep on going, my reckless driving not even registering with my mind.

How could he do that to me? How could he talk to me that way!?

Who does he think he is? I know exactly who he is, and it's nothing like what I originally thought ... if that makes any sense whatsoever.

Somehow, I find myself laughing through my tears, which then causes me to cry even harder. Even when that prick breaks my heart, he still finds a way to make me smile. That is positively not fair. The realization that this relationship is sure as hell over has my whole body feeling poisoned, straight to my stupid heart, for ever having trusted and allowing myself to let him in. God, Evelyn, you really are a stupid woman!

Deciding I need music to drown out the pain, I turn on the radio. Dierks Bentley's "It's Different for Girls" immediately filters through the speakers. Go Figure. I don't even try to stop the tears that turn into sobs and eventually turn into convulsions as the rain falls harder and the stupid radio plays a song that mirrors my sad, pathetic, now-broken heart and life. Turning the volume up, I let myself go, hitting the steering wheel as I belt out every last word, half in tune and half full of screaming anger.

Fan-fricking-tastic! I'm a hot mess.

I have no clue where I'm headed, but damn if I really even care. If I would have just stuck to my original plan in life and not fallen for Mr. Too Damn Good to be True, this would never have happened. The inevitable thought that I could have avoided this makes me feel even more pathetic. Damn it! I thought I was so much smarter than this.

Between the pouring rain and my pathetic tears, I'm not paying attention to the road and veer to the left. I quickly jerk my car back into my lane just in time to avoid a head-on collision. Even though it should, it doesn't even faze me.

Noah made me believe he was the right choice when I had spent my whole life planning for something more. We had actually started to build a life together … up until that jerk decided to pull a Doctor Jekyll and Mr. Hyde routine and completely destroyed my life, my world, and my heart. Stupid heart! How can love go so sour so fast? How can feelings so sweet flip you inside out in an instant?

The rain outside begins to pick up, and the sky turns darker in an instant. I turn my windshield wipers on full force, barely able to make out the road in front of me. My phone rings in my purse, and I know I shouldn't answer, but if it's that asshole that just ripped my world apart, I know exactly what I want to say to him. I want to make him hurt! Somewhere, anywhere close to how bad I hurt. I feel around on the passenger seat for my purse. Reaching inside, I try keeping one eye on the road. The damn thing is lost and still ringing, only making my irritation skyrocket.

I pass a construction worker holding a "slow" sign and subconsciously speed up. Like a girl can really slow down when she is running away from her heart and her mind. Knowing I can't escape either one, I begin to cry in a loud, pathetic sort of way I didn't even know I was capable of, all the while subconsciously pressing my foot down onto the pedal harder. I look to the sky and silently beg the one above for some sort of answer.

The phone's still ringing, and in a moment of desperation, I figure to hell with it. I grab my purse yanking it unto my lap. Alternating between looking up at the road then at the purse in my lap, I finally pull the phone out from its hiding place. Glancing at the screen, I notice its Gwen. A smile slowly creeps across my face as a few more tears roll down my cheek. Hitting accept, I turn my attention back to the road in front of me.

I don't blink. I don't breathe. My eyes widen as I hear my best friends voice coming through the phone. My foot hits the break, my ears hear the crash, and then there is darkness ...

Chapter 1

Evelyn

November
6 months earlier

Standing at the end of the pier, I take a moment and get lost looking down into the ocean's ever changing waters. Watching as they change from dark blue to green is hypnotizing, putting me at ease and calming every thought in my mind. I love how with every wave that crashes into the pillars, the ocean churns and gives way to light blue and then white. Releasing a sigh, I breathe in slowly and tell myself what I always say, standing at the edge of this pier: This is where I belong!

I continue to watch the seaweed swaying beneath the ocean's glistening glow. When the crisp breeze picks up enough, I can feel the mist from the waves dampen my skin. Orange County is home, even if my mailing address tells the world differently.

Overhead, I hear the seagulls out in full force. The birds call to one another as they fly out across the water to places unknown, their secret hideout safe from the people below them. Glancing around, I am suddenly aware that the pier is more crowded than normal; everyone has decided to gather tonight to watch the sunset. Tourists with cameras in hand gawk and point at the amazing sight. Locals might take the sunset for granted as the hurry around in their busy lives, but it still steals their breath when they slow down long enough to look at paradise around them.

I wouldn't label myself a tourist, more like a relocated local. I make sure everyone knows I was forced to leave what I view as Utopia, the end of the rainbow if you will, as a preteen. When my father got a job transfer he couldn't pass up. My parents moved me and my older brother to northern California to start a new life. It's something I vow to never let them live down.

I love it here in my hometown. The ocean is in my veins: the rise and fall of the waves, the salty mist that engulfs your body, the way the noise from the birds and people mix together in complete harmony. These things make up who I am and all I could ever want to be. When I am here, I can breathe, the deep soul-confirming, this is where I belong, type of breathing. Something I never feel up north.

I watch the last of the sun slip beneath the glistening horizon and gather my thoughts the best I can. With light disappointment, I reluctantly turn to leave the pier. It's later than I expected, and I had told Gwen I would meet her at Longboards, a local pub on the main drag, just a few minutes' walk from the pier.

Gwen and I have known each other since I moved north. The two of us bonded immediately, and there is nothing we don't share. We've absolutely been through it all: first loves and first heartbreaks, the experiential stages of high school and early college, Gwen's parents' endless fights and threats of divorce, even family tragedies like when death stole Gwen's younger sister in a sudden car crash a few years back. We haven't known each other our whole lives, but the bond between us is unmatchable. She's my best friend, my sister. The one person I know I can always trust and always rely on, without a doubt.

We both applied to the same college straight out of high school: Long Beach State. We had dreams of the beach life. We even looked for apartments and picked out a few contenders, positive we'd ride off towards SoCal and the new life we couldn't wait to start together. We were sure that the best was yet to come, and we were confident we'd conquer it all together. Gwen was accepted, while I got a rejection letter. We looked the same on paper, and there was no explanation. It was just one of those things. The rejection was not nearly as bad as the fact that Gwen got to live out my dream of moving south while I was forced to stay in the mud and dirt of northern California.

Still, it gave me added reasons to visit and move if I could ever afford it. Trying to survive in northern California was hard enough, the amount of money you needed to sustain a life in SoCal was insane. I had my savings and recently started taking steps to hopefully make a move possible. I took a gamble and applied for a position at the L.A. Times, and even though they responded saying they had found another candidate, I vowed to myself I would never give up on my dream.

My degree in journalism is the one thing in life of which I'm the most proud. The one thing I drown myself in when everything else around me won't stop spinning. The one thing I won't allow myself to give up on—nothing and no one can make me lose sight of what I've dreamed about since I was a little girl.

A job at the L.A. Times is all I've ever wanted. And even though I knew the odds were low and couldn't possibly be in my favor, I asked if they wouldn't mind keeping my resume on file or if I could follow up with them later to see if things had changed. Which is why I'm keeping it my little secret and not telling anyone for now. I won't even tell my hotheaded crazy best friend of mine, who's waiting for me at one of our routine meeting places.

It's packed when I walk into Longboards. That's what Saturday nights are like at any bar on Main Street. I train my eyes in the direction of the bar, searching the faces for a glimpse of Gwen. With no luck, I look around at the tables near the back and eventually see her cozied up in the corner with some bar hound I am sure she only met a few minutes earlier.

Gwen catches my eye and immediately waves me over. "Ev, Ev... over here!"

Maneuvering my way through the crowd, my annoyance thickens as drunken men and drunker women fill the room. It's only 7:30 and they have most likely have been drinking all afternoon. Orange County is a tourist destination that's for sure. Even people who live inland come to the beach on the weekends, making an already crowded location even more hectic—and most times insanely frustrating.

The bar life annoys the hell out of me, although Gwen loves it. She thrives on it. The thrill it gives her is enough to make me laugh and endure it at least a few times. I let myself suffer through it when we finally get the chance to hang out together.

"I was just talking to... What's your name again," Gwen asks her flavor of the night as I approach the table. She is already slurring, having taken no time starting the night off without me.

"Excuse me... I'm talking to you! What's your name?" she

CHAPTER 1

continues pestering the stranger, poking the poor guy in the ribs. His attention is already elsewhere, on some younger early-twenty-something batting her eyelashes at him from a table close by.

"Tom, the name's Tom," he says, barely glancing back at Gwen.

I throw my purse on an open chair at the table and then proceeded to take off my coat, sizing up the situation in front of me. Not exactly what I wanted to encounter on what was supposed to be girls' night out, but I'll go with it as long as I can figure out a way to ditch the stereotypical man-whore later.

"Nice to meet you, Tom." I try my best to hide my annoyance. Tom's attention still hasn't moved from the girl at the table next to us. Rolling my eyes, I look around the bar in the hope of catching the eye of a nearby waitress.

Bar hounds are all the same, preying on the easy and vulnerable, and unfortunately, there are many conquests readily available to such a sorry excuse for a man. Not my Gwen. She's the kind that's in the wrong place at the wrong time on a bad day.

Gwen leans in close to me and whispers, "I met him here last night. He bought me a drink, and you know how I can't say no to free drinks!" Holding up her nearly empty beer bottle, I smile sadly. Oh, I know.

After her sister's death, Gwen had gone on a downward spiral. She had some days, weeks, and months that were good, although some she drowned herself in substance abuse. I'll never hold it against her, and I'll never blame her. I have no idea what I would succumb to if I ever lost a member of my family, and I never want to find out. I'd probably lose my mind—or worse!

My best friend studies her bottle for a minute, and then I watch as she chugs the rest of its contents in a lightning fast rate. This is obviously a bad day. Time to put up a guard for the both of us since there is no way she will be thinking clearly.

A waitress finally appears and asks the table if we wish to order anything more. Her attitude and annoyance are evident as I try to raise my voice loud enough for her to hear me ordering a Tom Collins, my go-to drink whenever I need something on the strong side. As I place my drink order, I notice man-whore Tom waves his hand in a sense that he can't be bothered, still unwilling to take his eyes off the barely legal girl to the right of us. The waitress and I both roll our eyes in a silent acknowledgment of disgust. She leaves, and Tom finally turns his attention back to our table, meeting my eyes for the first time since I arrived—perhaps the only reason being the young bar slut he had been trying to flirt with got up and left the bar.

"So, what's your friend's name," he asks Gwen without ever taking his eyes off me.

"This is Evelyn, but we all call her Ev," she replies. Her attention is now on her cell phone, checking Facebook or texting someone, no doubt. Gwen loves her phone. It barely leaves her hand and hardly ever leaves her side.

Tom continues staring only at me, and I notice him lick his lips as his eyes graze over every inch of my body. I feel the pit of my stomach revolt by the idea of what must be going through his mind. His stare is enough to make even the sluttiest of woman uncomfortable, and I have to stop myself from getting up and leaving immediately.

I'm definitely not in the mood for nasty bar men who think

every girl that walks into a place is easy. Swallowing hard, I tell myself quietly that I'm here for Gwen, and from the looks of it, she definitely needs me right now.

"Ev, huh," Tom says slowly. He begins looking me up and down again like he is picking out a steak he's going to devour later. There's nothing I hate more than being sized up, especially by stereotypical bar assholes. Exhibit A: the guy standing right in front of me.

"I got me a friend too," Tom says, cocking his head to the side and scratching his chin, his gaze resting a little too long south of my face. "Hey, Bud! Bud over here!" he shouts.

Bud? Is his friend's name actually Bud or is he calling his buddy? The stupidity of it all has me silently giggling. Wingman buddy, no doubt. I doubt this situation can get any worse. Gwen is so oblivious. She must have drunk more than I first assumed.

Before I have a chance to think about looking towards where Tom gestured, I feel the breath of another person on the back of my neck. Stale and gross, it makes me break out in goosebumps of disgust. I feel hostile and nauseous. No doubt in my mind this has to be Bud.

"Well aren't you a pretty little thing," I hear Bud slur. His breath smells of whiskey. I don't even bother to look up at him. I keep looking straight ahead at Gwen whose eyes still haven't left her phone.

"Gwen," I plead. "Gwen!" Maybe I can get her attention and somehow find a way to talk her into leaving and getting out of what I know is a horrible disaster waiting to happen.

My severely intoxicated friend only glances up from her phone and gives me a drunken stare. "What?" she mumbles, annoyed, then looks back down again. Her phone is obviously more important than the situation she's just gotten us into. An escape is definitely not in the cards.

Turning around, I allow myself to meet the eyes of our new guest for the first time. He's about five-eight or nine, cleanly shaven and has muscles bulging out of his shirt, which is two sizes too small for him. The sorry excuse for a shirt is labeled with a surf brand. I have to stifle a laugh because I know this man has probably never surfed a day in his life.

My hateful stare further dissects this annoying little man. Tight jeans, impeccably clean shoes, and he has a few of those tribal band tattoos on each bicep. He's also wearing so much cologne that it almost overpowers the smell of whiskey seeping from his breath. Not entirely, but almost. Yup, very typical!

"I'm not your pretty little thing if that's what you're insinuating," I sneer at him, just as the waitress returns with our drinks. I grab my drink and take a long sip, hoping maybe he will get the hint and leave me alone. I try and emphasize this by swiveling in my chair so my back now faces him, but my plan fails.

Out of the corner of my eye, I see Bud hold his glass up to the waitress, signifying he obviously wants another, to which the waitress just rolls her eyes and walks away. Great, Bud is also an ill-mannered jerk. Not that I am really surprised. They tend to run in packs. He rounds my side and walks right in front of me.

Bracing his arms on the table behind me, he leans in close and whispers, "Why don't we just wait and see where the night takes us," and drunkenly teeters back when he takes it upon himself to cheers his glass against my own. Like a toast is all that's needed to seal the deal and change my mind. Men actually think women fall for this? What is wrong with my

CHAPTER 1

generation? Don't even get me started because I will never end that rant.

"How about we don't," I shoot back, swiveling my chair again in the other direction. I hate that I promised Gwen I would meet her here on my last night in town. I would rather be anywhere else in the world than here right now.

His irritating pickup line oozes out of his lips. "Hey, come on now. A sexy siren like yourself has to be used to all sorts of attention."

He tries to touch me, moving my hair off to one side and leaning in closer from behind. I shrug his hands off with all the force I can manage without actually getting up and punching him. Get the hint already and back off, Bud!

"I know you didn't step out of the house looking like that to not get noticed," he says, walking in front of me again, giving me an awkward looking wink. I have to swallow back the vomit that involuntarily starts to rise in my throat. Go ahead and touch me one more time and see where that gets you.

An unpleasant silence falls between us as we sit there and stare at one another. Rolling my eyes, I decide to stand up from the table and think of a way to lose Bud and leave this very stupid situation. Maybe I can claim to need to use the restroom. Maybe I should pretend I smoke so I could go outside and hopefully ditch Bud and his wingman in the process.

Tom, the wingman, who, along with Gwen, is now missing. A blank stare comes across my face as I stand there wondering when that happened and how I could have missed it.

Frantically, I begin looking around the bar for Gwen as Bud takes a step closer. It's as if he thinks standing up from the table is a signal for him to come closer. Moron. I roll my eyes for at least the tenth time since he approached the table, and then continue to try and put distance between us as I scan the room for any sign of my now missing best friend.

Leaning in, Bud takes a deep breath right next to my neck. "You smell good," he says, intruding upon my personal space.

I'm taller than him with my heels on, and it makes me have to look down on the tiny man. This must hurt his ego. How can my towering over him not make him feel like less of a man and make him want to retreat from his over-the-top, persistent mission to somehow make me his?

Irritation makes me snap. "Really..." I glare at him, my annoyance at an all-time high "...is that supposed to make me want you now? Make me change my mind and decide to let you take me home so I can spread my legs for you? I don't think so!"

I take a step away from the table and continue to scan the room, looking for Gwen. Unfortunately, Bud still persists, stepping up beside me and trying to grab hold of my waist. Shaking off his grasp, I shoot him a look daring him to try it again. And I do dare him! I want nothing more than to knee him where it counts right now and drop this loser to the floor.

"Don't be so cold!" Bud shouts and slams down his now empty glass on the table. He tries his best to focus back on me as he continues. "Pretending like you don't want it. If you're half as easy as your friend was last night with Tom," he says, reaching out to try and touch me again, "I shouldn't have to try hard at all."

His statement makes me step back. Pausing for a second, I let his words resonate in my mind. I honestly can't believe what I am hearing. First, the jerk has the audacity to think I can easily be picked up, and then he insults Gwen, thus obviously insulting me further. I know her shenanigans aren't always

CHAPTER 1

honorable, but damn it no one gets to say so except me!

"Excuse me?" I shout back. It's the only response I can manage as his previous statement has left me in a state of shock. Finally able to find some words, I glare at him as I sternly say, "I think it's about time you go to hell and take your friend with you!"

Grabbing my coat and purse, I turn to leave. I'll find Gwen wherever she is, but there is no way in hell I am standing here listening to this for one more second. Bud grabs my arm and swings me around to meet his eyes. He has a forceful and severely painful hold on me. I glance down at his hand holding my body in a vise grip and look up again with a hateful stare.

He smiles mischievously and moves in closer. "Don't be like that. We can take it slow ... if that's what you want." He licks his lips and moves closer, his voice now a grotesque whisper between the two of us. "Trust me, baby, I know you'll like it." He grabs me around the waist again, trying to grind himself against me, cornering me against the table.

"Let me go," I manage in the most assertive voice I can. My eyes glare into his as I push off him, a desperate attempt to break free and make a run for it.

"I'll leave you begging for more. Come on, you know you want to, baby. I know you haven't had anything as good as me." Bud tightens his grasp on me, leaving barely any room for a possible escape.

"I said let me go! Stop it!" I yell.

Chapter 2

Noah

Southern California ... Alright ... been here, done that. Can we pack this up and go home now? An insane world with endless buildings, endless people, and endless craziness. Two hours sitting in traffic to go five miles? No thank you! Are we done yet?

I glance at the time on my phone for the hundredth time in the last two minutes and then look over at Rex and the latest fling he caught this vacation. Beth the bar troll that's somehow made it to day three.

Wrapped around one another, Rex and Beth are totally unaware of the looks of disgust people are giving them. They continue groping one another in a way that I'm surprised doesn't make them feel uncomfortable. They're saying goodbye for what Beth thinks is just until tomorrow, but I know is permanent. Rex never holds a relationship longer than a week. Two tops.

I met Rex in college. A born and raised Californian that landed at Ole Miss. Rex was as far from a southerner as you could get and always stuck out in a crowd. Saying he was from California gave him a lot of attention from the ladies, which he loved.

CHAPTER 2

How we ever became friends, I couldn't tell you, but somehow, we managed to hit it off and have remained almost inseparable ever since.

He suggested I move out to California with him when he graduated last spring, and I jumped at the idea in order to put some distance between me and the one girl I can't seem to escape and never want to see again. The one that broke my heart and still won't stop haunting me. Lesson learned. Never break up in a small town. You can't escape it.

Moving to California sounded like a chance to live on greener pastures, so I signed up to take my senior year of classes online and followed him out west eager to make a fresh new start. I figured a new life, where no one knew my name or my past, was exactly what I needed.

Once we arrived in northern California, I liked the change of scenery. The hills and country almost felt like home. We signed a year's lease, and I started to stretch out and settle into a brand-new world. However, now my year was almost up and my time in California was ending. I hadn't agreed to renew the lease with Rex and honestly couldn't wait to pack it up and move back home. I thought I could find some sort of new meaning to life and freedom in the move, but the longer I stayed, the more I regretted it. With absolutely nothing to keep me here any longer, I knew without a doubt the California lifestyle, northern or southern, was definitely not for me.

This trip south was Rex's last attempt at making me change my mind, and actually, all it did was prove he might just be stupider than he looks. A country boy has no place in a cluster fuck like Los Angeles. The beach was pretty but overcrowded. All I can dream about is being able to go home to the beautiful countryside, have the space to breathe and think. Something you can't do with all the noise and chaos in southern California.

Yes, sir, as soon as Rex could kindly remove his tongue from that superficial girl's mouth, I will be hightailing it to the car. I can't wait to jump on the road and get the hell out of this concrete jungle and away from all the people in it. Trying to find something else to focus my thoughts on besides the two I'm sitting next to, I let my mind wander back to her ... that girl, the one standing on the edge of the pier, that I couldn't stop staring at. Hell, on a scale of one to ten, she was off the damn chart. Even from where I stood on the sand, I was drawn to her. She looked sad in the most gorgeous of ways. Is that even possible? And even through the ocean's glare and her apparent sadness, I couldn't help but be stunned by her beauty. Her long blond hair blew perfectly in the breeze. One look at her and damn it if it wasn't obvious she had to have broken a thousand hearts. I remember at one point she smiled, making me catch my breath. She was stunning! She was stunning in the way that everything about her made you want to know her. In that brief moment I first laid eyes on her, I felt myself wanting to be able to experience everything I could about her.

What she smelled like ...

What she talked like ...

What her favorite food was ...

Did we listen to the same kind of music?

I stared at her for what seemed like forever, and it still wasn't long enough. I took in every bit of her I could from the distance between us, trying to commit the moment and her to memory and subconsciously knowing I never wanted to forget her, and knew I couldn't even if I tried. She would haunt my fantasies forever. Why? I don't know if I will ever know.

Sitting in the bar, I thumb through my phone, not paying

attention to what I'm actually looking at as my mind races back to earlier. I stood there staring at her, noticing the way she ran her fingers through her hair, how she shifted her weight on her feet. I even caught the slow exhale of breath she gave as her thoughts slowly consumed her mind. God, what I wouldn't give to be the one she thinks about. The thought comes out of nowhere and shocks the hell out of me. Shaking my head, I try and refocus. Forget it! Girls like her are usually all sorts of trouble. Heck, any girl is trouble. I'm headed home to Kentucky in two short months, away from here and her. And that is just the way I like it.

My annoyance quickly returns as I am brought back to the here and now. I watch my best friend act like a horny, embarrassing teenager in public and try and think about how he managed to talk me into going for one drink before we hit the road. One drink that Rex has now turned into three—with a few added shots just for the hell of it!

He is plastered all over Beth in our corner booth, not paying any attention to anyone or anything else. I will no doubt be driving, which is why I'm sitting in the back corner of some bar off a side street in a town I can't wait to get out of and drinking a plain old coke when what I really want is a dark beer.

Glancing up from my phone, I make out the girl from the pier sitting at a table nearby and my breath immediately catches in my throat. Nervously, I pull my ball cap down lower and fidget in my seat. I want to get a better view of her but have an overwhelming need to hide my stare at the same time.

I must look like an idiot, but heaven help me because damn it if I'm not helplessly drawn to her. Looking away for a moment, she pulls me back to her like a fucking magnet. I feel like a drooling idiot, a prepubescent teenager myself who just bumped into their junior high crush. But hell, I can't help it, and somehow I don't want to either. She's more captivating up close than I could have imagined. I sit here in a damn trance, watching the way she moves, studying her every gesture. Never has a woman fascinated me like her before. She's addictive.

She's sitting with another girl, which I have no doubt has to be her friend. I watched her friend drink one drink after another before the girl from the pier arrived. She seemed as interested in the guy she was with as she was in the drinks she was drinking.

Shortly after mystery girl arrived, I noticed another man approach their table. I'm surprised as a surge of jealousy run through me, thinking this guy has to be her boyfriend. A girl like her is usually never single. Well, I guess I lost out on that one. The fact that I'm even considering mystery girl has me confused. I shake my head again, trying to regain some sort of sanity. Get it together, Noah! Don't let one drop dead beautiful woman make you feel what you're feeling. All chicks are the same. They'll just take and take until you have nothing left to give—and that's when they always leave.

Glancing back up, I continue watching the two of them, even though I feel sick inside doing it. Why can't I shake this pull she has on me? It doesn't take long watching the two of them for me to second guess myself. Maybe I'm wrong. Maybe pier girl doesn't have a boyfriend. I quickly see annoyance run over mystery girl's face. I sit and watch as the conversation escalates, both their voices rising higher. I look closer as the guy from the bar proceeds to put his hands on her and back her into an almost cornered position. If she does know the guy, it's obvious she wants nothing to do with him.

Before I can process the emotions and the thoughts running

through my head, I am on my feet and over at their table. Without hesitation, I grab the girl from the pier and swing her around towards me. God, she's gorgeous. I falter slightly as I take her in. Wide blue eyes, startled expression, flushed cheeks ... Damn it! I'm in more trouble than I thought!

Wondering what the hell I was thinking, and what I'm about to do next, I take a pause and swallow hard as I manage to say, "Hey, there you are! I've been looking all over for you ..." Without another thought, I pull her into me, kissing her senseless. I grab her tightly around her slender waist, feeling her crash into me and knowing I will never recover. From her ... from this ... She's priceless!

As my lips crush hers, I suddenly collapse into the magnetic force between the two of us that even she can't deny. I've never felt anything like it. Our connection is undeniable, hitting straight to my core. The spark is consuming, robbing every bit of me. I surrender to her, wanting to never return from wherever she can take me.

She never pulls away, and I hope that's a good sign as I unintentionally deepen our kiss. Too passionate and familiar to be a first as I feel her fall into me effortlessly, like this isn't the first time I have tasted her. Too fueled with desire for a person I don't even know, I have to stop myself from taking it further and stealing her away somewhere just to be able to take more of her. Holy hell, this girl tastes like heaven. Sweet as hell and in every perfect way breathtaking. I can taste her drink on her tongue, and it makes me crave her. It makes me need her even more. Pushing a little further and not letting up, I am surprised to feel her grip tighten around my arm, and I swear she kisses me back. She presses into me instinctively like she doesn't want to pull away. Either that or my head is more screwed-up than I thought.

When I can finally force myself to break free from the surprising ecstasy just created between the two of us, I am once again drowning in the most beautiful pair of blue eyes. A pair of blue eyes that are most certainly looking at me now like a deer in headlights, completely shocked, stunned, and wanting an explanation. Maybe I should start counting the seconds before her alluring eyes regain their sanity and tell her the smart thing to do is to slap me in the face.

Time to think quickly. I grab her arm and pull her to my side then shoot my hand out to the jerk from a few minutes earlier who was trying to get way further than the first base I just scored.

"Hey, thanks for keeping my girl busy," I start off, glancing back at the girl from the pier. God help me! Just looking into her eyes is the most thrilling thing I have ever experienced. Her lips are now swollen from our kiss, eyes still wide in astonishment. I'm amazed when I can even find the words to continue. Looking back at the man in front of us, I say, "I guess you succeeded in showing her what kind of scum hangs out in local bars and taught me never to leave her waiting!"

My hand is still extended towards him, and I'm not the slightest bit surprised that he never takes it. I look back at the girl standing next to me, and she still hasn't taken her eyes off me. The silence thickens. My throat goes dry as I try to find the right words to say. At any moment this could turn bad. I'm either the smartest guy in the world or the stupidest. And I'm about to find out.

"We should probably be going if we want to make our reservation," I nervously say to the girl, who not only hasn't stop staring at me but surprisingly also hasn't stepped away

CHAPTER 2

from my grasp.

Finally, after what seems like an endless nerve-racking minute, she blinks then smiles. Tearing her gaze from mine, she looks back at the man in front of us then speaks. When she does, the sound of her voice reaches a place deep inside me, igniting something I can't put into words. To hell if I know why, but it feels like coming home.

"Of course, dear," she states sarcastically, batting her eyelashes for extreme emphasis. She clenches my arm hard—any harder and I swear she'll draw blood. "That is unless our friend wants to have a drink with us. We don't want to be rude."

Her eyes flicker with something I am not quite sure of as she glances back my way. A flush grazes her cheeks, and she seems slightly nervous. I cock my head to the side and stare. A sly grin unintentionally graces my face. So, she's going to play along. A little shocked and very much relieved, I settle into the possibilities of whatever might come out of this.

The three of us all stop to look at one another, each one of us wondering who will make the next move. Seconds pass. Then a minute. Right as I begin to swear this was the worst idea I have ever had, the man in front of us breaks our three-way stare. He waves his hand as if to say "to hell with the both of you." Mumbling something under his breath, he then turns and walks away. I immediately exhale a breath I didn't know I was holding as I turn and look back at the beautiful woman next to me, and damn it if I can't help but smile to myself. Random jerk in a bar - 0. Noah - 1.

Chapter 3

Noah

The air becomes so thick in the moments that follow kissing a random stranger in a bar. Wondering what the best way to cut through the silence is, I figure the strongest knife in the world is perhaps even too dull to ease this tension. Standing back and having to now come up with an explanation, I'm beginning to think maybe running and hiding sounds like the best available option.

In the time it takes to find words to speak, a million thoughts run through my mind. Do I tell her how long I was watching her? Do I mention that I noticed her down by the pier? Do I say anything at all? How the hell have I now succumbed to starring, stalking, and kissing random women in bars?

Her beauty is mind-blowing. Her presence is overpowering.

As I stand here staring, I realize I'm completely helpless in her presence. Standing only a few feet apart, I can almost feel every thought I have fleeing my mind. Unable to find the brain power to form a simple sentence, I stand in front of her, searching for anything that holds any sort of worth to say to her ... yet I have nothing.

I'm amazed that she doesn't immediately turn and walk

CHAPTER 3

away. Her blue eyes dare me, and her posture, although standoffish, is enticing and sexy as hell. She's evidently expecting a great explanation; but with each passing moment, any logical explanation I can come up with seems to be just a stupid excuse to kiss a beautiful girl in a bar.

The fact that I find it impossible to form even one sentence in her presence is something that has never happened to me before. Sure, I have had my moments where nerves have gotten the better of me when starring into a pretty face, but actually speechless? Yup, I am totally losing it.

"I don't normally do things like that ..." I kind of stutter, finally beginning to find words. "I mean I've never done anything like that!"

I take my hat off and run my fingers through my hair, a nervous habit. If there was ever a time to be nervous, it's now—when I'm standing face to face with unquestionably the most beautiful girl I have ever seen and will ever see again.

I watch as I see something flash through her eyes as she watches me. What it is, I can't quite put my finger on. Whatever it was makes me slowly smile, and I watch as her cheeks flush the most adorable shade of pink once again.

She has to know how pretty she is. It hurts to even look at her. It's almost as if she was perfectly crafted just for me. I couldn't dream of a woman more beautiful if I tried.

She's entirely out of my league. I would be the luckiest man in the world to have a chance with a woman like her. Too bad I will never know if she'll give me the opportunity after the stunt I just pulled.

I notice I still haven't found anything more to say, and she still has yet to respond to my lame attempt at conversation. I can't decide if she's in shock from what just happened or trying to call bullshit. I need to say something, anything, just to keep her here with me because hell I wouldn't mind being able to look into those eyes just a little bit longer.

My gaze falls to her mouth and I lick my lips. Those lips, I'd do anything to be able to taste them again. She's the most intoxicating thing I have ever experienced. I know I could never get my fill of her. She's the type of girl you let yourself drown in any chance you get.

How is there something about this girl that renders me absolutely crippled in her presence? I can't leave, even if I wanted to, and hell if I'm in any rush to go anywhere. Where was she a few days ago when I really could have explored her? Explored this, whatever it is. I'm not sure I will ever be the same after this feeling. How can something you have never had before suddenly be something you know you don't want to try and live without?

"My name's Noah," I manage to say as I clear my throat. "Let me at least buy you a drink after making such a fool of myself. It's the least I can do."

She has to be trying to decide if I'm trustworthy enough to sit with or if I'm as bad as the jerk that just left. Although she just watches me, and as much as she looks curious, I see doubt there as well. Maybe there is a glimmer of hope she will give me a chance somewhere behind that doubt. By the looks of her, she's debating it.

She squints her eyes, and her nose scrunches up as she angles her head to the side. Adorable mixed with sexy. Yup, I am absolutely in trouble. I stand there and watch the wheels turning in her head, wondering how I got lucky enough to even get as far as I have.

All I want to do right now is grab her and show her just how much I'm nothing like she has ever had before or will ever get the chance to have again. When it comes to members of the opposite sex, confidence has never been my strong suit, but this girl makes me want to take that leap of faith. I resist even though I can feel the drive to do so vibrate through my body to my fingertips. I need to tug her into me and feel her against me just one more time.

"Can I at least know your name, before you walk away and leave me having to guess it for the rest of my life?" I laugh, attempting one last time to make her stay. I've never begged before, but desperate times and all that shit. I'm not above groveling for this girl.

She crosses her arms over her chest, still observing me. I glance down momentarily and notice her curves. Her body is the thing dreams are made of. Slender neck and shoulders, ample breasts without being overpowering, an hourglass waist leading to thick hips and long legs ... Could this girl get any more perfect? Her indecision makes me anxious, and I begin to remember why I don't have the confidence others have. Taking chances are nerve-racking as fuck, but I can't stop myself from trying if there is a way to make her stay with me just a little longer.

Hoping she didn't catch my roaming eyes, I glance up and meet her stare. Soon, a small smile spreads across her lips. She's not walking away. Maybe there is hope for me. As much as I had no plans for allowing myself to fall for anyone, let alone her, I suddenly know I don't want to watch her walk out of my life just yet.

"Evelyn," she reveals with a smile. The gorgeous girl also has an elegantly beautiful name. I watch as her smile becomes bigger and notice the twinkle in her eye when she looks at me.

Her eyes dance like I have never seen before. And I want to know what is behind them. I want to know everything about this girl who has me stopped dead in my tracks.

"Noah, is it?" she continues. "I think you owe me a drink and an explanation."

"Yes, ma'am. I suppose I do, don't I?" I beam at her. I know my grin has to be bigger than a five-year-old on Christmas morning, and I don't give a damn. She just gave me the chance I was hoping for, and there is no way I am going to screw this up.

Motioning towards the table, I quickly pull out her chair so she can sit down. I watch her body slowly lower into the seat and bite the inside of my lip, trying to get myself to focus on something else besides her amazing body that she carries so well. With curves any man would die to have his hands on, I feel my palms itch to touch her and almost can't resist the urge.

Focus, Noah! There is no way in hell I can try to make conversation when my mind is wrapped around the idea of where my hands want to be instead. I'm one lucky son-of-a-bitch for a chance like this, and I know it.

This trip down south is beginning to not be so bad after all. Now if I could just relax enough to not scare her off, I might have a chance at night two.

Chapter 4

Evelyn

Normally, if any guy walked up to me in a bar, swung me around, and kissed me, I would have slapped him into next week. Or better yet, kneed him where it counts and dropped that sucker to the floor!

So, what stopped me from doing that to Noah? Why did just the sight of him leave me weak in the knees?

When he spoke, my mind went blank. Watching him adorably stumble over his words only somehow made me more intrigued. I could tell he didn't know what to say, and yet I couldn't even begin to find the words myself to help him. My mind was still foggy from the sexiest, most electrifying, lustfully perfect kiss that I have ever had. The man took my breath away ... stopped my heart and restarted it all again with one mind-blowing kiss. What just happened between the two of us left me in a trance.

I can't think. Paralyzed, I feel as if I can barely breathe.

Sexy as hell, standing at about six-four or a little more, he has dark hair and the most crystal-clear blue eyes I have ever looked into. A perfect five o'clock shadow grazes the lower part of his strong chin and gives him just enough rugged appeal that's undeniably yummy.

He has on a ball cap with a symbol I don't quite recognize, no doubt for some sports team. Wearing a plain white T-shirt and dark blue jeans, he's dressed so simple yet looks handsome and altogether perfectly manly. He's also wearing boots, which is a very different sight in SoCal to say the very least.

Noah's fit without being to fit. You can tell he takes care of his body without obsessing over it like it is a trophy to show off. A very pleasing and very rare thing in my opinion.

My heart pounds in my chest, and my head feels dizzy. I feel anxious and nervous, not wanting to mess up and say the wrong thing. Being hit by a feeling I have never felt before, I can only stand here and hope he feels it too and that our kiss rendered him just as speechless.

In a moment of complete chaos, I've never felt so at peace. In a moment of violation, I've never felt so protected and secure. In a moment where I should have felt disgust, even anguish, I feel nothing but desire and passion.

Everything in me tells me to leave. Everything about this situation tells me I am crazy, that Noah could turn out to be the most terrible kind of trouble I have ever gotten into. But crazy has never felt so good, and trouble has never seemed so tempting!

Sitting in Longboards with a complete stranger, I find myself feeling more alive than I have in a long time. He has a way about him that makes me feel at peace, almost as if we have met before. There's an ease to our connection which scares and thrills the hell out of me all at the same time.

Even when my head tells me to run as fast as I can, I find myself not wanting to be anywhere else in the world but right here, sitting at a small table making small talk with a man I find myself slowly wanting and needing to know more about. I

CHAPTER 4

love watching him smile and adore hearing him laugh. I blush more than once when his eyes linger on mine. The way he looks at me is enough to make any girl feel wanted. And after all, isn't that what every girl dreams of? The lust in his eyes makes the air between the two of us electric. An undeniable spark between us gives me the best high I have ever felt, and a small part of me fears I never will again.

Our conversation is typical for introductions, consisting of questions generic to when you first meet someone. He asked me if I lived in town. I mention this was my hometown and left it at that. I had no clue how far he would dive into his world, and I wasn't about to give up to much of my own.

A waitress shows up and asks if we want a drink. I order another and can't help noticing Noah orders a coke. The mere thought that he is in a bar and not drinking makes him more intriguing and piques my curiosity even further.

"So, you're from here, huh? I wouldn't have guessed that at all," Noah confesses in a thick southern drawl that makes every good part of me tingle.

I watch as he slowly wipes the condensation off his glass with his fingers. Involuntarily, my mind starts thinking about how those fingers would feel running the length of my body.

Trying to focus back on our conversation and not read too far into his comment, I smile and say, "Is that supposed to be a good thing or a bad thing."

I debate telling him I don't live in southern California but see no point in giving up my truth. I'm sure I will never see him again after tonight.

He fidgets in his seat, obviously a little nervous. Something about that has me feeling accomplished. Nervous means he wants to impress me, which hopefully means he's interested.

"No, I mean, it's just ..." Noah stutters. "I've been here a week and I haven't met anyone like you. Well, no one ... umm, or ... well, you know..." he trails off, fumbling and stumbling over each one of his words.

I just raise an eyebrow at him, aiming to keep him on his toes. I can't hide the giggle that escapes my lips as I realize it worked and he is at a loss for words once again. The butterflies in my stomach are at an all-time high from his closeness. I can smell the mixture of sun, sand, and man—an aphrodisiac lighting up every single part of me.

"So, Noah," I say as I try and hide the nerves just under the surface, "where are you from that everyone is so much easier to talk to?" I finish asking as the waitress returns and deposits our drinks on the table. I quickly take a drink to slow my nerves before continuing. "I mean ... I can already tell you're not from around here with that long drawl of yours."

With a huge smile on his face, Noah's gaze meets mine straight-on. It's a heart-melting, toe-curling smile that makes me thankful I am already sitting down.

"No, miss. I'm from the south," he states, obviously very proud of the fact. "Kentucky to be exact. You know where the bourbon is strong and betting on horses is one of the oldest past times."

"Bourbon and horses, huh?" I say, not having ever given Kentucky much thought before. "I take it you're not that impressed with the West Coast, then. California not exactly everything dreams are made of?"

"I didn't like it all that much at first," Noah slowly says as he leans closer, "but you're making it hard to want to ever leave the table, let alone the state."

His comment startles me, his face now serious and smoldering. He intensely stares straight into my eyes, making his statement sink in, which in turn makes me melt right into the seat I'm sitting on. He looks at me like he could see right through me, and I can't help but falter.

God help me, how do I even come back from that one?

"I bet you say that to all the girls." I roll my eyes, smirking at him. When he doesn't say anything, I continue. Rambling like the nervous girl I feel like inside. "Kentucky must be great. I've never been further than Colorado, so I wouldn't know. Kind of sad, huh?"

"That is sad," he says. "I'd love to show you everything you've been missing." Noah seductively flirts, leaning in and nudging his shoulder against my own.

Just the smallest brush of his body against mine sends my head spinning and leaves me wondering how he has a way of making me feel like a nervous schoolgirl that has never been touched by a boy before? I smile, loving the effect he has over me. How, with just one small touch, does he have the ability to make me feel so alive?

My blood pumps at a rapid speed through my veins. Butterflies flutter in my stomach, and my head feels dizzy. The feeling he gives me is all kinds of crazy and all kinds of wonderful too. It's something I've never felt before, and I'm still not sure how to process it all.

"You keep laying on those southern manners nice and thick and I don't think you will have to convince me much at all." I flirt back.

The feeling doesn't last long, though, as we're both startled when Gwen suddenly hits the table, almost running it and us over. She's out of breath and looks a mess. I hate to admit it, loving the girl dearly, but this is no way to make a first impression. And I know her presence, both awkward and embarrassing, is about to get much worse. She's hammered drunk, sweaty, and her makeup is smeared everywhere.

"Ev, holy hell, we have to go! Like NOW!!" She shouts, rounding the table and grabbing me by the arm, almost pulling me down on top of her. We stumble before we catch ourselves from tumbling over. Noah rises from his seat to help.

"Now?! Like this second now?" I try to catch up to speed with what's going on. I barely pull my purse off the table next to me and end up grabbing my coat with so much haste it drops to the floor. Noah picks up my coat and hands it to me with a pleading look.

"I'm sorry, I guess I'm going," I say, feeling very disappointed. I attempt to pull back from the death grip that Gwen has on my arm to try and buy myself a little more time but fail miserably. I eventually give up and stumble backward as she continues towards the front.

"Thanks for the drink," I yell at him while being pulled further across the room. "And the kiss," I joke as an eerie sadness begins to fill me inside.

I see Noah say something and try to gesture like he wants to pull me back. Every part of me wishes I was just a little bit closer so he could. The noise in the bar makes it too loud to hear what he is trying to say, and I'm already too far away to feel his touch.

As we leave the bar, a part of me feels left behind. I struggle, trying to make sense of why I feel that way. I hurry alongside my best friend as we reach the outside. I can't help but hate her a little, something I don't do often but just often enough to make me wonder why our friendship has lasted as long as it has. We slowly start walking towards the parking garage, stopping occasionally when Gwen trips over her own feet. We start walking again only when she insists she doesn't need any help walking.

My mind wanders back to Noah. What would have happened if we stayed longer? Might I run into him again? I know it's a long shot, but hey a girl can dream can't she?

Every happy thought I have quickly dissipates as I turn around just in time to see Gwen throw up in the bushes.

Chapter 5

Evelyn

Fall finally arrived in northern California when I return home from Orange County. It's mid-November, and the trees are beautiful shades of reds and oranges. Millions of leaves line the streets and take flight when the breeze hits them just right. A late afternoon rain shower makes the sidewalks wet. The winter chill is slowly setting in after its long absence.

The rain feels so incredible. California had been in another one of its ever long droughts, and our state has barely seen rain in four long years. I catch myself sighing contently as I drive through my small town, realizing how my love for the fall grows more and more each year. Rolling down the window, I let in the smell of fresh rain and breathe deeply. The light crisp fall breeze mysteriously finds a way of always refreshing me.

Eventually, I pull up to my apartment and can't wait to get out and stretch my legs. The drive from southern California to Nevada City is almost eight hours and seems never ending at times, especially that torturous last hour as anxiety over wanting and needing to get home creeps in.

Jumping out of the car in relief, I walk around to the trunk

CHAPTER 5

and grab my bag before heading inside. My apartment is an old Victorian house at the top of one of the main streets in town. It has been renovated and divided into four units. Walls have been erected in the foyer of the old house to establish separate living quarters. There are two apartments downstairs and two apartments upstairs. Mine is at the top of the stairs on the right and is actually the largest of the four, having two bedrooms in addition to the family room, bathroom, and kitchen.

I take the time to grab my enormous stack of mail that accumulated all week while I was away and try my best to balance carrying it upstairs with my luggage. With each step, I wonder how I will even manage to unlock my door but somehow pull off this juggling act and make it inside. Dropping my things in the entry, I run to the wall across the living room to start the heater. The one drawback to living in an old building is no central heating or air-conditioning, at least not in this old house. I don't mind, though. One of the things that sold me on moving here is the charm of the old buildings. Growing up, I always admired this old Victorian town with its cute vintage houses and boutiques that line Main Street.

The wall heater soon clicks away, beginning to give much needed warmth to the room as I make my way to the kitchen and pour the biggest glass of red wine I can. Long car rides deserve big glasses of wine! Although, I wonder what some good bourbon tastes like?

Shoving the thought from my mind, and the memory of the one man if evokes, I take sip after long sip and begin the torturous process of I thumbing through my mail. Throwing bills and junk aside, I settle on a magazine and browse the pages, only half paying attention. As much as I try, I can't stop thinking of the one thing that has been on my mind since last night. Noah!

It's driving me crazy. Even crazier is the thought that it doesn't matter. I could go on thinking about him day after day ... after day and never see him again. For one, he's from another state! Two, we never had a chance to exchange any information to contact each other. Thank you, Gwen!

Or maybe I actually should thank her. Noah was a beautiful distraction. One I can't afford and don't need. In the short amount of time we sat at the table together, I found myself beginning to want him and that could be dangerous.

Having planned out my life many times before, I decided early on I would never let a man get in my way of accomplishing my dreams, and I'm not about to start now. I'm so close to what I've always wanted, and I cannot afford any distractions, no matter how tempting and delicious they might be.

After graduating high school and having my dreams crushed when I didn't get into a southern California college, I'm not going to let a guy come along now and stop me from attaining that one goal: moving home.

After graduating from college, I promised myself I would work a few years up north and put in my time as a new journalist, building a strong resume until the bigger newspapers would take notice. I'm so close I can almost feel it. All I need is that one shot at landing a big job, and I would be set.

No man is going to come along now and take the dream that I have had ever since my parents moved me up north—not even a southern boy with charm for days that has my head spinning and knees buckling in ways I have never felt before in my life.

Chemistry leads to feelings, which leads to sex. And sex typically leads to commitment, which obviously means a relationship, which leads to love and more feelings and screws

CHAPTER 5

up my plans and my future.

Luckily Noah doesn't live anywhere near here, which is a plus because what he ignites inside me without even trying scares the crap out of me. No thanks. Love can wait. I'm a girl on a mission. Love is not part of the plan.

But maybe ...

Just maybe ...

I let myself entertain the maybes and wonder how I might find him or if I ever could ...

Should I Facebook stalk him? Search all the Noahs in the great state of Kentucky and see if he pops up? Social media has to be good for something right? After that, I can check into an institution and kiss any opportunity with him goodbye because that's definitely crazy! He's already making me lose my mind. Best to keep my distance and my sanity! I'll be damned if I let anyone rearrange my priorities in life.

But maybe ...

Smiling, I shake my head as I actually let myself consider this "maybe." Butterflies flutter in my stomach as I wonder what I would even say?

"Umm, Hi! Noah was it? Creepy bar stalker here from California! How are ya?"

Or ...

"Hey, Noah. It's me, you know the girl you promised to show things about the south that would make me second guess any other plan I had in life? Whatcha' doing next week?"

Laughing out loud, I have to admit as looney as it sounds, it's actually kind of tempting.

But tempting is bad! Tempting means trouble. If he can tempt me so much just thinking about him, I wouldn't stand a chance face to face. Distance, Evelyn! Distance! Keep your damn head straight.

I'm rattled out of my thoughts as my phone rings on the counter and makes me jump. Glancing at caller ID, I see it's my mother and involuntarily roll my eyes.

"Hey, Mom," I say when I reluctantly pick up my phone. Normally I have a great relationship with my mother, though the holiday season turns her into Martha Stewart on crack! Everyone and everything has to be perfect, and I know this is just another one of those phone calls to discuss the upcoming festivities as well as my need to be present at her dinner party later this evening.

I should have ignored the call and played it like I got home late. Silently chastising myself for not having this thought before I hit accept, I blame it on the wine as I wait to hear the rambling of the one and only Cynthia Monroe on the other end.

"Evelyn! Are you home yet? Please tell me your home," my mother begins interrogating me frantically.

"Yes, Mother, I just walked in the door," I hiss back.

"You just walked in the door? Good Lord, Evelyn! You need to get ready and go right back out the door again! The Roberts will be here at five! You know how I hate it when you're late, Evelyn Anne Monroe!"

I know I'm in trouble. My full name only comes out when my mother wants to scold me—and this time for a crime I haven't even committed yet!

"It's fine, Mom. I'll just come like I am. I was only driving all day—"

I try and argue, but my mother cuts me off. "No you most certainly will not," she yells back at me, taking the time adding emphasis on the last two words. "Trevor is in town visiting his parents. He is coming to dinner too. You need to be looking

CHAPTER 5

and acting your best. I want grandchildren before I'm ninety, Evelyn!"

And here we go again. It's hysterical to me that before a woman is twenty-five, she's supposed to focus on a career. Once she hits her mid to late twenties, most people look at her like she's washed up and her prime is ticking by quickly.

"Mom! I already told you, this thing you think is going to happen one day between me and Trevor will NEVER happen. Drop it already," I say through gritted teeth. My body cringes at the idea of Trevor and me actually having ever been an item.

The Roberts and my family grew up together. My older brother Michael is best friends with Trevor's older brother. They did everything together as far back as I can remember, and Trevor always tagged along wherever the older boys went. Growing up, I thought it was just so he could act older. Now, I know it was so he could be near me any chance he could get.

Trevor's the same age as me, and for a brief second, I gave into his schoolboy crush when we were sixteen. What started off as a wild and hot summer fling, I later totally regretted. I was young and lonely and knew his feelings ran way deeper than mine ever could.

I started the relationship thinking maybe my feelings would grow and change over time. Everyone likes a summer romance, right? I quickly realized that starting anything with Trevor Roberts was one of the worst mistakes of my life. At first, it was fun, new, and exciting, like when you're climbing a roller coaster all the way to the top. Thrilled at what might come next, only to soon be jerked and bumped around through one disaster after another.

The more he confessed his undying love for me, the more I regressed into a little hole I never wanted him to pull me out of again. The more I pulled away, the angrier and more possessive he got. I left him at the end of summer with a broken heart that he obviously never recovered from.

My mother's voice breaks me from my past. "If you two had the hots for each other once before, you can find a way to get the hots for each other again!" I cringe again at my mother's use of the term "hots."

"Now get your little butt going," she insists in a pleasantly annoying voice, trying to get her way. "And wear the blue dress I bought you that you look so adorable in. You better not be late, Evelyn Anne!" With that, my mother hangs up.

"Goodbye to you too, Mother!" I snap into the already dead receiver.

As I set my phone down, I proceed to take long sips of wine staring across my living room and contemplate not even going at all. I laugh at the horror of putting my mother through anything like that and know if I want to live to see another day, the better option is to go.

Cynthia Monroe is as punctual as punctual could get. Growing up, my childhood home was immaculate. If you even sat at a chair in our front sitting room to put your shoes on, my mother would know the chair had been sat in and heaven forbid maybe moved.

Little annoyances like this are easy to laugh at now, which my brother and I do on a regular basis. Although living in that world day in and day out and having to be unnaturally perfect all the time was terrifying. I often wonder how my father puts up with it, but then I smile knowingly. One word: Scotch! Lots and lots of scotch!

I begin walking to my bedroom and dread every step I take, knowing it's leading me to a night I'd rather fast forward

CHAPTER 5

through. Right now all I want to do is slip into my frumpy comfy pj's and flop my butt on my couch. A fire in my fireplace, a big glass of wine, the cool fall breeze from an open window, and a chick flick marathon sounds more appealing than the night awaiting me at my parents' house.

Flicking on the light in my room, I start rummaging through my closet. I debate briefly doing what my mother requested and dare to wear that blue dress. Though always the rebel when it comes to her, I settle for a little black number that turns heads. It's fun and flirty. The glass of wine and call from my mother obviously left me feeling feisty. Maybe letting her think there is something between me and Trevor could be fun. Let the night begin!

Even though I don't like Trevor, I still enjoy the idea of making him drool all night. Plus, if I have to deal with my mother in her current state, I need to have a little fun. Not wearing what my mother so strictly tried to enforce will also give her the hint to stop trying to control my life. Not that I have much luck in that department; Mom hasn't stopped trying in twenty-seven years, and I know she probably won't stop anytime soon ... if ever.

Throwing on my dress, I grab some red heels to give the outfit a little extra kick. What the hell! What's the point in life if you aren't having fun right? My mother hates these heels; she insists they make me look like I'm asking for it. Totally a plus! One thing my twenty-seven years have taught me is to go big or go home, especially when it comes to annoying my mother. And tonight, between her and Trevor Roberts, this outfit is guaranteed to give me the upper hand.

Pulling my hair back in a ponytail, I start to freshen up my makeup and take a moment to savor my last few sips of wine.

Walking back to my kitchen, thoughts of a certain tall, dark, handsome southern gentleman consume my mind. I wonder what he would think of my tight black dress and "come get me" heels. Would it make him act a little less like a gentleman? Maybe he'd have the guts to pull another stunt like he did last night in the bar.

"Get over it, Ev. You're never going to see the guy again!" I say aloud, laughing at myself.

The brief fantasy makes me smile, yet pulls at all the wrong places and stirs up something I can't quite put my finger on inside of me. Even though I don't need a distraction right now, I can't deny the fact that I'd love a chance to be near him again.

I shake my head and tell myself to focus. Stick to my plan. Tempting distractions are not part of the plan.

Setting my glass down on the kitchen counter, I grab my keys, purse, and coat and start towards the door. Glancing back at the clock, I see I have exactly forty minutes to speed like mad towards my childhood home. Better not be late. I smile to myself as I lock my front door and head towards my car, knowing my mother can't handle my tardiness, the dress, and the shoes all in one night.

Chapter 6

Evelyn

My parents live in a town called Auburn, forty minutes south of Nevada City. Auburn and Nevada City are very similar to one another; both have a small old fashioned Main Street, surrounded by rolling hills and houses. Although Auburn definitely comes with many more amenities. Most of the drive to and from takes place along a two-lane highway through tall trees and endless countryside. Once I arrive in Auburn, a short drive through some of the old Main Street and up a few more rolling hills brings me to the home I grew up in.

My parents live in a suburban community called Ridge Crest. Huge houses sit side by side, perched up on hilltops, looking down on the people and cars passing through. Beautiful gardens and winding driveways bring you to the most beautiful custom-made homes. Each home is charmingly perfect in its own way and makes a statement of money, power, and prestige.

As I turn into my parents' driveway, I continued to feel smaller and more insignificant the further I drive up it. Glancing at the clock, I see it is 5:08. "Damn it!" I curse under my breath.

The house looms over me as I pull up to the front porch,

almost as if it is watching and judging my every move. Standing on the massive front porch, judging me right along with the house, is my mother with a glass of wine in her hand. She's reluctantly glaring at me as I pull to a stop.

My mother doesn't waste much time and is already descending the steps to meet me as I climb out of my car. I take a deep breath and exhale, readying myself for a battle that's obviously been brewing long before I even pulled up the driveway. Although I love my mother, I have already had a long day and don't feel like having it out with her tonight.

"What … are you … wearing?" is my mother's first demeaning comment. She reaches out and grabs a hold of my dress as I walk past, almost as if touching the dress will make her realization that I obviously didn't follow her strict instructions more obvious.

"Oh my God!" She gasps. "Those shoes, Evelyn!" she shouts as I walk up to the front door.

"I brought you more wine, Mother," I respond, waving the bottle in the air. I continue walking, trying to ignore the lecture that I know will pursue me if I dare pay her any attention. A smile spreads across my face as I quickly walk up each step. I know my mother is irate, but there is nothing she can do about it either.

"We always have enough wine, Evelyn," my mother continues to scold. "Is that why you're late? You took time for an unnecessary stop? Seriously, Evelyn Anne, you can be so inconsiderate!"

Ignoring the harassing comment with a roll of my eyes, I push open the front door and am immediately greeted by wagging tails and slobbery kisses. A black Pit Bull-Lab mix and Golden Retriever run towards me, the pair very oddly matched but very much a part of the family. I bend down and give each dog loving hugs and kisses. Reaching into my purse, I pull out treats I always keep on hand when I know I am coming to my parents. The dogs accept the treats enthusiastically and run off.

Frank Sinatra's "Luck be a Lady" fills the background, soft and low on the whole house speakers. It smells of Thanksgiving dinner and expensive scented candles. My dad comes out of the family room situated straight off the foyer. Scotch in hand, he's grinning from ear to ear.

"There she is," he says, almost singing.

"Hey, Daddy!" I smile back, hurrying towards him for the bear hug I know always awaits me. He smells like tobacco and Doublemint gum, a fragrance that I have grown accustomed to over the years. Like his hugs, it has also come to hold a sense of comfort for me. He gives me a kiss on my forehead, and I let him hug me tight like he did when I was a little girl.

"She's late, David," my mother snaps, closing the front door behind her.

She proceeds to stand there, tapping her foot on the tile, obviously waiting for my father to agree that being late is the most absurdly vile thing one could be. I roll my eyes and look at my father, pleading. He smiles, looking back with understanding.

"She didn't miss anything, Cynthia," he says without taking his eyes off mine. "Come on, now, let's get you a drink, Evie." He winks at me reassuringly and drapes his arm across my shoulders as he leads the way into the family room.

Once in the room, I notice most of the guests are spread out, already deep in conversation. Setting my purse down on the couch, I follow my dad to the bar in the back of the room. I sit down and roll my shoulders, trying to relax into the evening the best I can.

My brother, Michael, has brought a date and is busy talking between her and his best friend, Rex Roberts. Gloria and Don Roberts are in the corner talking to Trevor and raise their glasses to me in a hello gesture. Gwen's parents stand alongside them and wave to me as well. Trevor looks over, and I can't ignore the intense longing in his expression—so much so that it makes me uneasy. Although he seems more nervous than anything ... for what reason, I absolutely don't know. I nod in return and settle into my seat at the bar in front of my father.

"Pick your poison, baby girl," he says, picking up a bottle of Johnny Walker and filling his glass to the brim.

"Red wine, Daddy, and keep them coming!" I smile back.

He nods, setting my glass down and filling it almost to the very top. Winking once more, he leans in closer. "A little liquid courage to deal with that hotheaded mother of yours."

I laugh as I catch my mother's very disapproving glance from across the room. My dad immediately wanders off in my mother's direction just as I'm joined by my brother, his date, and Rex. Rex comes up right behind me, grabbing me tightly around my waist and kissing me on the cheek!

"Wow-eee, you get better looking every time I see you!" he hollers loud and obnoxiously, taking a seat next to me at the bar.

"Really, Rex, that's so gross! I don't know where your lips have been," I say, wiping his kiss away. "Besides, I'm like the little sister you never had." I roll my eyes and smack him on the arm.

"I just like to watch that one squirm." Rex laughs, jabbing his thumb in the direction of Trevor, who is now hatefully staring back at his older brother. He kisses the top of my head in the most brotherly of ways and takes a seat next to me at the bar.

"You're a twisted, twisted man, Rex Roberts!" I giggle. He winks knowingly and continues taking very long sips of his beer while his gaze surveys the room. He appears to be looking for something, or someone, which catches me as odd, and I wonder if he, too, might have brought a date—which would be completely out of character as I have only ever met one girl in the long history that I have known him. And to say that they were actually dating is a long shot.

Rex and I have more of a brother-sister relationship than the one I have with my own brother. We laugh and joke in ways Michael and I never do. When my brother disapproves of my poor life choices, Rex is right there for a shoulder to cry on, an ear to listen, and a best friend to kick anyone's ass that ever dared to mess with me. I have always thought our comradery was due to the fact that I was more like my father and Michael was more like my condescending mother, always ready to look down on someone that wasn't exactly up to their standards. I never could understand why, being so different, the two boys got along so well.

I cherish the brotherly love Rex gives me, especially when it lacks from my own brother. Rex is one of my most favorite people in the world. Nothing anywhere close to romance has ever happened between us, just pure love for each other in a best-friendship kind of way.

"So, Little Sister," my brother Michael says, clearing his throat with emphasis and putting his arm around his date, "when did you get home?"

"About an hour and a half ago," I reply, taking a sip of my

wine. "Who's the girl?" I ask, staring straight at my brother and his date.

I'm fully aware that the girl is, in fact, standing right in front of me and can hear me and answer for herself if she wanted to, but girls like her never do; they just stare off into space, completely dumbfounded.

"This is Amber," he replies, staring straight down into Amber's massive cleavage displayed so boldly I'm sure the neighbors can even see it clearly on display.

Amber just smiles, almost as oblivious to his staring at her fake boobs as she is to my rude question moments earlier. Michael has a similar taste in women as Rex does; their motto is the stupider, the easier, the more fake and plastic the better.

My theory is this is their protection against long-term commitment. The girls Michael and Rex date are momentary pit stops on their life journey. Neither one of them have any intention of making them last longer than a few weeks tops. This apparent comradery, I've decided after all these years, is perhaps exactly what makes their life-long friendship last.

"So ..." Michael continues his focus now back on me. "How was the OC?"

"You were down south?" Rex butts in. "No way! I was there too, just got back last night!"

"I just went down to see Gwen," I tell my brother. "Just a few uneventful days, nothing big ..."

Rex cuts me off almost instinctively, "Gwen! Really! How's she doing? Is she still dating that douche bag from a few years back?" He pops open another beer then goes through the motions of pouring me a water. He knows me too well; I pretend I can handle my liquor, but he's taken care of me on one too many nights where I ended up more talk than show.

"Since when do you care?" I ask and notice a subtle hurt expression cross his face. "We spent last night at Longboards …"

"What the hell! We were there last night too!" Rex exclaims, cutting me off again. The mention of "we" that escapes his lips doesn't slip past me. "I didn't see you guys, though!"

"Strange," I manage, wondering who he was with last night. "The place isn't that big."

"Well, I was kind of wasted," Rex confesses. A very annoyed expression comes across his face as he continues. "I spent most of the night shacked up with some girl in a back booth and now she won't stop calling my phone…" he almost shudders, closing his eyes, obviously now scarred from the experience "…but still, what the hell!"

"You already said what the hell." I laugh as Rex rounds the bar once more and takes his seat next to me. His back is against the counter as he surveys the room once more. Glancing back at me, he smiles a mischievous kind of smile that I have seen before, and it's one that always means trouble.

"We all could have hung out," he persists. "Three's a crowd, but four's a party!" He nudges me, trying to make a point, but I'm utterly and completely lost. I have absolutely no clue what he is talking about. It wouldn't be the first time, and it won't be the last.

"You, me, and Gwen would still only make three, Rex!" I assert, annoyed. "And who, do you presume, would be the fourth?"

Turning around, I face the direction Rex is, just in time to see the one person I never thought I would ever see again. A million thoughts rush through my brain, and I immediately feel my cheeks flush. My hands spontaneously start to tremble.

I whip around as fast as I can and sit down with my glass. With wide eyes, I stare down at the bar and wonder what's the best next move to take as my heart thuds against my chest and my palms sweat. Rex catches on as I glance up and see my brother, luckily caught up in some sort of conversation with his date.

"Hey, what's wrong?" Rex asks. "You look as if you've seen a ghost!"

"Noah?" I whisper.

Chapter 7

Noah

Standing in the Monroe family restroom, washing my hands, I look up at my reflection in the mirror and repeat to myself, "Just a few more hours, you got this!"

I turn around and dry my hands on towels that look way too fancy to even be touched. Shaking my head at how some people choose to live, I ready myself for the night ahead. Opening the door, I walk back to join the party in the living room, which is on the very opposite side of this very vast suburban house.

Rex had been trying to get me up to the Monroes' house for dinner since I had first arrived in northern California. Rex grew up with the Monroe family and wanted me to like them as much as he and his parents did. Every time he asked me to join him for dinner, I had politely refused. Spending time learning how the upper middle class enjoyed their liberties was not something I ever desired to do in my life.

Normally, upon invitation, I would have refused again. This time, though, Rex played the mother card against me, knowing that my plan was to decline once more. Rex hadn't even asked if I'd go but rather had me answer the door when his parents showed up unexpectedly. Rex's mom gave me such a hard time and promised a fun evening. When that didn't work, she gave me grief by saying how much she wished I would meet their family friends at least one time while I lived in California. I eventually caved, and fifteen minutes later, I found myself in the car driving to the house and the family I had tried to avoid since moving out here.

I had met Michael Monroe a few times before and knew he and Rex had some sort of bond. They've been friends since they were in elementary school. I can't say I mind the guy, but I wouldn't say he and I are destined to be friends—or even best friends like Rex and I are. Michael has an air about him that eludes to the fact that he thinks he's better than everyone else. I rarely spend time in people's company that hold such high opinions of themselves.

Entering the living room, I can hear banter and laughter coming from the bar at the back end of the room. I know Michael's younger sister is supposed to be at dinner, and if she is half as condescending as Michael is, I'll need something stronger than beer to survive the night.

Tell me again why I agreed to come tonight?

Michael, I can maybe deal with, but fake plastic chicks that flip their hair and bat their eyelashes at everything ... I thought I had escaped that last night driving home!

There is one exception, though. Her. Good Lord, I can't shake her from my head. And damn it, I didn't want to. She'll be the center of every fantasy of mine for a long ass time—and one I've indulged in more than I care to admit since she left me standing there, needing answers, in the middle of Longboards.

Our connection. Our chemistry. Hell, the way I saw and felt her body react to mine. The girl from last night seems only a dream, but I know it was real and find myself willing to give

CHAPTER 7

anything if promised one last chance with her.

Evelyn hadn't left my mind, and I wasn't expecting she would anytime soon. I hadn't felt anything like the way she made me feel in a long time, and the thought of where we could've gone given the chance is enough to shake me from my fantasizes long enough to regain a little sanity before she pulls me back under again.

Nothing could have prepared me for who I see sitting at the bar alongside Rex, laughing and joking and leaving me absolutely blown away. I stand for a moment, drinking her in and silently thanking God that I agreed to come tonight.

No way in hell! How could I get this lucky? I know I've just been handed the lottery of second chances and can't wait a second longer to collect my winnings.

As I approach the bar, she turns and looks me straight in the eye then nervously swivels herself back around, giving me a perfect view of how her slender waist gives way to perfect round hips that fit snugly in a tight black dress. My mind wanders as I imagine she wore it just for me.

I hear her whisper, "Noah?" And the way she says my name leaves me immediately more aroused in her presence. I begin to think of her sighing it as I do the things to her that I have been fantasying about since last night. I want to indulge in every curve and touch every sensitive spot on her sexy as sin body if only she'd let me.

"Lucky guess or is there something I should know?" Rex playfully asks, completely oblivious to the truth in his own question.

Once again, I find myself staring at Evelyn, not knowing who should speak first. Speechless and stunned, we both seem at a loss for words. Although, this time I don't feel like I'm the one that has any explaining to do.

Cocking up one eyebrow, I smile at her when she glances over her shoulder at me. Seeing her face blush makes me wonder how she would look breathless and flushed, on top of me, underneath me, hell even looking back at me— I have to stop myself from taking my thoughts to the next level as she looks me in the eye once again.

God, she's gorgeous. I'd take her any way I could get her if she would only let me.

Evelyn turns around to face me and time drags on anxiously as she sits, not taking her eyes off mine, which starts to make me a little nervous. I'm not one that suffers from anxiety, but I suddenly felt like the walls are slowly closing in. It's as if everyone else is sucking all the oxygen out of the room, leaving me lightheaded.

Last night after she left, I talked myself into the fantasy that she'd want to see me again ... but does she? Maybe I had misread our chemistry. Fear I may be right makes it impossible to think straight as I look back at her eyes.

"Oh no, we've met!" Evelyn says finally as a sly smile spreads across her face, one that instinctively matches my own. "Fancy meeting you here, Noah," she continues overdramatically. "You had to be the last person I thought I'd run into tonight."

"Likewise." I smile back, exhaling a breath I didn't know I was holding. It's not the greeting that I fantasized about and played over and over in my mind while lying in bed last night and this morning, but it isn't a slap in the face either.

I see Rex out of the corner of my eye, looking at the two of us in disbelief, his head turning to Evelyn first then to me then back to Evelyn. Obviously in an extreme state of shock, his mouth falls open as he tries to understand what's going on between two of his best friends.

"Noah, you want another beer?" Michael calls out from behind the bar, and I silently thank God for his tiny distraction.

"I'd love another beer," I reply, smiling at Evelyn, pushing between her and Rex to take a seat at the bar beside her. Not sure how I have been lucky enough to end up in this situation, but I silently promise myself I'll do everything in my power to not let this girl escape me again.

"This is that friend of mine that moved out with me after college," Rex starts to explain. He immediately changes the topic, obviously thinking our story is the one needing more explanation. "Excuse me, though," Rex says, shaking his head and sounding completely puzzled. "How and where have you two met before? I've been trying to get him over here for months now, but he always refuses."

Evelyn's eyebrows shoot up and her smile spreads across her lips. I stare a little too long at her mouth, remembering her taste and wanting to do anything just to be able to savor her once again. Looking up, I notice she is looking right at me, her blue eyes pulling me in like a magnet. Catching me in my fantasy, I can tell she knows exactly what I'm thinking I'd be lying if I said I even cared.

"So, you think you're too good for us huh?" she asks, teasing me. God, what I wouldn't do to tease her back, watch her body rise into a frenzy of need like the way she makes me feel. Slowing, I take my time torturing her senses in the best way imaginable.

"Well, if I would have known you'd be here, I definitely would have come a lot sooner." I wink at her, shocked by my own confidence. I take a sip of my beer, never breaking eye contact. I make it a long sip, hoping it will calm the nerves I feel rising inside me with each second that passes.

Her sexuality exudes back at me as she leans forward on the bar, and I unintentionally glance down at her cleavage pushed up just enough to make me want to see more. Glancing back up, she provocatively replies, "But then that wouldn't have given us that wild and crazy night in the bar now would it?" She winks slowly, licking her lips for an added effect that has my heart beating out of chest. I catch my breath. Damn it, does she know what a turn-on that is? I'd love to give her wild and crazy, slow and sweet, or any way that she likes as long as I'm the one giving it to her.

"Whoa ... whoa ... whoa! Now, what the hell did I miss?" Rex shouts, breaking my train of thought. He takes a few steps back from the bar and all of us, eyes wide in astonishment. If Rex was surprised before, our witty banter now must leave his head spinning.

Evelyn throws her head back, laughing at his comment, making me notice once again the unintentional way she captivates everyone's attention in the room. Every ounce of this woman is alluring, and I would do anything for the chance to explore every bit of her further all night long.

Rex's brother Trevor has made his way over to the group during our conversation and takes the empty seat on the other side of Evelyn. I watch as Trevor seems to respond the same way I do to her charm. I can't deny the jealous tug that immediately starts to build inside of me. What the hell is this? Back off, Trev! If I would have known this little brat was all over trying to get a piece of her too, I would have never declined a dinner invitation, making sure to have staked my claim a long time ago. The thought alone startles because it's been a very long time since I have let any woman have any kind of effect over me.

"Don't get too excited." She giggles. "Nothing like what you would consider wild and crazy, Rex. He saved me from ... shall we say ... your typical bar rat ..." She looks at me for confirmation, to which I nod and watch as Trevor scoots his chair a little bit too close to her for my liking.

"You know," she continues, "the type that can't keep their hands off. Thinks no means yes and that every girl is asking for it."

I close my eyes and remember the encounter well. The surge I felt to protect her then and the unexplainable draw to her, I still feel now.

"Want me to make you another one, Sis?" Evelyn's brother asks. She nods, and I watch as she finishes her drink. She pulls a cherry out from a dish on the bar and plops it in her mouth. As her mouth closes around the stem, I fight the urge to push her back against the bar and taste the cherry flavor on her tongue. The thought makes me more aroused than I already am, and I have to turn away slightly to gather my thoughts.

"I would have saved you," Trevor mumbles under his breath, low enough to only be intended for Evelyn's ears but loud enough for me to hear it as well. The comment jolts me back to the present as I turn towards the two of them. She smiles at him and Trevor longingly smiles back.

Yup, it's confirmed. This guy thinks he can just roll up and stake claim to what I intend to make mine. Game on! Sorry, Trev! This is one time I will make sure in every way I can that you don't have a chance.

"So, how's business?" Evelyn asks Rex and Michael.

Her brother and Rex had opened a nightclub in Auburn about a year ago when Rex and I returned home from school. The two of them had always talked about going into business together, and now that they both have degrees, and money isn't an issue due to their well-off family names, they pursued their childhood dream and recently opened up one of the biggest watering holes this side of the Mississippi River.

Gatsby's sits on top of a large hill in Old Town Auburn. It's an upscale lounge made to look vintage with an art deco edge. As if the town of Auburn always needed and wanted a place like Gatsby's, the club's popularity came quick, and word spread through Auburn and neighboring towns fast. Anybody who wanted to be seen and known about town flocked to Gatsby's on a regular if not almost nightly basis, drinking and schmoozing their nights away in a way that would make even Gatsby himself proud.

I made it a point not to frequent there often. I'd heard enough stories from Rex, when he pulled himself home in the early morning hours, to know that it wasn't anywhere I needed or rather wanted to be.

"I still love that you took the name I suggested," Evelyn says. "It's masculine with just enough lustful edge."

"Anything to make the ladies lustful," Rex jokes. "There was this one that came in the other night with the biggest ass and perfect—"

"OK, on another note," Evelyn loudly interrupts, making Rex laugh.

"Business is great as always," Michael interjects. "We're about to have our first holiday season. We've planned a lot of special events. It should be impressive. Maybe you should write about it. Put it in the paper and help your brother out!"

"We'll talk this week, and I'll get the details. We have the next edition of the magazine coming up, and I know Rob has been wanting to create more articles to bring in younger readers. I'm sure he would be all over it," Evelyn suggests.

"Wait, you're a writer?" I ask, intrigued and slightly turned on the more I learn about her, her life. A writer's sexy. I can imagine her in glasses, clicking away on her keyboard, deep in thought late at night and writing about things I know nothing about. I'll gladly show her some things to help inspire her.

"I am. Majored in journalism. What's your superpower?" she jokes.

"I work best with my hands," I tease, looking her deep in the eye then watch as her cheeks turn the loveliest shade of pink. She glances at my hands and has to be thinking what I'm thinking. I'd love to run them all over her body as much as she looks like she wants to feel them. Taking my time, I'd be sure to memorize every curve.

"Construction, mostly." I laugh and see her wiggle in her seat, trying to regain her train of thought. "Mostly odd jobs to keep me and my hands busy," I joke. "Although back home I worked at the local fire station."

Leaning in, she whispers, "Maybe one day you can show me just how skilled your hands are."

Holy hell. She has no idea. I'm seconds away from saying screw it and damn all the people in the room. I'll show just how these hands want to control that body of hers, but Rex cuts off my train of thought as he comes around the bar and pops open yet another beer. He does the same for Trevor, who is staring me down. If looks could kill, I'd be a dead man.

Man up, Trev! I don't know your history here, but there is no way I am going to let you be her future.

"Noah here is still finishing up his degree online back at U of M," Rex fills Evelyn in. "We're trying to get him to help with an addition at the club. He's majoring in business and wants to open his own construction company, but we can't talk him into sticking ..."

"Hey, Michael," I exclaim loudly. "Didn't you say Amber's parents might be needing to hire someone for an addition on their outdoor deck?"

I don't know what has come over me. I'm sure Rex was about to mention me moving home. It's not like I've changed my mind. No doubt about it, I'm moving back to Kentucky almost as soon as I can arrange for it. But for some reason I can't quite understand, I don't want Evelyn knowing. I want to keep that to myself, just a little bit longer.

Michael is about to respond when David, Evelyn's father, returns to the bar and huddles around the back of Evelyn and Rex. Poking his head in the middle of our group's endless chitchat, he looks at us with a wide lazy grin.

"Time to come and get it, kids. You don't want to make that wife of mine angry. I'm not running interference for you this time," he says.

I watch as all the "kids" in question quickly finish their drinks and stand, obviously ready to please in any way they can, especially if it means avoiding the wrath of Mrs. Cynthia Monroe. Even though this is my first time meeting the lady, she already makes me nervous enough to never want to step out of line.

Rex and Trevor head off first, and I notice Trevor looks back with jealousy as Evelyn stands up and walks alongside me. The air between us is electric. We fall into a comfortable silence. Every few steps, she glances my way. I haven't taken my eyes off her once. She smiles at me every time our eyes meet, and when she does, it adds another layer to the endless

CHAPTER 7

sexual tension that's been building between the two of us since yesterday.

Michael and Amber trail behind last. When we reach the doorway to the dining room, I pause and wait for Evelyn to pass through first. Half of the reason being my momma raised me to have good manners and the other, I'd be lying if it wasn't also to stare at the beautiful body of hers. Every one of her curves has me salivating and licking my lips.

"Ladies first," I say confidently as I place my hand on the small of her back and lead her through. I let my hand slip a little too far south and watch as she looks back at me, giving me a look that makes me dare to take it further. Whoever invented ladies first was definitely an ass man; my compliments to him as I watch the amazing view in front of me.

I feel a spark when I touch her—the same spark I first felt last night—and feel lucky as hell to have the opportunity to be able to feel again. Damn it, she has no clue just how bad I want her. All of her. The thought scares me. I promised myself I'd never again allow myself to feel like this.

"Chivalry. I like it," she says, leaning back a little into my touch, and that right there is almost my undoing. I can hardly contain the urge to grab her right here with everyone watching and push her and that tiny excuse for a skirt up as I hold her against the door frame.

"I don't get it," Amber says from behind us, bringing my attention back to the present. "I thought your name was Noah? Who's chivalry?"

Evelyn and I try to hide our laughs best we can, but they bubble over as we find our seats at the table. Michael looks embarrassed and quickly ushers his date away to find their seats as well. I settle in across the table from Evelyn and can't tear my eyes away from hers to even notice the people setting platters of food on the table. Oh, I am hungry alright, but the only thing that can satisfy me is staring right back into my eyes and making me think nothing more than tasting and savoring every last drop of her like it's my last meal.

Chapter 8

Evelyn

It's a very typical dinner in the Monroe house. My mother has hired help to cater to the family and our guests while they eat. I know my mother likes to do this for two reasons: one is to show off and the other is she's a traditionalist and secretly thinks times should have never changed; in her world, maids and hired help are always in style. After all, the help Cynthia Monroe hires assists her in maintaining her extremely organized, clean, prompt, everything-in-its-place lifestyle. There's no way you'd see this type of woman running back and forth from the kitchen, waiting on her quests while also trying to play the perfect hostess. But that sure would be hysterical to watch!

I sit across from Noah, next to Amber. From time to time, I try and talk to my brother's date, although the conversation never goes any further than one word responses. It's hard to carry on a conversation with another person if they are incapable of even having one in the first place. Women like Amber, who are all body, typically have no brains to go along with it.

Occasionally, I look up at Noah to find him already staring back at me. I smile at him and he smiles even bigger. I wonder what he must be thinking because he never seems to take his eyes off of me long enough to eat his dinner.

His look is so intense I feel slightly nervous under his gaze. It's like he's slowly undressing me with his eyes. Licking his lips from time to time and making the room feel hotter and hotter with each moment we lock our eyes. Even though I don't mind, it makes it hard for me to concentrate on anything other than the look he gives me and the way it makes me feel: sexy, excited, and thinking about things way too racy for a family dinner party.

At times my gaze drifts over to Trevor, who sits next to Noah and seems to be growing more and more irritated. He fidgets in his seat every time Noah and I hold a stare, obviously upset at whatever might be between the two of us. If Trevor notices the spark between us, maybe everyone else does as well.

If our chemistry is so obvious it can't be contained, even for a simple dinner, then maybe there is something more to the idea of Noah. Maybe this is something that I should pursue. After all, no one has ever made me feel the way Noah does. Like an electric current is running through my veins, vibrating and pleasuring me in a way that becomes more and more addicting with each passing moment.

Imagining Noah and I taking things further fills me with an excitement I am not sure I have ever felt before. I haven't been in a relationship with anyone in over a year and a half.

My last relationship ended as a result of it probably never should have started. I told the guy I had loved him, and we spent almost two years of our lives together. Although, the longer the relationship lasted, the more I wanted out of it. I finally came to the realization that the reason I hadn't ended it sooner was because of boredom. There were no other options

CHAPTER 8

available at the time. I came to the conclusion I was in love with the idea of love but not actually in love with the man himself. When everything finally hit the fan, he agreed, and the two of us separated and never actually spoke again.

And although I sense a pattern with my love life, my ex and then Trevor, I sum it up to being focused and not allowing anything to derail or deter me from achieving my goals. Some things are non-negotiable.

Single life is refreshing. It allows self-growth, maturity, and strength. I'm on a good path now and determined to see my dreams become reality. Noah might just be a curve ball that I am not sure I can handle. Taking things further might be too risky. But then why do I feel myself already needing my next fix?

Looking up again and admiring the man across the table from me, I start to feel my resolve crumble and tiny barriers start breaking away. Maybe a little fun is ok? How bad could it be? As long as I don't let my heart get too close, why can't I explore all the ways he drives me mad with need just standing in the same room as him?

As dinner comes to a close, plates are cleared and coffee is set in front of those who want or need it. I start to feel antsy for the opportunity to be alone with Noah for the first time. I quickly sip my coffee and watch as one by one people start to leave the table.

Noah still hasn't gotten up. He's in a lively conversation with Rex and has obviously said something hysterical because Rex almost shoots beer out of his nose, laughing. I want to be in on their conversation, but they are talking too low on the other side of the table for me to even pick up the slightest bit of what's so funny. Still, I keep my ear trained towards them, hoping to catch what I can.

"You all finished, Evelyn?" Trevor asks, startling me out of my daydream. I'd been so drawn to the conversation in front of me with Rex and Noah that I hadn't noticed Trevor still sitting at the table.

"Yeah, sure am," I reply, smiling, wanting to be polite but not wanting to give the impression that there could ever be anything between the two of us again.

"Your mom said she was going to have someone light up the fire pit on the back patio." Trevor looks down at the table and then up again. It's almost like he's too shy and embarrassed to even look me in the eye, which is silly because we have known each other since we were kids.

"Want to go and see if it's lit? We haven't done that in years. I can grab you a blanket, and we can snag some drinks from the bar on our way," he urgently and very silently asks, not wanting to be heard by the others at the table.

Normally on any other night I would have said no. Sitting around a fire pit, under a blanket, with drinks on a cool fall night is not your typical way of letting a guy know you're not interested. However, the thought of leaving with Trevor makes me realize it might make Noah notice me once again.

"I'd love to," I exclaim, rising from the table as if Trevor has just suggested the greatest idea that I'd heard all evening.

Noah immediately breaks from speaking and watches as I round the table and walk out of the room with Trevor. Rex is still talking, but it's obvious that Noah hasn't heard a single word.

Trevor must have been just as shocked as Noah. His mouth falls open at my response. Then he jumps from his seat so fast he turns his chair upside down. Quickly, he sets it back

CHAPTER 8

up straight and scrambles around the table to meet me, even having the guts to hold onto my arm as we exit the dining room and head towards the backyard. I'm tempted to look back and see Noah's face, but when playing a game, a true winner never lets the opponent sense any sort doubt.

As we reach the patio, Trevor's nerves are at an all-time high. "You go sit. I'll run and grab a few drinks and something to keep you warm," he says, fumbling with his words.

"Actually, I'm kind of wined out. Could you just grab me some hot tea or something?" I plead as I try to slyly look past him to see if anyone has followed the two of us. Disappointment hits as I don't see anyone in the shadows inside, and I try to hide it as I look back at Trevor, who is so obviously excited for this opportunity I'm quickly regretting.

"Of course, anything for you, Ev," Trevor says endearingly. "I'll grab the peppermint one you always drink. I won't be long, I promise." He backs up, falling over a chair, barely catching his footing before turning and almost breaking into a run. He doesn't even notice the slider door is shut but catches himself, quickly grabbing the handle and stepping inside, trying to cover up his clumsiness.

I giggle under my breath. Even if I don't like Trevor, he does mean well. He's always so attentive, and I feel sorry for the guy because I will never feel the same. His attention has always felt like a blessing, somehow reaching me when I feel my lowest. It's the very reason why I never completely say no but never wholeheartedly say yes either. It's hard to turn down something that helps boost your self-esteem, even if you never attend for it to go anywhere further.

Fumbling with my iPhone, I decide music is what's missing. The speakers had been turned off during dinner. Selecting a

Frank Sinatra station on Pandora, I snuggle down in the chair, wrapping my arms around myself to keep warm until Trevor returns. My thoughts drift, and I began to wonder how long it will take for Noah to find his way out to the patio—or if he even will at all. Maybe he doesn't play games and is on to sudden schemes.

What if I made a mistake?

Fear and anxiety rise up inside, and my stomach starts to turn sour. Fidgeting in my seat, I debate going back inside and almost get up, but then I hear the slider door to the patio open. Great! I can't leave now.

The realization there is no way I want to ruin any chance of something happening between Noah and me takes over immediately. The thought is scary and all too real, but I know even if I try to fight it, this is a battle I have a good chance of losing. Keep your head straight, Evelyn, I tell myself. If you're not going to get to close, why are you worried about ruining anything?

I stare at the flames in the fire pit and count the seconds until Trevor is at my side. I'm half in the moment and half back at that dining table as I try to think of a way to fix this—if I have in fact just screwed up my chances.

Hearing footsteps, I look to the left, out across the yard, and let out a big sigh. It's colder than I had expected, and I know just who I want to be snuggled up next to me to keep me warm—and it isn't Trevor.

"Has anyone ever told you how thrilling and gorgeous you look by firelight?" His low husky voice is a whisper as the wood crackles in the fire pit.

Turning, I see Noah hovering over me. His eyes dancing with desire, I immediately exhale breathing in an all too

CHAPTER 8

overwhelming sense of relief. It sure as hell doesn't look like I scared him off, and I thank my lucky stars for that. He doesn't say another word. Swallowing hard, I try to hide my happiness behind what I am sure is a very poor poker face.

"Want to sit down?" I say as I watch the light from the fire dance across his expression—as if he needs any more help in looking absolutely irresistible.

"Absolutely nothing I'd like more." He smiles. He doesn't take his eyes off mine, and I somehow manage to never take mine off his as he moves past me and sits in the seat next to me—the seat I know Trevor is hoping for but am beyond grateful that Noah beat him to it.

As if the music knows exactly what tune should be selected, ol' blue eyes starts singing, "The Way You Look Tonight." Half embarrassed and half impressed that somehow the music has lined up so perfectly, I glance down at my phone and noticed Noah do the same. Looking back up, we share a smile for a few moments before he glances down at my phone again. He raises his eyebrows and smirks at me.

"I can change it," I say, hurrying to grab my phone and growing more embarrassed by the second—not embarrassed that I listened to this kind of music, more at the idea that I don't want him getting any ideas I've somehow set this up.

He rests his hand on mine right as I go to grab my phone. "No, it's nice. Not what I would have picked myself, but … fitting," he says with a slight laugh effortlessly escaping his gorgeous mouth. He runs his free hand through his hair, and I sit still, realizing my need to be feeling his thick locks between my fingertips.

What is coming over me? How does this man make me feel this way?

I can't help but notice he continues to hold onto my hand and doesn't give the impression that he ever intends to let it go. Blushing, I look down at my lap and smile. Every time we touch, it's electric, shocking my whole body and only intensifying as he slowly starts rubbing his thumb across the back of my hand. His grip tightens slightly. God, I am in trouble. Big, gorgeous, irresistible, tempting man trouble.

"What kind of music do you listen to, then?" I ask, still not looking up to meet his stare. His confidence has made me shy and vulnerable. I'm not sure at this very moment I find it hard to take the intensity of his stare up close.

"Country mostly, although I have a brief knowledge of the classics," Noah says. His admission shocks me. I look up and meet his eyes just in time to see him nod towards the music playing.

"Country, huh? You telling me you're some sort of cowboy? Wouldn't have pegged you for that," I confess, raising an eyebrow.

As he meets my eyes, the butterflies deep down inside start to intensify once again, and I find myself quickly looking down, embarrassed and shy that I said the wrong thing. Eventually, my eyes catch sight of the shoes he's wearing: the boots I first noticed in the bar. I wonder how I hadn't noticed they were cowboy boots or how I hadn't put that together with the tight flannel shirt and dark blue jeans he's wearing tonight.

Maybe in my world cowboys always wore big brimmed hats and smelled like horses and sweat, not the woodsy, perfect kind of musky smell that makes up Noah. This southern country boy shocks the hell out of me and makes me question every first impression I ever had before. He's some sort of something I never expected, but some sort of something I'm beginning to

CHAPTER 8

crave, and that could be very dangerous.

"Oh, so now it's your turn to be surprised!" he says, smiling a little too big and leaning in closer. It's obvious he likes—a little too much—how he's able to hold one up on me for the first time since we've met. The very thought of which makes me nervous and undeniably unsure of myself.

Feeling like I said the wrong thing yet again, I realize I want more than anything to make a good impression on the type of man I always avoided and now suddenly want to know better than any man before. Maybe country boys aren't that bad. This one sure beats any city boy who ever tried to get my attention before. He could be just what I've always needed.

I eventually find words. "Well, I didn't say it was a bad thing. I've never been this close to a country boy before, but there is a first time for everything isn't there?" I'm still not sure if that's the right thing to say or not, and it has me nervously tapping my foot against the ground and looking around the backyard.

"You've also never been this close to a southern boy before, darlin', remember?" His accent thickens and his drawl slows with his response. God that's sexy. The way he pours on his thick southern accent heats me up and makes every part of my body tingle. He can make fun of me all he wants as long as he continues to talk to me like that again.

Not knowing what to say, I decide to give in to him as he wins this battle of wits. I look at him with a ruffled brow and a sly smile. A low seductive chuckle escapes his lips as his grip on my hand slightly tightens again. What I wouldn't do to close the distance between the two of us. All I want to do right now is crash into him and never look back. To taste what my body has been craving. To indulge in what I know it's wanted since we separated last night.

Why do I fight it?

Oh yeah, my plans, my future. Head straight, focus.

But hell if all I have to focus on is his eyes staring right back at me, wanting me as much as I am trying to deny that I want him, then this is going to be one hell of a struggle.

His lip curls up on one side when he notices me lick my lips. My heart quickens, and I can feel his warm breath against my cheek as he leans in closer.

"What did I tell you before? I can show you some things that would most definitely change your mind about us country boys," he suggests as his eyes drift to my lips and he moves in even closer. I can smell the alcohol on his breath and long to taste it on his lips. "We can get started right now if you're willing."

Catching my breath, I notice how my body involuntarily moves closer to him, like there's a force between us that makes us yield to its will—a force I know we will never have any control over.

"I might just take you up on that offer," I whisper back.

At this moment there is only the two of us. The music has even faded in the background as we close the distance between us, little by little, more and more. I breathe in slightly just as we become close enough that I feel the heat of his breath on my lips. I look up and catch him do the same. Our eyes meet as we are seconds away from a connection I know both of our bodies crave. Need. Want.

"Here's your tea, Evelyn."

Breaking away from our trance, I turn to see Trevor standing a few feet away. He has my tea in one hand and my blanket in the other. He looks hurt and disgusted like he's just been slapped in the face and punched in the gut at the same time.

CHAPTER 8

Immediately, I feel my heart break for him, and I feel horrible for having used him.

"Trevor, I'm so sorry." Ashamed, I snatched my hand from Noah's and rise to grab my drink. "Thank you so much. I really do appreciate it," I say, resting my hand on his shoulder, although he immediately shrugs it off. I can honestly say I don't blame him at all.

"Do you want to join us?" I feel stupid for even asking, not knowing if he actually would say yes or no but not knowing what else to say as well. Trevor looks at Noah for a moment, and I know he's debating it. I wouldn't blame him if he turned around and walked right back inside. His ego has to be bruised. He never got up the nerve to take his feelings to the next step with me, but for some reason, he sure has the confidence to do so tonight. And now I've made him regret it.

"I'm not trying to intrude," he says, directly at Noah. I can feel the hate in the glare the two of them exchange.

I don't know what else to do, so I just stand in front of him, as if not sitting back down next to Noah would make up for what he just walked in on. I wasn't trying to lead Trevor on, but given our history and our families' friendship, I don't want to hurt him either.

"Nah, grab a seat. There is plenty of room," Noah says.

I look back at Noah and can't tell if he's oblivious, cocky, confident, or maybe a little of all three. His eyes never leave Trevor's, his jaw set tight with an intensity that makes me question his reasoning for asking Trevor to stay.

Looking back, I make sure to look Trevor in the eye to emphasize my apology once again. I take the blanket from him as he chooses a chair across from me instead of the one next to me that I know he had his heart set. Sitting back down, I place my tea on the table next to me and then wrap the blanket around my legs. I smile at Trevor from across the fire; he sadly looks back my way before directing his attention to something off in the distance.

I take a moment before looking back at Noah, and when I do, I notice his attention is still directed only towards Trevor. Instead of the lust that washed over his expression minutes before, there is something else present. I can't deny the sense of irritation, jealousy, and challenge radiating off him.

Without taking his eyes off Trevor, Noah reaches back over and grabs my hand. He's marking his territory, and even though I'm startled with this sudden display of ownership, I let him, not only because I feel compelled to but because the possession that suddenly flashes through Noah's gaze leaves me feeling all sorts of weak in the knees and incredibly turned on. He's claiming me in front of Trevor like I want him to do in private. God if that isn't the sexiest thing.

Suddenly I notice Rex, Michael, and Amber making their way through the doors to join us, and I'm thankful more people will be around to break up the tension that has formed on the patio. The back patio at my parents' house is huge, although in the last few minutes it has felt like the smallest little box in the world. I'm usually good at breaking up awkwardness, but I have no clue what I would have done had it not been for their sudden entrance.

"I guess this is where the party's at," Rex shouts, stumbling awkwardly towards me. "Change that boring music! What the hell are you listening to, woman?" he says, making his way towards my phone and grabbing it with such force I'm surprised it doesn't fall out of his hands. It wouldn't be the first time Rex has broken one of my phones while he's been

CHAPTER 8

drinking.

    Closing one eye to focus on the object in his hand, he selects a classic rock station and starts dancing around like an idiot, doing his best air guitar impression as the patio slowly begins to fill with laughter. The tension starts to lift and my heart slowly returns to its regular beat. Although when I look back at Noah, he's still looking straight ahead at Trevor, deep in thought.

Chapter 9

Noah

Rex is in rare form as he dances around the patio, trying to do his best Peter Frampton impersonation to "Show Me the Way." Everyone laughs as he can barely stand and somehow manages perfect air guitar moves and electronic voices to complement Frampton's. Everyone joins in on singing the words during the chorus because Rex's enthusiasm for the song is just too damn contagious. Even if you didn't feel like singing, you join because he's clearly very into his performance.

I keep my eye on Trevor and wonder what kind of history he and Evelyn must have had. I'm slightly worried their past might be a threat to what I hope is my present or dare I dream ... future. I never disliked Trevor before. In fact, we've always gotten along well.

Although in the short time I observe him and Evelyn together, and whatever the deal is between the two of them, I instinctively start to feel threatened. The thoughts of his hands on her or his lips anywhere near the places I long to kiss makes me want to pummel the little brat right to the ground.

Returning my gaze to Evelyn, I watch how amazing she looks in the firelight. She laughs and jokes with everyone sitting

CHAPTER 9

around the fire. The ease at which she enjoys herself makes her that much more appealing, and I subconsciously find myself changing my mind about not wanting to get involved with anyone. I'm still planning on moving, but that move is two months away. Two months is a good amount of time to at least see where things can go and have some fun while doing it.

I don't know what came over me when I grabbed her hand or why I wanted her attention directed only at me. I haven't felt this way about anyone in a long time. The feelings of desire, lust, even jealousy, are emotions I long ago tried to forget. No one has stirred up these feelings in such a long time, and she has a way about her that makes it happen so easily.

The music slows and someone must have changed the station because "Let Me Down Easy" by Billy Currington plays low in the background. I'm consumed as I watch Evelyn, mesmerized by her every move and how easily she holds everyone's attention captive as she talks. I know without a doubt I have no self-control when it comes to her. Any amount of fighting will be useless. As long as I stay anywhere near her, I will always give in.

If trying not to feel anything for her feels this good, how much better would it feel if I gave in? And what if, just by some crazy chance, her feelings were the same? Could she possibly feel anything anywhere close to the way I do when I look her in the eyes? I need to know and I might have been moments away from knowing before Trevor showed up.

He might have won for the moment, but there is no way I'm letting Evelyn get away again—not without attempting to take things further. I just have to know if she'll let me see her again. I need to see her after this night, away from a crowd, like I need the air I breathe. I need to be near her more than I have ever needed to be near anyone before.

"How's work, Trev? I'd expect things to be more hectic what the holidays approaching. Any crazy stories to thrill us with tonight?" Evelyn asks Trevor, and I begin to feel the sting of jealousy burn through my veins. I tighten my grip on her hand and see the recognition of its tight grip flash across her pretty face as she tenses. She doesn't turn to look at me, but I know the message is delivered.

"Not too crazy. We do live in such a quiet town. My shift changes next week, and I will be back to working nights. Maybe I will have some stories for you then," he quietly replies, still obviously hurt from earlier.

Trevor's a police officer and it suits him. The man never breaks the law and even looks down on his family members for minor offenses like speeding tickets. He's annoyingly perfect and so uptight it's hard to make him smile most of the time. How anything ever happened between Evelyn and Trevor has me completely confused. I can already tell the two of them are as different as could be.

"Noah here has some stories!" Rex butts in, slurring and laughing at the same time. "Tell them about the fire we fought up Highway 50 and how you found the culprit running naked through the forest shortly after!"

Not one for bragging about the work I do, or even retelling too many stories from my time spent volunteering with Rex fighting wildfires, I just shake my head at his comment. "No one wants to hear that kind of stuff, Rex."

"You're a firefighter here too? I thought you said you only did that back home?" Evelyn asks surprised. "Do you ever rest? Work, school, firefighting! You're like a crazy one-man show!"

CHAPTER 9

"I like to keep busy." I shrug. "I love being outside. Never one for being cooped up inside an office all day." She has a point though; I'm extremely busy—a strategic plan I developed a few years back to help with my long hiatus between relationships. It's a plan that has succeeded so far but might be crumbling as we speak.

"This guy right here saved an old woman from a burning building!" exclaims Rex.

"What?" Evelyn looks shocked as she turns towards me and searches my face for the truth.

"Saw it with my own two eyes!" Rex continues. "He's rescued cats from trees, saves babies, helps grandmas cross the street, risks his life for those less fortunate. He's a hero. He's my hero." Rex fakes tears as his voice breaks, and he puts one hand over his heart. Evelyn finally catches on to the joke, and I'm definitely way less amused.

"Shut up!" She giggles playfully, slapping him in the arm. "You're so stupid, Rex."

I sit there growing more uncomfortable by the minute. I don't volunteer to look like any kind of hero. Rex likes to tease me because I take being a firefighter more seriously than he does. I also shy away from talking about myself under any and all circumstances, unlike Rex, who is always eager to use it to his advantage—mostly with members of the opposite sex.

"Come on now," Rex continues, "don't hold out on the lady, or I will be forced to tell her the truth about you since you seem so keen on holding on to her hand so tightly but not saying one word."

"I enjoy it." I reluctantly begin to talk about myself. "Like I said, keeps me busy. Maybe even busier if California doesn't start getting any rain," I say, glancing up at the sky. "We've been having a lot of lightning, and the ground is too dry. Could be a serious problem. But nothing crazy like this character keeps saying." I motion towards Rex, annoyed.

Holding up his hands in defense, Rex shrugs. "Just trying to help a brother out."

He becomes immediately disinterested in the two of us and focuses his attention, instead, on the conversation building between Trevor and Michael. They're discussing adding additional security for the upcoming holidays and several special events scheduled to take place at Gatsby's.

"Help you out for what?" I hear Evelyn ask and turn to meet her gaze. I question if this is the right time to pursue the matter, but figure to hell with it because I don't want to chance not having jumped in headfirst in case I never get the opportunity again. I saw how quickly my last opportunity was spoiled … and the one before that. Time to throw the cards on the table and see what we're both holding.

"What do you need help with?" She smiles, having to know the answer to her own question. I pause for a moment, taking her and this moment in. I've never been one to half-ass anything. If I'm going to go for it, I'll be all in and I will never recover.

"You wouldn't be interested in those details," I say, trying to buy more time to make sure I'm positive about my decision and ever so shyly trying to avoid the question. I suddenly fear her rejection more than I have since I first laid eyes on her, and I am not entirely sure why. Maybe it's because I am typically safer in my little fantasy and the truth might hurt too much.

"I don't know. I'm pretty inclined to like everything about you at this moment," she says, whispering and leaning in closer. "Try me. You might surprise yourself."

CHAPTER 9

Evelyn's confidence, an unforeseen bonus, both shocks and turns me on. Mind immediately made up, I'm ready to surrender it all if she'll have me. Hell, if I wasn't so tripped up on this girl, I'd realize she already half-answered my question.

"What if I was to say I'm liking everything about you the more I get to know you too?" I whisper back, countering her confidence with some of my own. I lean in and drown myself in the blue of her eyes. I'll never tire of looking in those eyes. A man can get lost in the depths of possibilities they evoke.

"I'd say maybe you need to get to know me even better, then," she says, leaving me thrilled with the ease in which we're having this conversation. I was hoping she wouldn't play hard to get but never anticipated it being this easy.

Without thinking, I open my life up for the first time in a long time and ask, "How about I take you out Friday and do just that?" Pausing, I take the time to speak my next set of words slowly, wanting them to sink in as much as they can. "There is nothing I want more than to have you all to myself. No group. No bar. No friends as a distraction…" I brush a strand of her hair out of her eyes and tuck it behind her ear, watching the shiver run up her body "…just the two of us."

Our conversation once again becomes whispers intended only for our ears as we lean into one another, attempting to drown out the world. It isn't that I wouldn't have asked her if everyone was listening, it's more the idea that privately she's all mine with no one's feelings to hurt and no one's opinion but her own to form her answer.

"I'd like that very much," she whispers back enthusiastically as she accepts an offer that has way more behind it than I think she knows.

"It's a date, then?" I ask, wanting to make sure that she

knows my every intention, not wanting to leave anything undefined.

"Oh it most definitely is a date," she confirms, smiling brightly.

I smile myself and ease back into my chair, enjoying that I just succeeded in getting her all to myself. Last night I felt crushed seeing her flee the bar, not knowing how to get ahold of her. The thought that I might never see her again was a nightmare I hadn't been able to escape all day.

Twenty-four hours ago, I had no desire to ever feel the way Evelyn makes me feel. Now, I can't get enough of her. All my ideas about never falling in love again died the moment I saw her sitting at the bar in her parents' living room. She's like a drug. Just being in her presence sends me on a high I have never felt in my life. I wonder if I could ever be lucky enough to be her drug, her high, her fix like she's quickly becoming mine.

I don't want this night to end. I want to stay with her, holding her hand next to the fire as long as I can. How will I even make it through the next week? Five days is a long time to go between fixes.

The only solace I find in the thought of saying goodnight later is that it's not goodbye. Sitting next to her on her parents' back patio, I feel myself start to wish the week to pass as fast as it can. I'm enjoying every second of every minute with her more than I have ever enjoyed a moment with another woman in my life. And as much as it should scare me, as much as I have done everything I could this past year and a half to never get too close, I find myself shocked that it doesn't seem to faze me one bit.

Chapter 10

Evelyn

Returning home after Sunday night's dinner, I collapse on my bed, feeling nothing but pure joy and absolute ecstasy. I'm happier than I've been in a long time. Actually, I'm probably happier than I have ever felt in the whole eternity of forever. I can't wait until next Friday and find myself giggling over the thought of it while I shower and get ready for bed.

I imagine every possible way Noah might plan our first date. "Our first date!" The phrase itself makes it impossible to wipe the silliest grin off my face.

This is different. I find myself wondering, for about two seconds, if I should be worried I'm getting too close and very possibly might be letting myself go too far. I quickly shove the thought away because I want nothing to kill this high Noah gives me.

We quickly managed to exchange phone numbers before the night was over while Rex was shouting obnoxiously for Noah to drive him home, and now I notice myself staring at my phone, wondering if I should text or call him first. I don't want to seem too excited. When he had asked me out, I was bold, almost egging him on to do it. As I sit cross-legged and stare are the phone in the middle of my lap on my bed, I quickly decide now I want to wait and see how eager he really is to see me again.

No one ever wants to be that girl, the overly needy one. I'm all for expressing my feelings, but not for seeming too desperate! Picking up the phone I almost cave but then decide to stand my ground as I set the phone on my nightstand and crawl under the covers, waiting impatiently for sleep—and hopefully delicious toe-curling dreams of the man I silently fear may be stealing my heart.

On Monday my week starts off slow. Work at the paper is tedious and unexciting. I find myself sending off emails and contacting people to form the same stories that typically run every week this time of year. I despise writing about upcoming events that the paper always covers. Racking my brain, I have to find something new to add to this edition that will intrigue the readers and doesn't sound the same as it did last year and the year before that.

I decide to write on Gatsby's. I've already contacted the editor at the Auburn Journal and got his approval that he'll run the set of stories as well. With most of the other towns close by, there are plenty of locals that would be interested in attending Gatsby's events. Michael came in Tuesday to give me the details I needed on what was already in the works. He never lets Rex handle any publicity for the club, and I absolutely can't blame him for that.

When Wednesday rolls around, I'm still surprised not to have heard from Noah. A funk settles over me as I get to work and turn on my computer. It's a funk not even a third cup of coffee and blaring rap music on the way to work will cure. The feeling has me slightly jaded, and I realize I might need to scale back my feelings because I'm totally starting to think he is not as

CHAPTER 10

into me as I am into him.

Around noon I'm absolutely feeling worse and find myself staring blankly at my screen. I had been stuck on the same article that needed writing for an hour and a half. I've been alternating between staring at the facts I had scribbled down and staring at my computer screen. Then I'd get up for a drink or use the restroom about every five to ten minutes, unable to find a way to push through my thoughts in order to get any work done. Now I'm back to staring at the computer screen and glancing at my phone, pushing the center button for the third time in one minute to make sure I didn't miss a call or text—though I already know I haven't.

My office phone rings. Turning to look at who's calling, I smile as I quickly recognize the number on the ID. This call might just be enough to break through the thick cloud that hovers over my thoughts. I need distraction more than anything right now, and this is just the person to do it.

"What's going on, lady!?" I say, picking up the receiver.

"I've been driving since 4:00 a.m. and I am telling you, every time I make this damn drive, I swear it will be my last. Next year I'm flying or I'm never coming home again!" Gwen proceeds to shout into my ear. I can hear her window is down and the sound of big rigs as she flies down the freeway. She curses at one of them before I can faintly hear her car accelerate.

"You're coming home?" I ask, shocked, excitement finally kicking in for the first time today. "You're not supposed to be coming home until Christmas!"

"Plans changed. My mom and dad are being ridiculous, saying I never visit." Gwen lets out an irritated sigh on the other end of the line. "I had the time to take, so I took it. I'm staying with you, though, because after last visit, if my mother and I spend longer than a few hours together, I swear someone will call the cops!"

I laughed for the first time all day because sadly her statement is very true. When first reunited, Gwen and her mother act like long lost friends. As time progresses, though, and more wine is poured, the two proceed to tear each other apart. Last time I had to intervene and restrain Gwen from grabbing one of her mother's expensive vases and hurling it across the room at her.

Gwen's mother was Irish, and her father Italian. The combination does absolutely nothing to calm the fight that's so naturally embedded on both sides of their genetic pool.

"Where are you at? Are you close to town?" I ask, excited that she'll be the best distraction I could ever imagine. She's sure to help me get my mind off of the one person I can't stop thinking about. She might be able to lend some good advice too, seeing as I am starting to think everything I was sure about when it came to Noah might not be the way I believed it to be after all.

"I think I'm going to take off the rest of the afternoon and just work from home tonight. My head is so not into it today!" I'm ready to be anywhere else but at work right now.

"What's the matter? Is your editor climbing up your butt again?" Gwen asks.

My editor is the definition of annoying, almost identical to the boss from Office Space. He throws work at me constantly and gets on my case for everything and anything. If it wasn't for my love of what I do, I would have quit a long time ago. He's a micromanaging, nitpicking, ready to through you under the bus every time just to make himself shine type of boss.

"Gwen, I'm not inclined to let anyone climb up my butt ever!

CHAPTER 10

It's a long story, I'll explain it later ... Maybe ..."

"Well, I'm about an hour out. I'll meet you at your place, and we'll drink wine and talk about whatever it is that has you all oppressed and melancholy!" Gwen says in a mocking, chipper tone.

"I do declare those are some big words for you, Ms. Gwen." I laugh.

"Hey, I went to college," she says. "Or if you'd rather, we can ignore it all and keep throwing glasses back until we are dancing on the dining room table. You know I'm down for anything. Now finish up and get your ass on home!"

"That's more like it." I laugh again. "I'll meet you at my place."

"Warm that damn place up before I get there too! Your place might be fabulously chic, but damn if it doesn't feel like the Antarctic in the winter and the Mojave Desert in summer!" With that Gwen hangs up and I start contriving a plan for my best excuse in order to get out of the office.

Normally I would claim an assignment and just take extra time off, making up for it later in the week, though I had already done that last week with my trip south. I managed to do some work on the road, but I know the boss won't be all too happy with me leaving again.

Leaning back in my chair, I glance at my editor's office and notice he was already gone. It has to be either an early lunch day or an assignment he's working on. Whatever it is, it's the perfect opportunity to escape.

Hurrying, I shut down my computer, stash my notes in my oversized purse, and grab the few things I toted into work that morning. I'll think up an excuse later. Gwen's always full of great excuses, and I have definitely taken advantage of using her expertise on the perfect alibi in the past.

On my way home, I stop at the local store and grab wine and snacks. If there's one thing bigger than my friend's drinking ability, it's her appetite, though I don't know where she puts it. She's a gorgeous redhead blessed with some amazing features that make many women jealous.

Hurrying through the local store, grabbing the perfect extras I need for the girls' night ahead, I quickly check out and return to my car eager to head home. Gwen's distraction is, in fact, putting me in a better mood. I had almost forgotten about Noah and how he hadn't even called. Almost!

As I round the corner to my street, my phone beeps in my center console. I glance at the screen and see it's a message from Rex. When I slow down at a stop sign, I pick up the phone and try to read the text before I accelerate once again.

Rex: Next time you give a guy your number, make sure you give him the right one. Noah's been trying to call you all week.

My heart drops. I can't even begin to imagine how I had done such a thing. Could I really have entered it wrong when he had handed me his phone? I've never done something like this before, but maybe the pure excitement of the situation clouded my thoughts somehow, making it easy to stumble over my fingers. Whatever the reason, panic builds inside as I worry he will think I did it intentionally.

As I pull away from the stop sign, I scroll through my phone and find Noah's name. I just hope he hadn't entered his information wrong. If he had, that's obviously my answer to how interested he is. But Rex said he'd been trying to call, so why am I even questioning it?

Selecting his name, I hear the phone start ringing as I pull up in front of my house. I hold my breath, waiting. After the

CHAPTER 10

first ring, my heart starts to beat faster. With the second ring, I can feel my heart in my throat. When it rings the third time, I swear I'm going to his voicemail and my heart sinks.

Then he picks up, and I have to remind myself to keep breathing.

"This is Noah!" comes what sounds like a slightly irritated voice on the other end.

"Noah! It's Evelyn." My voice is shaky, and I clear my throat, trying to buy time to settle my nerves. Of course, I notice he remains silent and that just makes me more nervous. "I'm so SO sorry I gave you the wrong number Sunday."

I wait for a response, but there isn't one, just more silence. This is going worse than I thought. I wouldn't be surprised if maybe he hung up on me. Stepping out of my car and grabbing my purse, I decide to come back later for the groceries after I hopefully don't have to stumble over my words, continuing my horrible explanation.

"I must have accidentally hit the wrong buttons. I swear I didn't do it on purpose." My voice is still kind of shaky, and I just hope my nerves won't get the best of me and I won't end up saying something stupid.

"I've actually been waiting, hoping you'd call all week. I didn't want to reach out to you first. I mean it's not that I didn't want to, it's more that I didn't want you thinking I was too forward." My nerves kick in as I start to fear what I might say next. I lock my car and grab the handle, jerking it twice to make sure it's locked.

Worried he had hung up, I ask, "Are you still there?"

I turn to start walking towards my house and am taken back to see Noah standing on my front porch. I stumbled with my next few steps. There he stands, three single stemmed roses in one hand and his other hand holding his phone up to his ear.

He doesn't move any closer. And he doesn't hang up. We both stand there with our phones, my mouth hanging open as I don't know what to say next.

He smiles. "You're adorably cute when you're flustered!" he speaks into the line. Then, ending the call, he starts to close the distance between the two of us. With each step, I can feel my body temperature rising. Breathing. Breathing would be a good thing right now. Would it look ridiculous if I started fanning myself? Yeah, it would be ridiculous. I take a deep breath and watch with anticipation the closer he gets.

"How did you know where to find me?" I ask eventually, returning my phone to my purse. The butterflies in my stomach are almost uncontainable. I suddenly feel so nervous, the mere act of looking up to meet his eyes seems nearly impossible. Finally finding the courage, our eyes meet and it takes me a moment to regain my thoughts. The three days apart have done nothing to lessen the effect he's had on me. It's only the opposite as I stand there, wrapping myself around how sexy he is.

Fitted blue jeans with black boots, a black shirt hugging his body in every perfect way possible, and a ball cap pulled down low, he looks like he's been working hard outside all morning but still manages to be put together nicely. His woodsy smell engulfs me once again as he comes to a stop in front of me, and I want nothing else but to be able to drench myself in it.

"When I finally realized I had the wrong number," he begins, "I debated all the reasons why that might actually be." Smiling, he tilts his hat back a little on his head. "I finally decided it couldn't have been on purpose, so I asked Rex for not only your right number but your address. You can't get away from me

CHAPTER 10

that easily." He winks, holding out the roses for me to take.

"Thank you," I say as I accept them, inhaling their beautiful fragrance. I look back up at him. Shifting my weight on one foot, I try to think of a response.

"Should I be concerned that you seem to be stalking me? First the bar, then my parents' house, now my doorstep?" I joke.

Disregarding the question and just gesturing towards the flowers, he says, "One rose for each day I haven't been able to be with you."

My heart immediately skips a beat at such an insanely romantic gesture. Is he for real? This is the kind of stuff that you only read about or see in the movies or you always hear happened to a friend of a friend, not what actually happens in real life. At least not to me.

"I was going to leave them with your landlord," he continues. "Or in front of your door. But I realized the landlord doesn't exist, and I have no clue what door is yours. Your coming home was perfect timing."

"I really am sorry. I didn't mean for any of this to have to happen." I try to apologize.

Shaking his head, he cuts me off. "No worries." He shrugs. "It gave me an excuse to see you before Friday." Smiling, he turns and looks back at my place.

"So, are you going to invite me in?" he asks, not missing a beat.

The question is a little surprising. Although, I guess it should have dawned on me, but I'm too flustered to think straight. The idea of Noah alone with me in my own house instantly takes my mind to a place where only naughty thoughts live and being able to contain myself might be impossible.

I decide, instead, to take this as the perfect opportunity to have a little fun and find out a little more about him. If he wants to get invited up, he's first going to have to offer up some info first.

"You haven't broken the law recently, have you? Any warrants I should know about?" I begin to teasingly question him.

Immediately looking back my way, Noah looks shocked. "No, not at all. Why?"

"Any drug addictions? Ex-wives? Psycho ex-girlfriends? STDs? Insanely annoying OCD habits? Recent aliments or sicknesses I should be aware of?" I proceed, halfway joking and half totally giving him the third degree.

Laughing and shaking his head, he answers, "Nope, I'm clean!" Holding his hands up in surrender for extra emphasis, he flashes me that insanely gorgeous smile of his. I almost melt right there at his feet like a silly little fangirl for her boyband dream.

Faltering for only a moment, I bounce back quickly. "Then, yes, Noah, I'd be delighted if you would come in." Batting my eyelashes for emphasis, I smile, taking his hand and leading him up the pathway to my front door, and it doesn't escape me how small my hand feels in his. The coarseness of his skin engulfing my own makes my mind go blank. Regaining my sanity, I silently ask myself what I am thinking and wonder if all this so soon is a good thing.

I stand at the door, fumbling with my keys, taking extra time to go over the way I left my apartment in my head and trying to remember if I had left anything out that might be embarrassing. Fully confident there are no bras hanging over the couch or boxes of tampons on the kitchen counter I forgot to put away,

CHAPTER 10

I open the front door to my apartment complex.

   I never would have expected this curve ball thrown into my day an hour ago, but I'm going to make sure I enjoy every moment of it. Fear be damned! I've never heard anyone complain about too much of a good thing too soon, and I'm not going to be the one to start complaining first.

Chapter 11

Noah

Once inside, Evelyn starts climbing the stairs. "I'm at the top on the right. It's the largest of the four units," she says.

I look around the foyer and take a deep breath as I begin climbing the steps after her. I can't help but notice that she puts a little extra swing in her step as she climbs, knowing very well what I must have my eyes on as I climb the steps behind her.

And good Lord what a view it is! Her pencil skirt hugs her curves like a second skin. Nylons with a line climb perfectly up the back of her legs, directing you to a heaven that's every man's dream. Red high heels make me drool at the many different ways I want to see her wear them when I have those legs of hers wrapped around me.

Her blond hair falls in soft waves down her back, and the closer I get, I take in the slightest hint of her perfume. A vanilla dream that makes her smell like the perfect dessert that I can't wait to devour over and over again.

Unlocking the door to her apartment, she lets me enter first. "After you, sir," she says.

I smile as I pass by nervously. Should I jump her and go

straight to the reason why I came here? I need to taste her again, need to feel her again! It's been too long. And now standing here with her within arm's reach makes me want to throw all self-control out the window.

She enters her apartment and puts her purse down, along with the roses I brought her. Setting them on the counter, she makes her way across the room and clicks on the wall heater. Turning, she timidly starts to straighten a stack of magazines on the coffee table.

Sticking my hands in my pockets to keep from grabbing her, I begin to walk around the small little living room. The place is not what I expected at all. I expected something out of a magazine. Maybe something more city and showy.

There are some newer looking items, like the couch and coffee table. But then there's a rustic, warn and old feel. It's the kind of space you want to stay in, a place that feels well lived in. Warm and inviting. I notice her watching me as I survey the living room and kitchen and then start to make my way down the hallway, glancing in each room I pass.

Two bedrooms? I wonder if she has a roommate. This is quite the place for one person to have all to themselves.

Turning and making my way back to her, I ask, "Only one bathroom?"

"Yeah, but it's only me. I mean, it's not the best when I have company, but it works, you know?"

Question answered. Finally! A place with no distractions or interruptions between the two of us. Maybe I should satisfy my appetite, close the space between us, and take as much of her right now as she will allow me.

Instead, I just nod and continue my walk around the living room once more, absolutely chicken to do anything about the fantasies that roll through my mind daily. I can see her studying me, wondering perhaps what I was expecting to find in her place. She begins to look nervous, and I let her. Something about the way she squirms under my gaze makes me imagine how she might squirm in a few other positions that I have in mind, wiggling with pleasure as I make sure she's undeniably satisfied.

"Do you want something to drink?" she asks, making her way towards the kitchen and looking in her fridge. She bends slightly at the waist to gaze inside.

I take full advantage of the view as I walk over to the kitchen counter, cocking my head to the side to admire a few of the things my hands itch to touch. She has a slender waist that gives way to thick hips and an ass that would make any man drool. I'd give anything, even the air I breathe, to be able to learn and memorize every curve of her body, every inch of the perfect way she was designed.

"I have wine, beer, soda, water ... milk?" she continues, furrowing her brow as she says the last item. "You're taking your chances with that one, though. I have no clue how long that has been in there."

"Nah, I'm good," I say, leaning against the bar that separates the kitchen from the living room.

Picking up one of the town newspapers she has on her counter, I examine it for a moment. "Is this the paper you write for?" I ask, trying to make conversation.

"Yeah, it's not much, but it's a start," she says, coming around the counter. "Allows me to do what I love while working close to home." She tenses as I read her writing.

"You're good. I like the way you write," I say, trying to calm the tension evident in her posture.

CHAPTER 11

"This stuff is mostly repetitive news. It's not that exciting to read," she says, defending herself when her writing needed no defending. "I prefer the magazines I freelance for. The people I meet and the stories I write for them ... everyone I meet touches my life, reminds me of why I chose the career I did, ya know?" she confesses, stepping closer and looking over my shoulder.

I lean into her slightly, not being able to even focus on the words I'm pretending to read now that she has my attention. The smell of her drives me insane. I brush up against her and she settles in next to me. Looking up, I smile at her, and she quickly returns the smile as well. The silence adds to the undeniable surge of sexual tension rising with each passing second, and God if that isn't a turn-on itself.

"You know, every time I'm near you I fight the urge to want to kiss you," I blurt out without even thinking, obviously catching the both of us off guard.

Swallowing hard and taking a deep breath, she says, "Well, why fight it?"

"Because," I whisper, leaning in close, waiting until her eyes flutter and land on mine before I continue, "if I start ..." I moved the hair off her shoulder, trailing my fingertips down her arm. She shivers, and that only makes me want her more. "I'm never going to want to stop."

She licks her lips and I watch, wanting so badly to be the one tasting and savoring those lips. I grow more impatient the longer I have to hold out.

She has to be the one to make the first move this time, I've decided. I flung myself at her once before. I need to know she needs me as much as I need her. It's time to decide, and she sure as hell is taking her sweet precious time.

Damn women! They know just how to make us men crave,

want, and need until we drive ourselves absolutely insane.

The side of her lip curls up on the right, and she smirks at me, egging me on, tempting me and having more patience and restraint than I thought possible. Hell, that's sexy. The anticipation of having her does nothing to quench my thirst. It's only made me salivate more as the seconds stretch out in agony.

Suddenly, she fists my shirt in her hands, pulling me close, and rests her lips against my ear. She nibbles once, making me start to lose all self-control.

"Then don't," she whispers.

In a rush, I grab her hips and spin her towards me, pinning her against the counter. I crash into her so forcefully I'm afraid I've hurt her as she lets out a slight moan the second my lips met hers. One of her legs comes around my thigh, pushing me further, urging me to take more, and I don't hold back.

Fisting her hair in my hands, I pull her head back and devour her mouth like a fiend, making sure to breathe in every last drop I can from her lips. Her hands grab me around the waist as she pulls me into her hips, grinding against her finally like I had been dreaming about. I pull her other leg up, and she instinctively wraps both her legs around my waist.

My right hand begins its journey up her thigh, knowing exactly where it needs and wants to go. On instinct, I'm ready to feel whatever she'll let me. Reaching the hem of her skirt, I pause. She hasn't stopped me yet, so I force it up higher. Another moan fills the room as my lips find their way to her neck, and I nibble and suck my way across her collarbone.

If she doesn't stop me, I'm ready to strip her bare right here. Grabbing my face back up to her, she rests her forehead against mine as I reluctantly come up for air. I meet her eyes and

CHAPTER 11

she bites her lip seductively. I proceed to grind into her again without thinking. I can't control myself around her and damn sure don't want to.

Her head falls back, and she slowly looks up at me. I keep my eyes focused on her. The sight of her is just as addictive as the feeling of her. She's soft and tender with just enough edge to make me lose my mind. I silently watch, waiting for her to make me want her more like I know she will.

"I thought you said you'd never want to stop," she teases, testing my will power, turning me on and making me want her even more. She grinds against me, and it's my turn to wince with the rising need growing inside. I want to claim her. Take her. Make her never want any man again except me.

Breathing heavily and laughing quietly, I respond, "Oh, darlin', you have no idea. I don't think you can handle what I have planned for you."

Cocking her head to the side and flinging her hair over one shoulder, she smiles. "Try me!"

Letting out a groan, I force both sides of her skirt up and grab her at the waist, raising her up onto the counter. I yank her close until she's right up against me. Her hands greedily feel for my belt as I continue my assault on her neck, down her chest, licking the top of her cleavage. I fight the urge to go further. I want to take my time with her. I want to make sure I taste every inch.

Hell, she is more delicious than I could have ever dreamed. I raise my hands, ready to grab and caress. She whimpers my name as she fumbles with the buttons of my jeans, and it only urges me on more.

"Excuse me, don't let me interrupt!" comes a voice from the doorway.

We immediately stop dead in our tracks, hands frozen in their spot, heads still hanging low. Embarrassed and not knowing how to proceed, we just stand there like two teenagers that just got caught when their parents come home from work early. Damn it, didn't she say she lived alone? What the hell is this?

Evelyn eases off the counter, and I meet her eyes as she tugs her skirt back in place. She has a smirk on her face like this is funny. I, however, see no humor to this situation. I adjust myself and take a deep breath before turning around to greet the intruder.

"No, please continue!" says the redhead standing in front of me. "I missed the mating display on Nat Geo last night. This is good, maybe even better." She sarcastically smiles at me, knowing damn well the embarrassment I feel.

Whoever she is, I don't know. All I know is she can turn around and leave the way she just came in. Wait … I've seen her somewhere before. In the bar that first night! She's starting to have an annoying habit of breaking up a good thing. I wait for one of us to say something, to move, to do anything but stand here in silence.

Evelyn lets out a laugh, and I watch as her company seems rather unamused with the situation, just like myself. Well damn, this is awkward. The redhead glares at me, making all sorts of judgments before I even have a chance to speak. Great! What the hell have I just stepped into?

Chapter 12

Evelyn

After no one says anything for a minute, which seems more like an hour, I decide to break up the silence with some introductions.

"Noah, this is Gwen. She's visiting from SoCal and staying with me for a few days." I have to admit, it falls on deaf ears as neither one of them seems to acknowledge me. "Gwen, this is Noah." Her facial expression deepens as she continues to glare at the man in front of her. "Noah and I actually met last week … when I was down south." Still nothing. "You met him too." She finally glances my way then looks back at Noah.

Nervous and slightly annoyed, Noah shifts his weight on his feet and adjusts his ball cap. I know the woman in front of me well, however, he isn't used to her and the way she conducts herself. I'm not sure he can handle her overpowering ways, but I guess I am about to find out.

"Well, I guess I should be going," Noah mumbles. I can't blame him. I don't want to be standing here any more than he does.

Gwen walks past us to the far corner in the room and drops her suitcase on the floor, which gives us a little privacy so we can say goodbye. He grabs my hand and squeezes it tight. I let myself lean into him, not wanting to let him go. I try my hardest to ignore Gwen's presence on the opposite side of the room.

"I'll call you later, ok?" he says quietly, and I nod. Then he leans in and brushes his lips softly against my cheek, only making me want to go right back to what we were doing before our intruder arrived.

I grab his belt and tug him into me slightly. I can feel him tense against my body and know I've gotten my point across. Our earlier encounter did nothing to satisfy our hunger for one another; it's only made us hungry with need.

"God, woman, you know how to drive a man crazy," he whispers in my ear before backing away and slowly walks to the door.

Gwen makes her way back over to us, and Noah pauses briefly in front of her. Extending his hand, he says, "It's nice to meet you, Gwen."

She takes it, shaking it slowly, continuing to size him up while staring him down, not ready to give up on making him feel like the one who was intruding instead of the other way around. She never fails to make people she is unsure of or doesn't like extremely uncomfortable in her presence.

"We've met, remember?" She responds coldly as if she's questioning the validity of it herself. "Will I be seeing more of you while I am here?"

Glancing back my way, Noah looks apprehensive. I can tell he doesn't want to assume anything but also doesn't want to answer wrong either. I think for a moment that he won't answer at all. Maybe he'll try and play it safe and change the subject. What's going on between us, as thrilling and breathtaking as it is, it's also fresh and new. Even I don't know exactly what to make of it.

"I sure hope I'll be around more often," he answers confidently. Smiling shyly at me, I realize how he warms my heart in a way that's unexplainable. Hope, in the beginning of anything, is addictive and perhaps the only thing that keeps you coming back for more.

"Hmm ..." is Gwen's only response. We both turn back to look at her as she narrows her eyes and crosses her arms, not saying another word, leaving him once again a little shaky.

"Well," he says, shifting his weight on his feet one final time. "Nice to see you again, Gwen. We'll talk later, Evelyn." And with that he leaves quickly, closing the door behind him.

Still delirious and completely in a euphoric state of mind, it takes me a moment to reorganize my thoughts and focus back on my best friend in front of me. She still hasn't uncrossed her arms and is waiting for an answer that I don't want to give. I walk past her into the kitchen and grab two wine glasses.

"Thirsty?" I ask, hoping to distract her thoughts though knowing it's a long shot. I know that until I spill and tell her everything, this night is not destined to progress any further.

The silence is deafening. I choose to continue to ignore her rather than cave. Grabbing a half-empty bottle of red wine, I divide the rest of it between the two glasses. Drinking from my own glass as I return to Gwen in the living room, I try to quickly plot a way to avoid the topic.

I know there is no way she will let me do that. Still standing in the same spot, arms still folded, and still waiting for an answer as to who Noah is and what's going on between the two of us, Gwen judgmentally stares me down. Extending the other glass to my best friend, I'm not surprised when she refuses to take it and remains in her stance. I begin wondering who will break first as I proceeded to take sip after sip of my wine and debate starting on Gwen's glass if we stand there long enough for me to reach the bottom of my own. Gwen breaks first.

"So ... who's the sex on a stick that was groping my best friend harder and faster than a horny thirteen-year-old boy?"

I choke on my wine, spewing some out into the air. Gwen grabs her glass angrily, waiting for my response. Her eyebrows shoot up, eyes wide, waiting for an answer. She purses her lips. Crossing her arms again, she waits for me to answer.

"It wasn't that bad," I say, wiping my mouth with my hand and looking to make sure I haven't spit the wine out on my shirt.

"Evelyn, if I hadn't walked in when I did, you'd be working on baby numero uno with Mr. Sexy Tall Dark and Handsome! Oh my God, Ev, the man is gorgeous!" she squeals. "Like almost too good looking! So not cool, girl. It's not like you to not tell me stuff! You've always told me everything, and I didn't know about this!" she shouts, starting the lecture I knew was scratching at the surface the moment she walked through my front door and found me practically baring it all for a guy she does not remember.

"Like how new is he?" she continues as I begin to walk towards the living room. "I mean, I know it's been a while for you, but ... girl, that doesn't mean you can be stupid! THINK! STDs! Screw that! Babies ... babies with strangers! Strangers that won't stick around to play house, or daddy, or make an honest woman out of you!"

I roll my eyes and walk further into the living room as Gwen follows. Calming a little bit, she finally takes a sip of her wine before continuing.

CHAPTER 12

"Who is he? And why the hell did I not know about this? This is incredibly important and very valuable information you've been withholding from me, especially if you're debating getting serious with whoever he is! What did you say his name was?"

We circle around the couch and take a seat side by side. I debate giving Gwen the long answer, though settle for the short, hoping the less information I give, the shorter this interrogation will be.

"His name is Noah," I answer, taking a bigger gulp of wine than necessary and waiting for the next round. I can take a guess at where this is headed and need to self-medicate if I'm right.

"Noah! Like who is named Noah anymore anyway. Or ever for that matter! I've never heard of that kind of name. Noah!".

She drinks her wine, and we sit there in silence for a moment. I start to think maybe she will let up, but the wheels in her head are still obviously turning. I know I have no chance at this ending anytime soon.

"This means ... I don't think he can be trusted. With a name like Noah ... honestly! Like, does he build boats too?" Gwen says, pressing the issue.

"Oh, stop it! You're too damn judgmental of people all the time." I snap, annoyed and not wanting to discuss the matter further.

"Fine, then." The irritation is evident in her voice. "Well ... what do you know about the guy? Where did he go to school? What's his favorite color? Favorite band? Favorite food? Best friend?" Her questioning continues.

"He's best friends with Rex!" I quietly answer into my wine glass, needing a little more help with what I know is coming next.

"Hell no! Rex! That has all sorts of wrong written all over it! Rex of all people? Evelyn, you should know better." She's shouting now, and even though I've never fully understood why, I know enough that Rex is a sensitive topic with her.

"Come on! He's not that bad." I try to smooth things over. "Talk about me withholding information. You ever going to tell me why you've almost always had this hatred towards Rex?"

Gwen shoots off the couch and walks into the kitchen. "We are talking about you, remember? Not me! Stop avoiding the questions."

"Me avoiding?! That's the pot calling the kettle black if I ever heard it," I yell over my shoulder.

"I'm not listening," she shouts back as I hear another bottle of wine being opened. She returns to me sitting on the couch, filling up her glass first and then mine.

"Be nice, or I won't tell you anything," I say quickly, succeeding in shutting her up. If there is one thing that gets her to stop it's the threat of being shut out from gossip. Gwen looks down at her glass and takes another sip, drawing out the moment she takes time to think before responding.

"It's just been a long time since I've seen you with anyone. And hell, I've never seen you with anyone like that," she says.

I laugh. She's right. We've seen each other in some pretty compromised situations, but I am sure that topped them all.

"I'm serious, Ev," my best friend continues. "I'm talking more than just the raging hormones and groping that I walked in on ... I'm talking about that spark!"

My eyes shoot up and I look at Gwen, who is already staring at me.

"Holy hell, lady! I could feel that shit and I wasn't even the one that started the fire." She fans herself and lets out a whistle. "Even when you guys stopped, it was like you were still going at it! I was uncomfortable just being in the room with you two. Like I was still intruding."

"You were!" I laugh. "How long were you standing there watching?"

"Long enough," she says, looking me in the eyes. Something in her expression has changed. A sadness fills her face, and for the first time, I see heartbreak there. Something I haven't seen since she lost her sister. "I just want to make sure that you're not getting in over your head. You're a strong woman, lady, I know that. But you have dreams and plans. I just don't want to see a guy come along and make you change your mind. Even if the guy might ooze more sex appeal than Justin Timberlake and Ryan Gosling combined!"

I laugh knowingly as she reaches over and squeezes my knee. "Good Lord, woman, I'm not joking. It's like Paul Newman's eyes on Channing Tatum's body with James Dean's rugged good looks."

I giggle, taking another sip of wine.

"I'm not gonna lie, I would totally take even like the smallest slice of that three-way." I begin to laugh even harder when she doesn't ease up on her comparisons. "I mean hell, he's like Chris Pine mixed with a little Tom Hardy then rolled into Elvis Presley's 'it just comes natural to be this sexy' kinda swagger." I laugh even harder. "I'm not lying! I saw the way he rolls his hips girl," she continues, starting to giggle herself. "Shit, he could 'love me tender' all night long! Or rough! Hell, beggars can't be choosers!"

I'm now laughing hysterically, and she joins in right along with me.

"Lord, I missed you, lady!" I say, catching my breath.

She smiles at me as we sit there silently, knowing how much our friendship means to one another without having to say another word. My mind slowly drifts back to the words she's just said. Not the long list of ways she compared Noah to some of the amazing men we have always admired, but her words before that ... I reluctantly find myself letting them play over and over again in my mind.

Sure, he's sexy, and God only knows how bad I want him. But I have never let anyone or anything stop me from pursuing anything before. I don't intend to stop now. I have no intention of letting this beautiful distraction stop me from the plans that I have had in place a long time before we ever crossed paths, no matter how strong our chemistry is.

When I still haven't spoken after a few minutes, Gwen decides to switch speeds. Getting up from the couch, she starts once again towards the kitchen.

"So, are we going out? Because I'm starving!"

"Oh my God, the groceries," I exclaim, remembering the groceries are still sitting in my car.

Jumping to my feet, I'm thankful it's cold outside and they most likely haven't spoiled. I grab my coat and keys and hurry out the door, down the stairs and to my car. Opening the trunk, I grab the few bags I had bought and rush back inside. The night has cooled off quickly. Even with a coat, it is much cooler outside than it was in So Cal was a week ago.

Setting the bags on the counter, I begin unloading the perishables into the fridge when Gwen slams the cupboard door she was looking in and turns around to face me.

"Screw this!" Gwen exclaims as I put the last of the items in the fridge. "We're going out! Get dressed!"

CHAPTER 12

"Gwen, I can't go out! I have to work in the morning." I try to reason with her.

"Whatever, stop being such a grandma." She makes her way towards the living room, grabs her bag, and heads down the hallway.

"If you're going off the market soon, I'm making sure to enjoy every last second until then."

"I never said I was thinking about getting serious—" I start to say.

"Save it! I already contacted Uber. Fifteen minutes, lady! Is that club of your brother's still as swanky as I remember?"

I can hear her rummaging through her bag and roll my eyes as I make my way down the hallway. Not only do I not want to go out tonight, but I definitely am not in the mood for Gatsby's. Glancing into the spare room, I see Gwen holding up a scrap of fabric that can hardly be called a dress.

"You know it is November in northern California. Have you forgotten you're not at the beach?" I ask.

She ignores me, grabs some gold stilettos out of her bag and turns to start dressing. Continuing down the hallway, I have no idea what to wear and no desire to be anywhere near an environment like Gatsby's. Opening up my closet, I pause briefly as I start to realize that maybe Noah is making more of an impression on me than I thought.

Chapter 13

Evelyn

One drink ... maybe two max! A couple of dances and then I promise I am pulling Gwen away from this place as fast as I can. Staring out the window as our driver nears Gatsby's, I watch the trees' silhouettes in the moonlight. Glancing up, the stars barely shine through the clouds in the sky. The air is crisp enough outside to cause goosebumps on my skin even though there is no window open.

It is 8:45 pm and I would rather be in bed, not dressed up midweek, about to brave the largest watering ground for singles typically only looking for a one-night stand. Gwen's face is plastered to her phone as she sits next to me in the backseat of this little car. She barely notices when we arrive and finally looks up, surprised, as we come to a stop in front of the club. Paying the driver, I brace myself before stepping out into the November evening.

Gwen rounds the car and links her arm in mine quickly. Squealing like a schoolgirl, she looks up at the big neon sign flashing across the top of the building. Two bouncers flank each side of the doors and a line of about seventy-five people wait in the cold to my left.

CHAPTER 13

"Hells yes, let's do this," Gwen exclaims as we walk towards the front. I'm a little timid while she's much more enthusiastic.

The bouncer, Troy, another one of my brother's longtime friends, walks forward to greet us. Even though he is not as close to my brother as Rex, he's always been around. They were sort of like the Three Musketeers when we were all in high school.

"Hey, Ev," he says. "Gwen, it's been a while. How long are you visiting?"

Ever the flirt, Gwen jumps at any chance to warm up to Troy. I can't say I blame her. If he wasn't such good friends with my brother, I'd be doing the same. Troy stands at almost six-six, blond hair, blue eyes, and the time he spent in the service as a Navy SEAL enhances all of the rest of his best assets.

"As long as you want me to be, handsome," she says and wraps him in a big hug. "Missed you, big guy. Glad to see you aren't off on another tour."

He kisses the top of her head in a brotherly type way before saying, "Nope, not yet. I'm sure it won't be long before I am called upon again, but for now, I get to look at you gorgeous creatures come and go all night."

"Very funny," I say, swatting him playfully as he steps back to open the doors for us. I hear annoyed muttering behind us that we don't have to wait in line like the rest of them. "Is my brother here yet?"

"Haven't seen him. Although, he could be in there somewhere," Troy says.

"Ok, thanks. I'll keep my eye out," I say as Troy grabs one door handle and the other bouncer, a new guy I haven't met yet, grabs the other door. He gives me a shy nod, and I smile back.

"You ladies have fun," Troy says while he winks at Gwen and she proceeds to blow him a kiss back. I ignore them both as the doors open and all other sounds quiet to the deafening beat of the music that begins to fill the night around us. Taking a few short steps inside, I decide to at least try and have a good time as the doors close behind us.

The air is thick, and the smell of alcohol and expensive perfume hangs in it like a fog. Steps cascade in front of us, down onto a dance floor already busting at the seams with people. The largest of three bars sits in the back of the lower level, and I can see at least five bartenders hurriedly making drinks for a line that's three people deep and extends down the whole massive bar top.

A DJ spins music directly across from us, above the bar on the second floor in one of the most elaborate booths anyone had ever seen. The floor wraps around the building, creating a balcony for the second floor to look down at the first. Behind us are stairs on both sides leading up to a third floor held mostly for VIP events.

The third floor is lush with expensive couches and even more expensive decor while the second floor has cozy little sitting spots tucked away throughout. The bottom floor is where most of the people hang out and remains standing and dancing room only.

A remix to the Justin Timberlake's song "Lovestoned" blares through my ears, loud enough where if I didn't already know the words, I wouldn't be able to make them out. I descend the steps slowly as Gwen turns it into a scene from a music video, dancing her way down each one with almost too much energy. Laughing, I try to shake my annoyance off and ease into the atmosphere. Maybe a night out is just what I need.

CHAPTER 13

"Drinks first," she yells out. "Let's go!"

Grabbing my hand, she pulls me out onto the dance floor and pushes our way through the crowd. Not caring and oblivious to the annoyed looks of strangers, she continues through as I apologize to everyone we bump into. Making it to the other side of the dance floor, we stop for a moment and take in the line for drinks in front of us, debating what the best course of action is. We both stand there feeling defeated, and the night has barely even started.

"Well this sucks," she says. "Maybe we should order two or three at one time so we don't have to come back."

No sooner had the comment left her lips that I feel a hand slip around my waist. Gwen obviously feels it too because we both jump and look towards one another to see Rex's face emerge between us.

"Don't touch me with those hands," Gwen yells, swatting him away. "I don't know what whore they were on last!"

He laughs, grabbing her hand and pulling her back to him. "You know, if you want my hands all over you, Gwenie, you don't have to beg in front of company, sweetheart," he says, winking suggestively at her. She rolls her eyes, looking back at me, unable to form an immediate comeback.

"When are you going to stop hanging out with this loser? His pickup lines get worse and worse every time I have the unfortunate pleasure of seeing him," she tells me. "And I thought I told you to stop calling me that ridiculous nickname years ago," she sneers at him.

"Behave yourself, Gwenie. I'm all you need tonight to quench your thirst," he says, gazing down her body. "Come on." He grabs us both and starts towards the bar.

The music changes, and Pharrell and Jay-Z's "Frontin'"

remix fills the room as we follow Rex around to the back of the bar. He lifts the side counter and ushers us behind the bar with him. I notice as he leaves his hand a little too long on Gwen's back, and she shoots him an evil glare, which makes him laugh and eggs him on even more.

Pushing his way into the mix, the workers behind the bar clear for him. The power of being an owner is unmistakable as he grabs two tall glasses and turns back to face us.

"What's your pleasure?" he asks us both, but only locks eyes with Gwen.

"Not that I will ever let you be the cause of my pleasure, but make mine an old fashioned," she says.

I laugh at the way Gwen acts like a child, knowing full well that Rex is eating it up like candy. He loves this type of behavior in a sick way. Smiling, he glances my way.

Knowing I better stick to what I was drinking before we left, I say, "Red wine, thanks."

He mixes Gwen's drink, and I notice he makes it a little stronger than he should. He then pours me a more than decent size glass of Cabernet. Glancing up, he starts flirting with a brunette across the bar, and I notice Gwen shift on her feet next to me, clearly annoyed.

"Are you finished yet," she snaps at him.

Pausing a moment, he slowly picks up the drinks and turns towards us. Gwen snatches hers and turns to walk away.

"Didn't know you preferred it fast and quick, Gwenie. I'll remember that for next time," he says towards her back.

"Behave." I laugh as I hug him and follow after her.

I take a drink and let the warmness of the alcohol mix with the bass coming from the music. I slowly feel some tension leave my shoulders as we make our way to a corner not far from the bar. I see Gwen locking eyes with a stranger and watch as she flashes him her "I'm available" smile. My phone vibrates in my clutch, and I pull it out to see I have a new text from Noah.

Noah: I wasn't kidding when I said you know how to drive a man crazy. Have dinner with me on Friday?

Doing my best juggling act, I try and balance my drink in my arm so I can type a reply. I pause for a moment because I have no idea how to come back with any kind of witty "I want you too, but I still want to make you chase me" kind of response.

Me: Are you sure dinner with me is the answer to your madness?

I smile as I notice he reads it right away and can see that he is typing a response. Taking another sip of my drink, I look up as Gwen's stranger makes his way over to us. I smile at him as he starts to talk to her, and I focus my attention back on my phone.

Noah: Darlin', at this point I don't care if they lock me up as long as I get my fix before they take me away.

I giggle a little too loud, which gets Gwen's attention. She rolls her eyes and goes back to her conversation. Switching gears, butterflies start to rise in my belly as I type my response.

Me: Friday sounds perfect. I get off work at 5.

Noah: Pick you up at 6. Dress casual.

Me: Can't wait.

Noah: Likewise. See you then.

Putting away my phone, I see Gwen take a few steps back from the guy she had been chatting up, annoyed. Quick to notice when to step in, I grab her hand.

"I love this song," I exclaim about the music that I have never heard before. "Let's dance. Sorry, buddy," I yell as I pull her onto the dance floor, and we make sure to push our way further into the middle and away from the guy who's quickly approaching creeper status.

"Thank you," I hear her say behind me.

Turning around to face her, I smile. We finish off our drinks so as not to spill and hold the empty glasses while we laugh and dance for a few songs. Maybe I will get out of here as planned, but for right now, it's nice to let the world go and dance with my best friend—a girl that knows me better than any sister ever could.

Chapter 14

Noah

Getting ready to pick up Evelyn, I hadn't thought I would be as nervous as I am. Grabbing the items I planned to take with me, I take one last look at myself in the mirror and try to get ahold of the emotions I'm feeling.

"Get a grip, Stewart," I say out loud. "It's just a date."

Then why do I feel like it's so much more, I silently plead with myself. Shaking my head and shutting that thought down, I head out the door and towards my truck. The sunset a little while back and the weather has turned much colder than I expected as December nears. Backing out of the driveway, I try my best to suppress things—and people—I haven't thought about in a very long time as I make my way out to the main road.

Turning on the heater in the truck, the anticipation to see Evelyn grows almost unbearable. A familiar tune on the radio fills the truck, reminding me of another time I allowed myself to feel the same way about a woman—a woman I forced myself to forget a long time ago and swore I would never let myself think about again.

Becky.

Rebecca Brown to be exact. It was my senior year of high school and she had caught my eye faster than any girl I had yet to meet before, much like Evelyn. I debated long and hard before asking her out, seeing as she was only a junior, a year younger than me, and I had already accepted a scholarship at Ole Miss—a full ride, playing baseball for the Rebels. Having lived with less rather than more, growing up on the family farm and working the grounds as soon as I was able, I knew passing up an opportunity like that would kill any chance at building a better future for myself.

The more I allowed myself to think about her though, the more I began to cave, and the harder I began to fall after our first date. She was addictive as well, just like the woman I'm headed to see tonight and one I can't seem to get enough of.

Becky's family came from old southern money. She looked and even smelled like the kinds of things I could never obtain in life, and boy did her parents let me know that.

Looking back, I have come to accept that was the only reason Becky probably even wanted to be with me—rebellion against her prim and proper life. I remained blind to all the reasons and stayed, love-struck like a fool, all the way to the end. And what an end it was.

I ignored the reasoning of friends saying it could never work, even when I gave up my scholarship to stay behind with her because she couldn't bear to see me leave. I even took a job with her father's company to prove I could fit into her world after graduation.

He came from a long line of upper-classmen that had built somewhat of an insurance and bonds empire in the south. Trading in my usual duds for a three-piece suit and tie, I tried my best to show her and her father that I could provide for her.

CHAPTER 14

That I could and would fit into a world I knew nothing about. To prove them wrong and to be the man she deserved.

I even continued to ignore the feeling in my gut when she showed up in tears, swearing she was pregnant, even though we hadn't slept together in over a month because I had been out of town on business. I was planning on proposing anyway but popped the question that night and wasn't surprised when she said yes. With a baby on the way, there was no way she would shame her family name. I made myself believe that in some way giving up everything for her, because of how much I loved her, would make everything ok. It would always be enough because the love we shared would always be enough. She was all I ever wanted. And as long as I always showed her that, then we couldn't fail.

It was the tears that she cried when I walked in to find her having sex with her father's partner, a younger man only about ten years older than the both of us, that finally broke the spell she had on me. It was the tears of her heartbreak over how he was a mistake she promised to never make again that slammed the door shut for me, never wanting to allow another woman in.

When I found out the truth that it was her father's partner's baby and she had told me it was mine because she knew the bastard would never leave his wife to make an honest woman out of her, I was already long gone. Having packed my bags and changed my number, that was the moment I had headed out west to live with Rex.

Feeling the way I do for Evelyn is exactly what got me into trouble the first time. It's what had me giving up a life for someone who didn't love me the same and lied about everything I thought was true between us. It is exactly why

I don't want to have the feelings I have been trying to fight since I first met her ten days ago. Maybe cutting things off now would be a good idea. After all, I'm still going home in six weeks. I don't belong here, and I'm not about to change me and change my life on the chance that what we're building could and would be all we'll ever need.

But this time, as I think about leaving, there's a nagging feeling in my gut. The thought of not being near her makes me feel sick—homesick almost, knowing that a part of me may always be missing. That part of me that feels whole when I am with her. A part of me I surprisingly never realized I was missing before.

Pulling up to a stop in front of her house, I notice there is no light coming from the windows in her part of the building. Maybe I should just leave, text her some lame excuse that I am sure she will never buy, and call it a night. Maybe go drink some beers with Rex and try and forget about her before I am in over my head. More panic hits as I realize I already am.

Grabbing my phone, I begin tapping my finger against the screen a few times, thinking. Maybe distance from her is a good thing. I promised myself I would never let a woman take control of my life or my feelings again after Becky. Walking away now could possibly save me a lot in the long run. If I walk away now, it will make it easier when I leave at the end of December.

Then why does my heart sink just thinking about leaving? And why am I, after everything I've promised myself, suddenly debating not moving home at all?

Moments away from typing out a text message, I jump to the sound of someone tapping on the window. It's Evelyn, bundled up in a coat, scarf, and beanie. Her cheeks are rosy from the chilly night air. She looks beautiful standing there, smiling, and it takes a moment before I come to my senses. Opening the door, I step into the freezing night air alongside her.

"You have to be chilled to the bone! How long have you been out here?" I ask, grabbing both her arms and rubbing them up and down, a sorry attempt at trying to warm her.

"Just walked out," she answers, bouncing up and down to keep warm. She bounces in a way that's so adorably attractive, I can't help but grin as I reach out and pull her closer to keep her warm.

"I was watching from the window," she confesses as I feel her warm breath against my shirt. "What were you thinking about, sitting in your truck so long?"

Pulling her back and looking her in the eyes, I smile before lying. "Football."

Her eyebrows knit together, clearly expecting a different response. "Football?" she questions back.

"Uh huh! Titans lost their last game. I need to make some adjustments to my fantasy league." I'm such a bad liar. Hardly ever having watched much football—baseball is more my sport—I hope she doesn't catch on. She shrugs like she couldn't care less, and I smile knowing that I'm in the clear.

"Come on," I say, pulling her in closer and kissing the tip of her pink nose. "We're wasting moonlight."

I looked down into her big blue eyes and start to feel her winning the war that's raging inside me. Pulling away, I immediately feel cold without her near me and walk her around the side of the truck, opening up her door and helping her climb in. Settling into the driver's seat, I put the car in drive and turn to face her, noticing she is already watching me, anticipating me telling her where we are headed. I stay silent and watch her start to squirm as I know the many ideas of where we might be headed are dancing around in her head.

"Where are you taking me?" she asks.

"I want to show you something," I say. "Tonight's just for us. No bar, no party, no outside friends for distractions," I joke, and she giggles knowingly. Pulling away from her house, we settle into a comfortable silence as a Luke Bryan song quietly plays in the background and my thoughts invade again.

Her eyes sure did seem to sparkle in pure excitement over the idea. Maybe she wants to be alone with me as much as I need to be alone with her. All I've wanted since I set eyes on her is to have her all to myself, but allowing that to happen means I'm slowly allowing her in. Being near her makes me question my future. Makes me want to rearrange everything just to allow room for her to stay, even if it's just for as long as she will want to.

I have spent so much time strategically putting up walls so as to never let any woman have the smallest amount of control over me. I still have no idea as to why I am hopelessly allowing her to break holes into those walls. I never intended to let anyone in again. As we merge onto the highway, I crack the window for a little fresh air as anxiety starts to build inside me.

"So," I hear her say, bringing my thoughts back to the present. "Since you won't tell me where we are going, let's play a game."

"A game." I laugh. "What kind of game can we play right now in the cab of my truck?"

She adjusts in her seat so she is sitting somewhat Indian-style, facing me. I glance over at her and see her smile at me mischievously. This might not be good.

"Well, I could think of a few things actually, but first ..."

she trails off, laughing. "I ask you a question and you have to answer with the first thing that comes to mind," she says. "Then you get to ask me and I have to answer. Then, again and again, vice versa, you know. That way we get to know more about one another than just the way it feels to be pressed up against each other."

"But pressed up against you is my favorite place to be," I tease, resting my hand on her thigh, my tension finally slowly leaving.

I look over and see her roll her eyes as she smiles and swats at me playfully. I grab her hand and hold it, smiling back at her while I drive. I notice her cheeks blush and more tension seems to lift as I realize I needed this. I needed her and there is no other place I would rather be in the world right now.

"Come on," she says. "It will be fun."

"Ok, who goes first?"

"I do," she exclaims, excited, and sits up a little straighter. I laugh at her enthusiasm as I glance at her again and see she is in deep thought, making me laugh harder. She gives me a playfully hateful glare, and I can't help but snicker at her.

"Stop it. I am trying to think ... Ok, I got it," she says after a moment. "What is your favorite color?"

"Orange." I smile and pull her hand up to kiss the top of it, noticing her smile. "Although, I do love I it when your cheeks turn that adorable shade of pink ... like right now."

She looks down, embarrassed. "What's your favorite food?" I ask.

"Oh, that is easy," she says. "Anything southern style BBQ."

"Really?" I ask surprised. A girl after my own heart. "Well, I can definitely help you out with that, sweetheart."

"I bet you can." She laughs. "What is your favorite hobby?"

"I'm a southern boy, miss. I'll let you guess that one. Shouldn't be too hard," I reply.

"I'm not sure," she says, thinking hard for a moment. "Maybe hunting?"

"Good guess," I say. "Throw in a little fishing and sports, my momma's front porch and some good sweet tea, and you got it darlin'."

"Well, I don't know much about those things," she says. "But I could learn." Her eagerness to try something that I love makes me smile.

"Your turn," she says.

"Hmm," I say, trying to think about my next question for a moment. "What made you want to be a writer?"

Smiling, she says, "That isn't really a one-word answer." When I don't respond, she continues, "I don't know, really. It is just something that I have always done. When I was little, before I could ever really write, I would make these books with scribbles for words and pathetic stick figures for people. I would staple them together and be so proud of my little creation. Over time, it has just morphed into more. I love the catharsis I get reading something really well written, and I love the idea of being the one that could write that for someone else."

Speechless, I just look ahead at the road in front of me, not quite sure how to answer such honesty.

"Good answer," I finally manage.

"So what about you, then? Have you always worked construction, or is it something you fell into?" she asked.

Cringing a little inside at the thought of my past, I try my best to shrug it off as I reply, "I worked briefly in the nine to five suit and tie world..." I glance over her way "...wasn't my

CHAPTER 14

thing."

"Gotcha," she smiles.

We talk more, trying our best to dig into each other's nooks and crannies without prying too much. This being our first date, it's never too polite to dig deep into someone's closet.

I find out her favorite color is blue, favorite holiday is Christmas, she never watches scary movies, and just the smell of green beans makes her want to vomit. I admit to having a guilty pleasure now and again to a good romantic comedy, and she's shocked to find out that I've never gone swimming in the ocean.

I slow my truck as I reach the top of the hill. Looking at Evelyn, I see her eyes are wide in amazement. Backing up, I turn the truck around so we can sit on the tailgate and take in the breathtaking sight.

The night sky is mostly clear and the stars are endless above. In the distance, clouds roll over far away hilltops and lightning can be seen as a thundershower approaches. Below is a valley with just the slightest twinkling of lights from a few houses.

I grin as I put the truck in park and kill the engine.

"Want to sit on the tailgate?" I ask. She nods, unable to speak as she looks out the back window of the truck.

I jump from the truck and run over to her door. Opening it, I help her down and grab a backpack from the backseat. Setting the items down, I lift her up onto the tailgate of my truck. Running back to the cab, I grab the two blankets I had stowed away as well and quickly return wrapping one around her to keep her warm.

"This sure goes down as one unforgettable surprise," she says as I hop up on the tailgate to join her.

Shrugging, I let a few moments pass before I answer her.

"I'm trying to make it hard for anyone to follow in my footsteps, is it working?" I ask.

"Oh, so you don't want someone else to come and sweep me off my feet, is that it?" she nervously asks looking out in the distance.

"Not if I can help it," I confess, shocking both me and her. With no idea where to go from there, I open the backpack I brought with me.

"Seeing as I had no idea your favorite food was my home state's staple, I did the best I could when I packed us dinner."

"You packed dinner," she asks, shocked.

"I made a promise to feed you, didn't I?" I say with a smile. "Now pickin's are slim when it comes to what will keep and pack away easily, so I did the best I could."

Pulling out some containers of food the lady at the store suggested, I nervously watch her as I open them.

"Here we have ham and cheese roll-up sandwiches," I say, opening the first container. After setting it aside, I open the second. "And here is some fresh fruit, pineapple, strawberries, grapes ... that kind of stuff." Opening the third container, I add, "And here I did my best attempt at what you might like for dessert. I stumbled across some store while in Auburn today and stopped in. I hope you like fudge or English toffee?"

Grabbing some toffee and taking a bite, she smiles up at me as she says, "Its perfect."

Pulling a bottle of wine from the backpack and a few cups, I say, "I did my best to pick you out a nice red. That was what you were drinking the other night, right?"

"Very good. I'm impressed," she says, taking the cup. "None for you?" she asks as I don't pour myself a drink.

I pull out a flask. "Kentucky bourbon." I wink at her. "Sure to warm you right up."

"Got enough to share," she asks.

Surprised I hand her the flask. She stares at it momentarily before tilting it back and taking a swig. Her face tightens momentarily before she opens her eyes and looks back at me.

"That's good," she says licking her lips.

I smile brighter, "I'm glad you like it."

She tilts it back again before handing it back.

"I could get hooked on that stuff," she chokes out. The second swig clearly a little bigger and stronger than the first.

"Ninety-five percent of the world's bourbon comes out of Kentucky," I say. "If you ever come out my way, trust me you will be in no short supply."

Smiling, she makes my heart race faster as she replies, "Maybe I will just have to come out that way then."

She has no idea. I would love to take her home and show her my world. Although I doubt she would ever want to leave California and the home and life she has built up here for herself. Maybe I could convince her to take a trip back with me if whatever is happening between us goes much further, but even then I'm risking more heartache when she would eventually leave so why even go there.

As the night wears on, something about Evelyn makes me want to gamble, though, just one more time in my life on this crazy and stupid thing they call love. Maybe she will be different. Maybe whatever this is between us, given the right chance, could work. Maybe it's worth a try.

After we've talked and had our share of food and drink, I watch as she gets down from the tailgate and wraps the blanket around herself tightly. She turns and faces me, smiling mischievously, the bourbon obviously giving her a new found confidence. Taking slow steps towards me, she comes to a stop in between the middle of my legs. My heart races, wondering what she's up to.

She says nothing, just looks into my eyes, smiling at me and waiting. For what, I have no clue. An invitation of sorts? Hell, she needs no invitation. I am always wanting to hold her, touch her, feel her, be anywhere near her. She leans in, teasing me, and then backs away before I can close the distance.

I reach up and brush a few strands of hair out of her face, watching as she leans her head into my hand, only extending the time I take to touch her. This, right here, is the moment time pauses. I stare at her knowing that I need to make the decision. I'm not someone to inch into the swimming pool. I always choose to dive in headfirst. And right now I need to decide if my heart is strong enough to take that plunge again because Lord knows if I ever do, I want it to be with her.

Somewhere between kissing her in that bar the first night we met and this moment, I know I have lost any will to guard myself. Taking this brief second, I wait. As much as I know my heart might not be strong enough to drown in love, as long as it's her love killing me softly, it won't even matter. I know it would never feel right letting her go either.

The only future I want to see now has to have her in it. To hell with my past and swearing off love. Being with her gives me life, and my life would be dull if I ever had to walk a day without her by my side again. I just hope that she feels the same way ... or could grow to in time.

"I don't want to be without you, Evelyn," I confess in a whisper. "I'm not sure how or when that happened, but something about you captivates me. Once you walked into my life, I haven't been able to stop thinking about you. You consume me."

Giving up and caving in, I close the distance between the two of us and kiss her before she has a chance to pull away. I have to have her. I have to taste her. I have to feel her against me to ease my nerves and calm the madness and doubt ragging in my head.

When I'm with her like this, there is peace. When we are together, I know I don't need anything else in the world.

She pulls back, and I do my best to resist, kissing her harder and pulling her back into me. Giggling, she finally breaks free.

"What? You think you can just say something like that then kiss me senseless and I am not supposed to say anything," she asks.

"I think we were just talking better than words could ever express," I say, pulling her in and going for her neck. Kissing her softly a few times, I see her skin prickle with goosebumps. I smile against her skin and continue my assault on her body, pulling her shirt off her shoulder, kissing and nibbling my way across her collarbone.

She moans into me. "You're making me lose what I was about to say."

"Good," I manage through kisses as I start to pull at the hem of her shirt, lifting it slightly under the blanket when she stops me and pulls away completely.

"Noah, whatever your middle name is, Stewart!" she says, flustered and slightly upset.

"Ryan," I say, smiling back at her and pulling her closer again. Flustered and playfully upset works for her and does nothing to stop the need building inside me to have her.

She falls back against me, giving up and falling into the pull we have on each other.

"Don't you want to hear what I have to say," she asks, pushing out her bottom lip in a pout.

Grabbing her ass forcefully, I lift her as she wraps both legs around me. Her blanket rests on the tailgate of my truck. Leaning my head against hers, I watch as her eyes cloud with desire when, I say, "No. I want you to show me!"

Chapter 15

Evelyn

I try to mask my nerves as Noah lifts me in his arms and spins me around so I am sitting on the tailgate of his truck. His hands come up to frame my face and he holds me there for a moment as his tender eyes gaze back into my own. His thumb runs across my bottom lip and I shiver in anticipation of what comes next. What happens after he decides to make his move? Because Lord knows I have wanted him to kiss me and push the limits between us, taking us over the edge and to a place we have never explored before.

He smiles at me shyly. "You nervous?" He teases, as his hands lower and he forces the blanket to fall off my shoulders.

My sharp intake of breath is my only response as his face lowers and he takes my lips in his. Tender at first as his hands grab my hips tight and pull me towards him. I open up and allow him access and the way his tongue caresses my own has my center begining to throb and my body trembling with need. I hook a finger through his belt loop and pull him closer as he bites my bottom lip and I let a moan.

Releasing me, he pulls away slightly and sternly says, "Lean back." The look he gives has me following orders immediately.

Scooting back into the truck bed, I watch as he climbs up and crawls towards me like a predator about to savor every inch of what is in front of him. My heartbeat quickens. My body shivers in anticipation. My need to feel him any way I can is almost unbearable. His eyes go to my jeans and I bite my bottom lip as I watch him admire what he longs to see, feel and touch just underneath.

His fingers graze over my sex, as his eyes rise and stare at me with passion. "I won't make you, Darlin', but I will push your limits. You tell me if I go too far, and I'll stop." He unbuttons the top of my jeans and my hips rise instinctively as he slides them down exposing my thin lace panties underneath. His eyes dance over my center before rising and meeting my own. His look is a mixture of emotions, but the most transparent of them all is concern. Concern I might stop him? Concern I might hurt him? Concern I might not respond to him the way he desires? But all of that is lost the second he forces my panties to the side and traces a finger across my folds.

The sensation has my head falling back before he even attempts to enter my body. He stops, and my head snaps forward and meets his stare. "God, Darlin'. There is nothing sexier than you. Nothing more beautiful." He pushes a finger inside me and I gasp out from the sensation. With wide eyes, I stare at him while he pleasures me. He never looks away and that only adds to the passion building between the two of us.

I grip his free wrist at my side as he continues his assault. I watch as he breaks our stare and licks his lips. Glancing back up, the urgency in his eyes to take what he wants is evident before he even speaks. "I want to taste you, Darlin'." He pleads. I nod my head and his sexy smile has me almost losing all restraint because all I want is to tell him to take me right here

CHAPTER 15

and now in the back of his truck. Lowering his head, I suck in a breath as I feel his mouth make contact with my wet center. His moan sends a sensation through my heat that I have never experienced before. I watch as he licks up my folds and sticks his tongue deep inside me before starting all over again. I say his name and it makes him groan with pleasure as he sticks a finger inside me and his mouth finds my clit.

Sucking it between his lips, my head falls back as he enters another finger inside and starts to pull both of them in and out in a way that has me frantically trying to not cum too soon. "You taste like heaven," I hear him say before he licks up my center one more time. "I could get drunk on your taste, Darlin.'"

Suddenly, his fingers pick up the pace. His mouth starts a demanding assault as he urges my body to climax. I call out his name, but that doesn't stop him. His fingers curl and hit that beautiful spot deep inside, just as his mouth sucks my nub in his lips with such need my body can't take anymore. Crashing over the edge, I pull at his hair as my screams fill the night around us. Still, he pushes my body further as his tongue licks and takes what he wants and my climax reaches new heights I didn't even know where possible. Once I start to come down, he slowly removes his fingers and licks up my center tenderly. With hooded eyes, he glances up at me and smiles. Sticking his fingers in his mouth, be licks my juices off with a sexy groan of approval.

"God, Darlin', you're sweeter than I dreamed." Climbing up my body, he kisses my stomach before pulling my shirt down and cupping my breast through my bra. He looks up at me and smiles as he lowers his face to my hard nipple. Sucking it into his mouth through the lace fabric, I moan out in pleasure and grind my hips up against his own. I can feel how hard he is as his massive length strokes the inside of my thigh when he pushes back against me. My hands lower and I grab his jeans, debating if I should go for it now, or wait. Before I can decide, he makes the choice for both of us.

Stilling me, he looks up in my eyes and says, "Not yet, Darlin.' The best things in life are worth waiting for. And our first time is not going to be in the back of my truck." He winks at me and lowers his face to my own. Kissing me sweetly, I sigh into him and wonder just what I did to score a man as amazing as him.

Chapter 16

Evelyn

"And then what happened," Gwen asks, wide-eyed, as she sits on the edge of the couch.

It's 2:30 in the morning, and we have been rehashing my night with Noah ever since I arrived home about an hour ago. Ever the night owl, I wasn't surprised when I came home to find her on the couch, still watching some late night infomercials. She has a strange addiction to home shopping networks, always buying what others only think of buying before they come to their senses. I know deep down it's because she never sleeps well. She's had sleeping issues since her sister's death.

"He drove me home and walked me to the door," I answer, trying to give away the least amount of information I can.

"And ..." she pries.

"And what?" I say, dodging the obvious.

She eyes me but I don't cave. I just let my smile widen, knowing all the toe-curling details and not giving up any of them.

"Come on!" she yells, chucking a pillow at me from across the couch.

Laughing, I throw it back at her while I take the time to choose my words wisely. "Let's just say that it took every ounce of my will power not to pull that man in here and finish what we started." I blush.

"That's it! He didn't even try to get to home base? Geez, what kind of guy is he?"

"A rare breed, I guess," I answer. "I believe they used to call them gentlemen. He pushed a hard third base though!"

"I'd have more respect for him if he rounded all three bases and stole home!" she exclaims. "Maybe he's gay!"

I laugh as I stand from the couch to make my way down the hallway to bed. "I can assure you that he most definitely is not."

"I'm not sure of anything yet until you come home barely able to walk. The verdict is still out on boat man," she yells after me.

Shaking my head, I slip out of my clothes and into a nightgown. Normally never forgoing a shower, I decide to wait a few more hours since my skin still smells like him. Crawling into bed, still buzzing from Noah and the bourbon, I let my mind remember all the events of the evening, still feeling his touch lingering on my skin as we lay in the bed of his truck for hours, exploring each other with such a carnal need.

I'm as surprised as Gwen is that he did not try and take advantage of the situation. Being respected that way makes me want him even more. Knowing that he didn't push for his needs but respected mine instead makes me want to give. He pushed as far as I did and never asked to take it any further. I know full well the need he had, though, as he pushed me up against the door at the end of the night, barely able to pull himself away from me as we tried our best to satisfy an appetite I'm most certain will never be sated. I felt the same need as we hungrily felt every inch of each other, breathing one another in and memorizing as much as possible ... as if we would never be together again.

Watching him leave was torture, and I stood there for a few moments, regaining my composure from the mind-blowing evening before walking inside. Never has a man been able to make me feel the way that Noah did.

When I stand next to him, I grow tingly and numb. The chemistry swirls in a force so strong I can barely think. The draw to touch him can barely be stopped. And once I do, I am at peace. I feel connected, like I am home. Something I have never felt before.

I just only hope I am not in over my head on this one. As much as this man can make me feel in ways you only dream about late at night or read about in books, I can't get distracted. I can't let myself give up by giving in. At the end of the toe-curling night we just spent together, that is the fear that overwhelms me as I try to focus on the events of the evening instead.

Noah

Walking in the front door of the house I share with Rex, I set my keys down on the counter and have to adjust myself as I take a few deep breaths again, standing at the counter. I have never been as worked up over a woman, and I have absolutely never stopped myself without going for a home run before either.

It's taken everything in me to try and think about other things, but just as I start to have control over both my heads, I smell her perfume lingering on me or remember the way she felt under my hands, and it all starts all over again. My manhood continues to stand at attention, needing like hell to release what has been building up inside of me while lying in the back of my truck with her for the last few hours.

I hear laughter coming from the back patio and grab a beer from the fridge. Popping the top off, I head out back to find Rex and Michael still in their suits from the club. Both are a little better or a little worse from the more than half-empty bottle of Jameson I see sitting on the table in front of them.

"Hey there, Romeo," Rex starts off. "How was she?"

"Fuck off, Rex. Don't be talking about my little sister that way!" Michael starts in.

I pull up a seat and take a long pull off my bottle, readjusting myself again at just the mere mention of her. Damn it, this is not good.

"That bad huh," Rex starts.

I set my bottle down and smile, not one to kiss and tell as they say. This crowd proves even more difficult, seeing that both men would happily kick my ass if I dared to screw with her.

"You honestly expect me to sit here and answer any questions about my date? You're crazier than I thought, asshole." I laugh, picking up my bottle and continuing to take a gulp, not a sip. Something has to work to lessen the spell she has over me and the way everything about her seems to follow me home.

"You know, if you even think for a second you might screw this up one day, you better back out now," Michael says. "I have no problem making sure to find a way to make you disappear if need be."

Normally I would respond with some sort of joke to break the tension, but the look the two of them are giving me makes me back up. I know that the protectiveness of a sibling is nothing to be messed with. Hell, I would never let anyone on Earth mess with my own.

"Understood." I nod at the two of them.

"I've heard about your past, man," Michael begins, filling up both his and Rex's glasses more than normal. "As much as I'm sorry about that, I don't want to be the shoulder she's crying on if you decide for any reason that you can't be the man she deserves."

I look at Rex, surprised. He was the only one that knew anything about my past with Becky. He wasn't sworn to secrecy, but I never thought he would go blabbing about it to anyone.

"I confess," Rex says, slurring a little bit. "I told him. But listen..." he continues, leaning forward and resting his arms on the table. "I did it because I know that if you are even thinking about anything again with any woman, then it must be legit, and I wanted him to know that."

"Legit or not," Michael starts, "you fuck with her, I fuck with you. End of story! You got that, southern boy?"

Trying not to glare but failing miserably, I nod. "Yeah! Got it." The thrill of the night is gone. I guess I won't need that cold shower after all with this unexpected confrontation.

"Good!" he says, slapping Rex on the back, which forces him to sit up straight and then proceeds to pour me a glass. "Now that we got that out of the way. Take a shot!"

"I think I'm good," I say, lifting up my beer.

"To hell you are!" he exclaims, pushing the brown liquid towards me. "I saw the way you walked in here. Something has to quiet the sting of getting left high and dry."

Rex laughs as he and Michael raise their glasses.

"To ..." Michael begins, and I just raise an eyebrow.

They both look at me, waiting. I start to sweat a little under their glare, knowing that I have to come up with something good or I am about to get pummeled right here and now. I raise my glass and say ...

"To not fucking up."

"Damn straight!" Michael says as we all cheers and take the shot.

"Speaking of which, you still planning on moving back to Kentucky at the end of December," Rex asks.

"Yeah ... about that," I say. "I don't know, I heard of two club owners that might want a little work done on their club. I'm thinking I might make this move permanent ..." At least for now, I think to myself.

"Good answer," Michael says as he fills our glasses one more time. They both shoot theirs back, and I just sit with mine for a while, contemplating the decision that I just realized I made. In only a few weeks' time, I have allowed a woman to have a pull over me that I swore to myself I would never let happen again. And even though I should probably feel anxious and sick to my stomach, I actually feel relieved and secure. There is a peace I have not felt in the past few years settling over me. As eerie as it seems, it almost feels like home. And I've heard that a wise man once said if it feels that way, you should follow it and never look back.

"Speaking of killing the sting, Rex here is well on his way to erasing a ghost that reared its ugly head this last week," Michael says, breaking my train of thought.

Rex pushes back in his seat, slumping low and closing his eyes.

"I thought you promised not to mention her name," he says, wincing at the thoughts obviously running through his brain.

CHAPTER 16

"Did you hear a name in that sentence? Shit, you're drunker than I thought." Michael laughs.

Rex just raises his middle finger but keeps his eyes closed. A few moments pass, and I am not sure if he is passed out, trying to stop the room from spinning or dealing with the shit in his own head.

"What is all this about?" I ask.

"A certain redhead has haunted him for years," Michael explains, and my mind immediately goes to Evelyn's friend. "Poor bastard screwed that door shut on his own a long time ago, and no amount of banging has ever inched it back open again."

Being the first time I have ever heard anything about it, I look at my friend and see him open up one eye, glaring at Michael.

"If I wasn't seeing double of you right now, your ass would be on the floor," he slurs, raising his glass and taking another sip of whiskey.

"Sure, lover boy." Michael laughs. "She's moving back home, you know."

Rex sits up straight. "Shut the hell up," he yells.

"I heard her say so to Ev at the club the other night."

My stomach turns as I take in what I just heard. Evelyn was at the club the other night? What night? As much as I know we haven't discussed being exclusive, those are definitely my intentions, and I do not like the idea of her anywhere where some other guy could put his hands on her. Hell, I could hardly stomach the idea of any man looking at her, knowing what they would be thinking. That first night I met her was proof enough.

"She was at the club?" I try and ask without drawing attention to myself.

Michael smiles as if he knows what I must be thinking, "Yup, two nights ago," he tells me as I let it all sink in. "That is where this all started," he gestures towards Rex.

I think about Rex's issue for about two seconds before being dragged back into my own thoughts about a certain blond that has rocked my world and turned it completely around in such a short time.

Evelyn has succeeded in thrilling me in every way imaginable. Strangely enough, somewhere in losing myself to her, I feel as if I am finding myself too. Knowing that I made a life-changing decision tonight, I take several minutes contemplating if I will grow to regret it. Even if the thought of her in the local hookup spot has me a little twisted, I know without a doubt that I won't. A smile slowly spreads across my face as I raise my glass to my lips.

Chapter 17

Evelyn

A few weeks and several dates later, Noah and I are inseparable. If we aren't texting each other, we're calling each other. If I'm home, he's there with me, and most winter nights we fall asleep on my couch in each other's arms with the fireplace crackling and popping in the background.

I always feel him sneak out from underneath me in the wee hours of the morning, kissing me softly before he leaves for work. Each night Noah swears he's going home early at least once that week, but night after night he always fails miserably; trying to let each other go seems far too difficult when we are both so eager to soak up every second together we can.

Deliriously smitten, I'm obsessed with finding out everything I can, mentally and physically, about the man slowly stealing my heart whenever we're together. I have never felt this way about a guy before in my life. In an attempt to not break my heart, and being entirely new to this kind of feeling, I decide it's best to only show as much emotion as Noah does towards me. Guarded, I fear showing too much too soon but have let myself let go of the fear that consumed me a few weeks back.

Just because I feel this way about him, doesn't mean I have to give up anything. If he feels the same way I do, and if he is falling for me as much as I am for him, he will understand my dreams and won't want me giving up on them either. The risk is just knowing where we stand.

Gwen moved in with me around the middle of December, after bombarding me with the news of her sudden move during our brief night out at Gatsby's a month ago. Because she would rather die than live with her mother, and I did happen to have a spare bedroom, the choice seemed obvious. Although her move did put a damper on mine and Noah's late night couch sessions. Since I never venture anywhere near Rex's, not wanting to bump into any of his latest conquests or hear their late night escapades, Noah and I spend the nights in my room, which makes holding out on letting him bring it home that much harder.

I still have not given him the green light to go all the way and to be honest with myself, I'm not quite sure why. Never labeled a slut, I'm also not a prude.

"I'm telling you, the man is gay!" Gwen exclaims one Saturday night over a bottle wine.

Typically, by now I would be curled around the tall, dark, handsome man that I have quickly begun to feel like my other half, but since Gwen's move, we haven't had much girl time. She sure has given me hell for it since most of all the other people she used to know around town either don't live here anymore or are already married with children.

"Stop it already." I giggle, well into my third glass and having no intention of slowing down. We had talked about getting food after glass one, but two more glasses and neither of us has made a move for the door or the phone, which could prove to be a very bad idea soon if we don't come to our senses.

"Well, then give it to me. Tell me why you know without a doubt that the man isn't just using you as his beard?" she says, winking at me with a wide smile as she takes another gulp—not sip—of wine.

"He has very skilled hands." I laugh into my own glass.

"Hands?!" she exclaims. "That's it!!! Hands! Geez, Ev, that is something you can do on your own!"

Rolling my eyes at her, my smile widens, remembering a few nights prior.

"His mouth is better, though." I wink.

Slapping my knee, her eyes widen. "I knew it, you little vixen. You've been holding out on me," she says.

Giggling, I wait until she's settled back in her seat. "And when he uses them both at the same time, Good Lord," I say, fanning myself and laying my head against the chair.

"Well hell," she confesses with a look of shock. "He might not bat for the other team after all."

I smile knowingly and let a silence settle over us. As much as I find myself more and more obsessed with the man every day that we are together, and as much as I have given up on the idea that falling for him means giving up me, I still have this feeling deep in the pit of my stomach that I fight with, and I am not fully sure what exactly it is yet.

I'm not scared or anything—at least I don't think so. It's more the unwillingness to hand over my life, to surrender to him and except that this might be it. Even if I won't surrender all plans and dreams to a man I have just met, knowing that if there is a greater future there between us, that typically means building a new set of plans and dreams together. The focus I tried to gain when I first met him is beginning to blur. And even though I try not admitting it to myself, a world without Noah is a world I'm not sure I want to live in.

But am I ready to build new dreams and somehow manage to keep my own?

The ill feeling in the pit of my insides creeps into reality every time I think about it as if holding me back from ever jumping over that edge. From ever allowing myself to feel completely the way that I imagine other people feel.

What if there is so much more that I'd be giving up by giving in? What if I find myself slowly compromising each day, each month, and what if our relationship goes further each year? What if in the end I'm left with a shell of what I used to be and our world has hardly anything to do with me?

Gwen gives me a questionable look, sensing something is up with the long silence. "What is it?"

"I'm not sure," I admit honestly. "I mean, I should be on cloud nine. I should be so excited and wanting to shout it from the top of my lungs. I should be giving in and doing things like going all the way, not holding back, and yet ..."

"And yet ..." she echoes.

Shrugging my shoulders, shaking my head, I force a smile. "Nothing," I lie. "I'll figure it out or it will figure me out. Besides, there is always more to life than love and romance right?" I ask, more making a statement than questioning the validity of what I had just said.

"Damn straight, lady!" she exclaims clanking my glass with her own. "It only burns you in the end anyway."

She gets up and makes her way back to the kitchen to grab some more wine, and I am left with my thoughts. Deciding best to push them down where they came from, I straighten myself up a little taller on the couch and raise my glass to my lips and take a sip.

"Burns you in the end ..." I say aloud, echoing her this time. How about burns right now? I know all about the burn in the pit of my stomach, and I'm not sure how to fight it. I'm also not sure I'm strong enough to fight the feelings that I have for Noah that grow stronger and stronger every day, and that makes it burn more.

Chapter 18

Evelyn

It's ten days before Christmas, almost a month after Noah and I became inseparable. Since Gwen has moved back home, I decided to throw her a house warming/holiday party. She's, of course, all about the event, except for the fact that Rex will also be in attendance because it's simply just too hard to keep him away. Plus, knowing Rex, he'd probably show up anyway, invited or not.

An hour before guests are set to arrive, Noah, Michael, Rex, and Trevor come over to help set up. When everything is just about right, Gwen and I slip into the back room to get ready while the boys head out to the balcony on this unusually warm December evening in California, enjoying a beer.

After a quick shower and freshening up my makeup and hair, I put on a little red dress that hugs my curves in all the right places. If the weather is going to bless us and feel more like spring than winter, I'm taking full advantage of it before January hits and it's typically wet and cold until spring.

"We're ready!" I exclaim as Gwen and I step out of the back bedroom and make our way down the hallway. The boys have moved back inside and are now gathered around the countertop

CHAPTER 18

in the kitchen.

"I can see that," Noah says, grabbing and kissing me hard the second that I come within an arm's reach of him. I kiss him back in a hurry then push away slightly. Grabbing me tightly, he lays an overabundance of kisses all over, first on my check then lower on my neck and collarbone.

"Stop, you'll mess me all up," I say, holding on to him as his weight pushes me slightly backward, giving him better access to my neck just like he likes. I know he does it to make me absolutely defenseless, and it works. He could mess me up all he wants as long as he keeps kissing that one spot right there.

"You know how hard it is for me to take my hands off of you once I start," is his muffled response.

"Oh my God, get a room," Gwen shouts.

"No problem," Noah exclaims, picking me up by the waist and hauling me over his shoulder as he makes his way to my bedroom.

"Noah!" I giggle, slapping him on the back. "Put me down."

He eventually obliges, setting me down softly in the hallway and leaning into me.

"Your all mine later, baby," he growls. "I have plans for you and that sorry excuse for a dress you're wearing."

"Oh, you like it do you?" I tease, pushing my hips forward and feeling him growing hard with need.

"I do, and so will every other man here tonight," he says, looking me up and down. "Not sure I like that."

"You're silly," I manage, an absolutely ridiculous response but I am unsure what else to say.

"Baby, if they have half the thoughts that I have running through my mind, and I know they will, I will have to fight them off left and right," he says. "I don't like other guys thinking any kind of thoughts about what's mine and only mine."

"Oh, I'm yours, huh?" I tease. "You own me, do you?"

I push away, smiling, and he grabs me from behind, holding me as we walk back into the kitchen. He nuzzles my neck a little. I feel the stubble of his five o'clock shadow, which only adds to the sensation of him pressed against me from behind.

"I'm planning to make you all mine later tonight. You can bet this sorry excuse of a dress on that," he says playfully as he tightens his grip around me. "God you smell amazing," he whispers in my ear, sending chills through every part of me, nibbling my earlobe.

"Your relationship cuteness is on overload." Gwen pushes past us with a glass of wine in her hand.

"So, Noah, next month's the big move huh?" Trevor hisses out, which stops me dead in my tracks and causes Noah to bump into me forcefully.

Move? Where? I've been with him practically every day and night since we met almost two months ago, and this is the first that I am hearing about any type of move. Looking up at him, I find myself unable to contain the slight tremble that takes over me as the sick burn in the pit of my stomach returns, and I hear Gwen's voice in my head ... "In the end, you always get burned."

"Actually ... I just signed a year's lease at a studio right in downtown Nevada City. Move in two weeks," Noah says, trying to reassure me and looking nowhere else but in my eyes. His stare holds me steady when I feel like everything else comes crashing down around me.

A small sense of calmness washes over me briefly from his reassuring eyes, but that burn inside still has not diminished. I grab his arm trying to find relief. He grins at me, but I can

CHAPTER 18

tell he's trying to search my eyes for how I'm feeling. Looking away, I try to hide the trembling I feel inside and the burn that is still there from having almost lost him when I didn't even know that was a possibility.

"I thought you were going to stay at my place?" Rex asks.

"I thought you might be kinda sick of me by now." Noah laughs. "Plus, a place of my own offers a little more privacy," he says, looking at Gwen.

"Thank God," Gwen exclaims. "These old walls definitely have ears."

"You got a place downtown? How close is it? Why didn't you tell me?" I ask warily. Still shaken, I haven't caught up on the conversation yet. Normally, I would have some retort for Gwen's comment, but I'm still stuck at not understanding how losing him was—or rather possibly is my new reality.

"I wanted to be closer to you," Noah says, staring into my eyes. A small smile breaks out on my face, but behind it, I feel that burn and start to feel myself holding back. Something has changed and something isn't right. Normally, I can push the burn down. Normally, I can push it away. But there it sits inside me all while my mind refuses to be quiet, rushing through a million scenarios I know are probably false but I listen to anyway.

"Plus, it's cheaper," comes Gwen's abrupt commentary. Everyone's attention immediately shoots towards her, astonished she has made such a comment in a moment that was supposed to be so tender.

"What!!" she yells. "It is!"

"I know someone else who's cheap ..." Rex starts to say.

"Oh shut up!" she says, shoving him slightly.

"If you wanted to touch me that bad, Gwenie, I can come a

little closer," he says, walking directly towards her, trying to cage her in between him and the counter. Huffing a little, she pushes around him and makes her way into the living room.

"We're still on for you to help with that addition at the club right?" Rex asks.

"Sure thing!" Noah says, laughing. "As long as you spread the word about who did the work."

"Well this calls for a toast," Michael suggests, raising his glass. "To friends! The old and the new! Glad you're sticking around, buddy!" He cheers Noah, and everyone moves forward to have their glasses meet in the center of the small room.

Noah continues to thank his friends and one by one they tell him how happy they are that he is staying. I escape to the balcony where he quickly follows behind me. As I turn around to meet him, he swoops me up in a big hug and doesn't let me go. At first, I giggle in his arms, fighting back playfully, trying to ignore what I felt inside. Soon I quiet and grab hold of him tightly.

"I didn't know you had plans to leave," I whisper into his chest.

"Now how could I ever leave you." He kisses me on the top of my head.

"I'm glad you're staying. I never thought you had any intention of leaving." I pause for a moment, hoping that statement sinks in a little. "It would have broken my heart if you left," I admit in a whisper, more to myself than to him.

"Just the thought of leaving you broke my heart... That's why I knew I had to stay. I can barely leave your side for less than a day. How could I be thousands of miles away?" he confesses, breaking away long enough to look me deeply in the eyes.

I smile. "I know the feeling."

CHAPTER 18

I lean in to kiss him sweetly and lovingly, but I could still feel my heart shaken from the thought of him possibly leaving and having to find out this way. I obviously hadn't thought him leaving me was ever an option, only me leaving him.

There is something different in the way I kiss him. Something's different in the way I am suddenly holding back. The burn, the sickness inside. For a brief moment, I don't feel the same in his arms. I try to ignore the presence I feel, the presence of something hiding deep inside. I want to know what it is but want to ignore it at the same time. Something has changed, and I want desperately to change it back. But how? How can you undo what has been done? And even though he isn't leaving, something inside me has started to shift, and I struggle trying to figure out what that is.

The thought of Noah leaving rattles me so hard I remain quiet most of the night. I hadn't even noticed I was standoffish until most of our friends start asking me what's the matter. Still unable to find words, I shrug and eventually say something like, "I'm tired, that's all," and hardly recognize myself how abruptly my mood has changed.

The trio—Rex, Michael, and Trevor—leave shortly after 2:00 am after everyone else has managed to clear out and get safely to their cars. Noah and I sit in silence, nestled into one side of my couch. He strokes the top of my head as I stare off in deep thought.

"Well," says Gwen, pushing herself out of her seat in the chair across the room. "I think I have had all I can for one night." She steadies herself on her feet, glancing our way. "Thank you for my party, my dear. I believe I will drag myself off to bed and leave you two love birds to it."

"Goodnight," I call.

"Don't do anything I wouldn't do," she says as she walks to her room.

A million thoughts rush through my mind, so fast they make me feel nauseated. It's hard to grab ahold of just one. My thoughts come with such force and intrusion, I can't even begin to think which is more important than the other. And the fact that I've been left alone with them all night has made them multiply like the plague—a mind plague that has prevented me from enjoying any ounce of the evening as I should have.

There is a void, and all I want to do is break it down. I had put up a wall between the two of us without even knowing. My heart broke. I need to find a way out, back to our happy place. With the speed in which my thoughts are happening, though, I find myself struggling even more as I try to find a way to break free.

"Your silence is not anticipated," Noah blurts out, interrupting the latest thought I have.

I begin silently cursing myself for having reacted the way I did, causing the silence which is now serving as a horrible intruder. I sense hurt in his voice and even though he never gets up, and never stops running his fingers through my hair, I know he's also scared.

"I'm just tired. That's all," I manage to respond, attempting to make light of the situation and hoping that he will drop it. Tensing, I wait for his response. I'd been in situations like this before and know most men wouldn't take that response as the truth, not if they really cared.

I want things to be great between us and sensing that we might be upon our first argument makes me sick to my stomach. Everything before now has been better than I could have asked for, and I don't want to ruin our new relationship buzz. Even though I know everything can't be perfect forever, I don't want our kind of perfect to end.

I have no idea how Noah handles himself in tight spots or frustrating situations. The fact is I will find out sooner or later, although I have no desire to cross that bridge tonight. If Noah has as strong feelings for me as I think he might, the matter will be pressed, and I'm on the verge of finding out just how our personalities might match in a fight.

"When I signed that lease, I was happier than I have ever been. I couldn't wait to share the news with you," Noah starts, obviously fully aware of what caused my sudden change in mood. "I walked around the apartment and thought of no one else. I actually saw us in every corner, in every space." He laughs nervously. "For many reasons, I never let myself imagine things like that. But I did with you. I couldn't fight it because it is all I want. Now I feel like that was stupid ..."

Listening to his slow, heartfelt confession, I don't move an inch from his side. I wait, wanting to hear everything he has to say, hoping it will shed some light on the thoughts that I can't get straight in my own head. Hearing him refer to himself and us as stupid, my head shoots up from his shoulder, I quickly cut him off.

"You're not stupid. Don't say that. I just ..." I trail off, collecting the thoughts I have been trying so hard to make sense of that cloud my mind. Taking a deep breath, closing my eyes, and looking up, I pause. I pause for seconds that turn into minutes. Noah sits, staring at me. I hope I'm ready to say what he wants or needs to hear.

"I never thought ..." I say, meeting his eyes, as tears roll down my face.

"Why are you crying, darlin'? Don't cry!" Noah grabs hold

of my hands, worried and just as shaken as myself.

Laughing, I wiped the tears away. "Let me finish!"

Noah sits taller and braces himself for what's coming next. As he squeezes my hand, I can tell he doesn't want to let go. With hope and fear in his eyes, he looks into my own and mirrors what I feel inside. I'm not even sure what I'm about to say, but I know that whatever this is, it needs to be worked through.

"I never thought," I repeat, smiling at him and pausing for a brief second before continuing, "that one day you might leave. When we first met, you told me you were from another state. Well, I threw away every idea of seeing you ever again. And even though the thought of you tugged at my heart, and hope consumed me, I thought I knew deep down inside you would never be in my life again. Seeing you at my parents' house, I was so excited and I just assumed you had to live here. I let myself fall for you, thinking you would always be around. Tonight when I heard you were leaving, my heart broke in a way I never thought it could. And I never ever want to feel that way again."

"But I'm not leaving," Noah asserts sternly, trying to break my train of thought from wherever he fears it might be headed.

"I know that now, but the fear shook me so badly ... I've never experienced anything like it. I can't explain it. And in a weird way, it still hurts," I try to explain. "I don't want to keep you from anything. I don't want to make you regret anything in life! I don't know what you had planned before you met me, but I don't want to be a regret and a reason why it didn't work out!"

"Evelyn," Noah says sternly, "you would never be something I would ever regret." He reaches up and touches my face. I

CHAPTER 18

can tell he's apprehensive in his touch, but I needed to feel him more. Something in his touch stifles that burn. When he touches me, it doesn't hurt anymore. When he touches me, there is peace.

Still needing answers though, I continue. "You say that now, but what about later? I mean, it's only been a little over a month, Noah! Can you honestly tell me that you know enough about me that everything you thought you had planned or thought you wanted can wait ... or possibly NEVER happen? I know I've had dreams! I have plans! I've placed my whole heart on the line in hopes of obtaining them! It's hard to let go and give up, Noah! That's a big decision to make! If you had hopes and dreams back home ..." I trail off, not knowing where to go from here having revealed more than I thought I would in this moment.

Noah searches my eyes, and I try my best to keep up my guard. I try to look mad enough to make him take me seriously but soft enough to hopefully see my heart. Above all, I want him to know that he has an out. If he's going to take it, it has to be now, before I invest any more of my time. The thought of him leaving has affected me so profoundly, I have been forced to face the reality that someday he might want to. I find myself wanting that day to be now before I let myself go any further.

"I made my choice," he says so simply, hurt and anger hurling out at me on the tail end of his response.

"But what if it's the wrong choice," I ask quietly, looking down at our hands laced together. I won't dare look him in the eyes. I'm scared and want to stand my ground. Looking him in the eye, I might break and give in to my feelings. I want nothing more than for him to stay, but I feel like I have to guard my heart and not let him know so he can be free to make whatever decision he needed to.

"I love you," he whispers. "And if loving you is wrong, I'll take my chances."

Startled and surprised, I look up quickly and hold his gaze. I'm searching for honesty and want to know if his words are real. It's the way Noah looks at me, the way he holds my hand, the electricity in the air between us.

I wait for the burn. I waited for the sickness. I wait for the thoughts, for any reason why I shouldn't trust him or continue to deny myself from feeling the same way, knowing that I started loving him the day he swung me around in that bar and kissed me senseless.

This man is amazing ... my man is amazing. My man has just beautifully told me he loved me in such a simple way, I know it will never be matched. He's willing to risk everything to take a chance before he even knew if I loved him too. He has thrown all his plans aside and moved his whole world around just to be with me. What he has done took courage, and I only hope I can manage the same.

"I love you too," I whisper back, looking in his eyes and wanting to see how he responds to my confession.

A smile breaks out on his face, his eyes glistening. I see relief and excitement like I've just given him the best gift ever. Pulling me close, he pauses briefly, before playfully saying, "And what if that's the wrong choice?"

Smiling, I respond, "Then I'll take my chances!"

He doesn't kiss me. He only stares into my eyes, lust building with each passing second, and I begin to tremble with anticipation and longing. He pulls me to my feet, and I stand willingly. The building silence between the two of us tells me one thing: we're done talking about the bull shit from earlier. Grabbing my waist, he hoists me up, and I jump, almost anticipating his move. He holds me there in his arms, in my living room, for a moment and somehow, somewhere in the quiet that surrounds us - I can feel it.

The love we have for one another will never be matched.

My eyes fall to Noah's lips—lips that have kissed me many times, and suddenly I know I'm about to experience them in a different way than I have ever before. I bite my bottom lip in anticipation and feel his touch tighten. Slowly, he starts his walk towards my bedroom, still not saying a word and letting the silence between the two of us speak volumes.

My heart quickens, and my body feels euphoric as I anticipate what awaits. I want to give Noah all of me. I want to show him how much I need him. And I want to let him possess me in a way I have never let any man possess me before.

Chapter 19

Noah

Entering Evelyn's room, my heart is beating out of my chest knowing that I can finally love her, all of her, and not hold back. I know she feels it too because the look in her eyes is a mixture of emotions telling me not to stop. Never hold back. Love her the way I have longed to love her - and damn it if that doesn't turn me on even more. Kicking her door closed, I take the few steps towards her bed and toss her down lightly. She giggles a nervous little laugh, before propping herself up on her elbows and staring at me.

"That's it?" She teases. "I thought you were going to do more than just take me to bed?"

"Oh, Darlin', I plan on taking you to bed," I growl as my eyes scan over her body. Her sorry excuse for a dress is now pulled up her thighs giving me a glimpse of what is underneath. My manhood begins to rise as my mouth waters thinking of all the ways I am about to devour her. We've waited long enough, but tonight - she'll see another side of me- and I won't be such the southern gentleman she's come to know.

Unbuckling my pants, I look at her sternly before saying, "Take off your dress." Her eyes lock with mine and a fire, a passion, builds as she rises to her knees and does what I say. Her body, something I have seen many nights and days before, is more intoxicating than ever as she shimmies out of her little dress in front of me. I let out a groan in approval as she tosses it to the floor and eagerly stares back at me. Kicking off my shoes, I grab a condom from my pants before losing them on the floor. Grabbing the hem of my shirt, I pull it over my head and toss it to the floor with a hungry need building inside me. Evelyn's hands roam up her stomach before reaching behind her back to unclasp her bra.

"Not yet," I say. "I'm the only one allowed to free you, Darlin'." She eyes me with challenge but drops her hands to her sides. She goes to speak, but I stop her. "Lay back on the bed." She looks at me with a mischievous grin, before seductively falling back against the sheets. "Spread your legs," I say, as I push my boxers to the floor and my throbbing cock springs forth. Her eyes flash to my manhood, as I stroke it a few times in front of her. She licks her lips and does what I say. Good girl.

Her center glistens in the dark, wet, greedy and hungry for me. It takes everything I have not to just take her right now. Building each other up over the last several months have been agonizing and I've dreamed of being right here with her spread out and ready for me so many times. But, as much as I need to be inside of her, I'm going to take her slowly and enjoy every inch of her skin.

"I need you to touch me," she whimpers in the dark. I smile at her feeling the need and desire radiating off her like it is me. "I need to feel you," she says as her hands lower down her stomach.

Rolling on protection, I come two steps forward until my legs hit the side of the bed. She looks up at me with challenge, and

I know if I don't take what I want, she will do it for herself. My hands roam the inside of her thighs as I hungrily feel my way towards her heat. Her eyes widen waiting for my tough. Just before my fingers get to the place they long to be buried in, my large hands quickly roam around her waist and I suddenly grab her ass pulling her towards me.

"Damn Noah," she cries as I position her wet center up against my cock. In one move, I tear her lace panties from her body and throw them to the floor. Her eyes widen as she stares up at me.

With a grin, I lower to my knees and watch as her eyes follow my descent. "What do you need, Ev," I tease. I run a finger along her opening and push slightly at her center. She gasps out in response. "Do you need this," I say as I push one finger inside her slowly. Her head falls back and moans fill the space around us. God, she is breathtaking. She's everything I could ever want and more. And she is all mine right now to take how I have longed to for far too long. "Or," I grit out as her wetness coats my fingers and runs out of her heat beautifully. "Do you need this," I say, entering another finger inside her.

"God, yes!" She hisses out in response as her hips rise and she matches my rhythm each time my fingers thrust up inside her. I curve my fingertips and hit her spot deep at the back of her heat. She lets out a slight scream of approval and my dick throbs wanting to be inside her. "Or," I say, lowering my face and taking in her mouth-watering aroma as my breath dances across her center. "Do you need this." My mouth falls to her folds as I lick up them tenderly. She moans loudly and I think I hear her say my name, but damn it I am too lost in her sweet heat to know for sure. I take my fingers out of her pussy and replace them with my tongue. Licking from her center to her clit, I start an assault that I know always pushes her over the edge. Just when I hear her start to cry out, I take her nub in my mouth and suck it as I moan out my own approval at the way she tastes. The vibration sends her over the edge, and I quickly push both fingers back inside her as I feel her body clamp down when her orgasm rips through her. She screams out as her body shakes and she comes undone for me. I lick and suck up her juices like it is my last damn meal, and hell if she doesn't taste fucking perfect.

I look up as her body begins to relax and see satisfaction on her face when she lets out a sigh. Her eyes lock with mine and she smiles. "God, you southern boys sure do know how to please a woman down south." She teases.

Rising up her body, I position myself at her opening and watch as her face clouds over with hesitation. This changes everything, and we both know it. Reaching behind her, I unclasp her bra with one hand and peel it off her body. My head falls to her breasts and my length pulses with need as I take one of her nipples in my mouth. She moans out as I suck and caress her hard peak with my tongue making it hard to hold back from pushes deep inside her like I need to.

"I want you, Ev," I say, looking up and trying to calm her nerves from the hesitation I saw in her eyes. "I've never wanted anything more. I want you every day, for as long as you'll let me, Darlin'. I'm not going anywhere." The last sentence gets her. She smiles and her hesitation from moments before is lost as she stares in my eyes.

"Then show me how much you love me," she whispers.

With a grin, my eyes look down at her lips. I begin to push inside her and watch as she takes me in. I glance up and see her eyes, wide as she tries to adjust to my length. Her tight center is pushed to its limits as I attempt to fill her completely. Just before she looks as if she can't take anymore, I capture her mouth with my own and forcibly push the rest of the way inside her. She takes my kiss with passion, with urgency, as I come completely sated inside her. I stay there as we both get lost in the moment. Pulling away from her, I look in her eyes as they glisten over with tears.

"Am I hurting you," I whisper. She shakes her head no, and I pull out of her slightly. She gasps, and I still. "Darlin', I need you, God how I need you. But if I am hurting you.."

"Never," she whispers as her hands clasp around my neck. "You'd never hurt me, Noah. That is one of the things I love most about you." Her eyes stare back at me with the love I feel for her matched in her gaze. I pull out of her the rest of the way and push in slowly. Her head falls back and she gasps from the sensation. I hiss as her tight wet heat perfectly wraps around me. Again, I pull out and dive up inside her harder. Her head falls forward and she stares into my soul as she takes my next thrust.

"Don't ever leave me," she whispers between us with tears in her eyes.

I shake my head at her and smile, knowing I never could. "Never," I say as I drive up inside her again. She looks at me with such passion as I begin to pick up the pace. My need to please her and my chase for my own pleasure builds inside as I watch her eyes while I make love to her. "I love you, Ev," I say as she holds my gaze. "There will never be anyone for me like you."

She goes to speak, but I cut her off with a kiss. She moans into my mouth as I thrust up into her wet center harder and faster the more her tongue glides across my own. I bite her bottom lip and she whimpers as her nails scrape up my back and dig into my flesh. "God, Darlin'. I am so close, I don't think I can hold back." I admit once I release her lips and start chasing my release like a man on a mission.

Her moans are all that fill the room as I continue my assault. Her nails dig into my arms as I pull back and watch as my hard cock pulls in and out of her tight wet channel. My thumb comes up to rub her clit and instantly sends her over the edge. She screams as her pussy greedily begins to grip and squeeze my rock hard length. Moments later, I find my own release while she is still coming down from her climax. My own groans fill the room as I empty myself inside her. I thrust into her folds a few more times as we both come down from our high. Falling down lightly, I gather her up in my arms and hold her close while I am still inside of her.

"Noah," I hear her quietly say. "Thank you. For taking the chance."

I laugh out in response as I prop myself up on my elbows and stare in her eyes. "I love you," I whisper.

"I love you, too." She smiles. Her hips thrust down on my half-hard manhood as mischief lurks in her eyes. "Now, show me again just how much." She playfully says as her lips capture mine and she forces herself on top. I stare up at her, with her blond hair cascading around her shoulders and know there is no other woman in the world who could ever take her place. She is it for me, and I made the right choice in staying here to be with her - that is for damn sure.

Chapter 20

Noah

Waking up, I take a few moments letting my eyes adjust to the light that fills the room. At first, I had expected to be in my own room, surrounded by my own things. Turning on my side, I see my beautiful woman sleeping on her stomach, blond hair cascading down her bare back that I kissed in a million places the night before, over and over again. The thoughts immediately make me want to wake her and go for round four—or is it five? But watching her sleep is oddly just as satisfying. I want to touch her, but don't want to wake her. She's so peaceful and beautiful, and just the gift of being able to wake up next to her is more than I could have ever asked for.

I brush my fingers slowly up and down her back and move her hair off to her shoulders. She stirs momentarily, and I slow my movements. I lean forward and kiss down her spine as I move out of the bed. I need a hot shower and coffee to regain some strength and start to feel human.

Taking a quick shower, I pull on my jeans from the night before. It might be time for me to start packing a bag and leaving it in the car. I hadn't before because I didn't want to assume too much of what was building between the two of us.

CHAPTER 20

But after last night, I doubt I will ever spend another night without sleeping next to her again.

I make my way to the kitchen, thankful that Gwen has already left for the day, and rummage through the cabinets to find coffee. I hear Evelyn stirring from the back room and hungrily anticipated her joining me. I might just be inspired to have my way with her in here as well and start imagining all the ways in which we could make that happen, completely forgetting what it was I was supposed to be doing. My phone starts vibrating on the counter across the kitchen, snapping me back to reality.

Annoyed at being jolted from my fantasy, I reach for the phone, forgetting I had silenced the ringer the night before. I'm taken back when I see that I have twelve missed calls and five new voicemails. Glancing at the time, I notice it's not too late on this Sunday morning and my heart slightly speeds up, hoping nothing was wrong.

Looking further, I notice two text messages from Rex. Both urgent. Both needing an immediate response, which I haven't given and hope I'm not too late once I have a second to digest what they are saying.

Fumbling with my phone and my train of thought, I finally find Rex's number and hit call. I wait impatiently for him to pick up, if he even will, and pace the kitchen a little. From the little I put together from the text messages he had sent, I wonder if I've missed my opportunity and wish like hell I haven't. It has been too long since my last fire, and hell if I am about to pass up my chance at another one. Adrenaline begins running through my veins at the thought of getting out there and doing one of the things that I like best.

"Noah! Where the hell have you been!? Never mind, don't answer that question!" Rex says.

"Yeah, yeah, put my phone on silent. Am I too late!?" I ask.

"I just got here. Chief said if you're not here soon, we're leaving without you!" Rex says urgently.

I know I have to leave fast. I hear Evelyn coming down the hallway, and for the first time, I feel a tug of regret having to leave her not knowing how long I might be gone.

"I'll be there! Try and stall as long as you can, but I swear I'm coming!" I hope Rex hears the insistence in my voice. I don't want to leave Evelyn, but I don't want to miss out on this opportunity either.

A forest fire from a lightning strike is raging in a town called Truckee, about two hours from here. Since the ground and surrounding trees are so dry from the drought, the forest is now engulfed in flames and is nowhere near contained. It's spreading fast and homes are beginning to be threatened. It has grown so rapidly overnight, they are now pulling any available firefighters from local towns to help go and battle the flames.

I had fought a few over last summer, but I haven't had the opportunity to fight one in winter. The forecast looks clear for the next week and temperatures have remained abnormally high, making fire season extend in northern California well past normal. With still no sign of rain, the drought seriously threatens the idea of any containment if we and any other firefighters, full time or volunteer, don't work overtime and long hours to put it out.

Evelyn comes into the kitchen, sleepy-eyed and looking sexier than I have ever seen as bare curves stick out from all the right places under the robe she has just thrown on. I curse myself silently for the news I'm about to break to her.

I won't even have time to indulge in what is standing right in front of me as she puts on the most beautiful early morning display that would make any man weak in the knees. The thought of it almost makes me want to stay and say to hell with the chief and Rex, but I know an opportunity like this may not come again for a long time, and I have to take it while I can.

"Kiss that girl of yours goodbye and hurry your ass up! We might be out there for a while. I'll do my best stalling, but you know the chief, he waits for no one," Rex says, bringing me out of my thoughts and quickly hanging up the phone.

I stand silent, staring down at the phone in my hand. Evelyn has obviously noticed the difference in my demeanor and doesn't come any closer when she first enters the kitchen. She stands, tightening the ties on her robe, already knowing what we both anticipate happening this morning is not in the cards.

"Is everything ok?" she asks.

"Yeah," I answer, swallowing hard, still not looking up from my phone. I don't think she would be mad, but I know she won't be happy either. I don't want to leave her and already miss her while I'm still standing just a few feet away from her.

"Are you sure?" she asks, not buying my first response. Looking up, I reach out and grab her hand, pulling her a little closer.

"Baby, I gotta go." I manage. She looks at me stunned like I've just hit her with the worst response possible. She takes a step back, her expression becoming a dangerous place to look, and I know I better hurry and explain better than that.

"Darlin', no, it's not like you're thinking." I laugh nervously. "A fire broke out overnight and it sounds pretty bad. They're calling all available volunteers. Rex is already there and said the chief won't wait long, so I got to hurry." Evelyn's face relaxes a little, but not enough to make me feel like I am out of hot water.

"Is it really dangerous?" she asks, sounding scared.

"Well, I'm not going to lie and say no, but I wouldn't worry," I say, trying to calm her nerves. It obviously doesn't work from the look on her face, so I continue as best as I can. "Don't even start thinking that way baby girl. I'll be back before you know it. I don't know how long they will keep me out there, but it can't be too long if they are calling in so many reinforcements."

Evelyn searches my eyes. She's not buying what I'm saying. I can tell she's still scared, and I hate the fact that my choices have now shaken her twice in the last twenty-four hours. I hope her heart is strong enough to withstand this part of my lifestyle and that our love is the kind of love strong enough to go through anything, only making us stronger. I know I sound sappy in my own mind, but I don't care. The woman standing in front of me is quickly becoming my whole world now, and I don't want to do anything to jeopardize that.

"I'll miss you," she whispers, looking down at the floor. I know she doesn't want to look in my eyes, so I tilt my head down trying to catch her gaze. She's trying to be strong and looking me in the eyes would make her fail miserably.

"I won't be gone long. I promise! And when I get back, you better clear your schedule because I plan on making love to you for hours. At least one time for every day I'm away, so save your strength."

That gets her. She looks up, smiling beautifully. Her eyes dance and desire builds from my comment still lingering in the air between us. Her hands grab the top of my jeans tightly as she pulls me closer and traces the top brushing her fingertips across my bare skin. She knows just how to tease, and I almost lose control, wanting nothing more than to pick her up and have my way with her up against the fridge, the counter, the cabinets, hell even the floor.

"Promise …" she whispers, looking up at me longingly. I swear I'm about to cave. The way Evelyn looks at me, grabbing me closer, almost forces me to the point of no return. I need to find restraint now before I make good on all the images running through my mind.

My phone buzzes in my hand. Looking down, I see a text from Rex and know if I don't break free now, I'm not going to make it in time. I step back briefly to read the message and then shove the phone in my pocket.

Looking back up at Evelyn, I grab her face in my hands. Brushing my thumbs against her cheeks, I look her in the eyes, not wanting to move an inch closer to the door but knowing I have to. Slowly, I lower my mouth to hers, taking extra time to keep my eyes locked on hers and watch the way she responds to my movements. Her breath quickens, and she tenses slightly, waiting for my lips to touch hers. The way she always responds to me turning me on like magic.

Kissing her slowly and passionately, I draw out every second of the kiss that I can. I want to remember the way she tastes, the way she feels, and how we feel together. Truth be told, I don't know how long I'll be gone, but I know it's going to be the longest we have been apart since we first met. Being without her is going to be torture, but knowing she's waiting for me and all the things I have in mind to do to her when I return proves to be worth it.

Backing away, I see a tear fall down one of her cheeks. I wipe it away with my fingers and hold onto her hands tightly. We look at each other, not wanting to let go but knowing it's necessary.

"I love you," I whisper with a smile.

"I love you," she assures me. "Come back to me in one piece, and I promise to show you just how much."

I smile and know without a doubt that Evelyn Monroe is the most amazing woman I have ever or will ever get the chance to love in my entire life. She's smart, witty, beautiful, spontaneous and full of life. Slowly making my way towards the door, I look back briefly before turning the handle. Exchanging a brief smile, she blows me a kiss just as I close the door. And damn it, as corny as it sounds, I already can't wait until she's back in my arms again.

Chapter 21

Evelyn

When Noah leaves, I tell myself I can make it a few days without him, and I'm crazy if I think I can't. People go a lot longer without one another and are perfectly fine. I almost have myself convinced, until he texts me saying he's leaving the fire station. He tells me he might not get good reception up in the hills and would call when he could.

I fill with fear, realizing I haven't even thought about not being able to talk to him. Not touching him or being with him is enough torture. Knowing he's out in the fire, and I have possibly no way of contacting him, makes me feel sick. I feel all the joy for life I always carry leave my body, and I begin walking around in a haze of anticipation and worry for the man I've only just realized I love so much.

Sunday passes and then Monday. Come Tuesday I still haven't heard from Noah, and my anxiety is going through the roof. I need to hear his voice. I needed to know he's ok and not lying hurt or dead in the flames engulfing the hillsides just a few hours' drive away.

I'm so consumed with concern for him that I call into work sick and tell my editor I will work from home. Instead of work,

I find myself staring at the television, not even aware that I've been watching the same infomercial for two hours now and sill have no idea what the hell they are selling, my mind too worried about Noah.

My phone rings, pulling me out of my trance, and I jump off the couch, grabbing it from the coffee table. I fall short and land on the floor instead. Gripping the top of the table, I hurriedly feel for my phone. Breathing out a breath I didn't know I had been holding in since Sunday, I finally relax a little when the screen shows me one name.

Noah.

"Baby, baby is that you?" I ask into the phone. It still rings in my ear, and I realize I never accepted the call. Cursing myself out loud, I hit the green button and wait impatiently to hear his voice.

"Noah!" I shout. "Noah, are you there?"

"Hey, darlin'," he says. Though the reception is weak, I'm so happy to finally be hearing his voice, I can't help the tears that begin rolling down my face. I cover my mouth with my hand, scared to let him hear. I'm so excited to be finally receiving the call that feels like I spent forever waiting for.

"Noah, are you ok? I've been waiting to hear from you for three days. You've had me so concerned. I'm new to this kind of thing, and I just couldn't stop worrying about you!" I start rambling, unable to contain the words that tumble out before I can even stop myself. I don't want to worry him with how much I've been concerned, but I need to know he's ok. I find myself feeling protective in a way, and right now the only thing that matters is knowing he is alright.

"God, Ev, it's so good to hear your voice," he responds. He sounds tired, and I wish so badly I could be with him to help him in any way I can.

"When are you coming home?" I say, hoping I don't sound as desperate as I feel.

"Not sure. We're making progress, but not what they would like. I slept out by the fire the last two nights, taking shifts with the other workers. Tonight they let us go to a nearby hotel. Hopefully soon, though. God, darlin', I miss you."

"I miss you too," I say in a whimper, starting to cry a little more but trying to hold back the tears I want to flow. I've become so endeared to the way he calls me darlin' in the deep southern drawl of his that it makes the distance between us hurt even more. I wish I could touch him, kiss him, be with him instead of being miles apart and missing him like crazy.

"I should be able to call you more now. We're taking more regular shifts, and I should be coming in and out from the hotel every day," he says, reassuring me. The few short days we were unable to talk obviously have a taken a toll on him as well.

"I love you," is all I can manage. I don't know what to say. I want to say everything, but find that those three words are everything I have to give and somehow they seem perfect.

"Aww, darlin', I love you too. I'm so tired. Rex is already asleep. He passed out the second we walked in the door. Didn't even make it to the shower," Noah says, somehow mustering up the energy for a small laugh.

I smile, listening to him. The sound of his laughter makes me feel closer to him somehow. I want to be as close to him as I can and find a strange peace in the little things that make me feel this way in this time that we're forced to spend apart—however long that will be.

"Do you need to go? I want you to get all the sleep you need? I don't want you tired out there. Remember, you have to come back to me," I laugh, teasing him and also feeling my heart pull at the thought of anything bad ever happening to him.

"Oh, I remember. Come back to you in one piece and then you'll show me ... what was it again?"

"I'd rather show you than tell you, Mr. Stewart." I laugh. "So make sure you get yourself back here in one piece."

The line fills with laughter, and I smile, knowing very well what we both have in mind. Even though his teasing is welcome, it makes the days we're apart harder and the nights colder without his touch. After we had spent the night together, before he left, I knew no man would be able to satisfy me the way he had. I replay that night in my mind over and over again since he's been gone.

Everything I want, he gives. Everything I need, he provides. In perfect harmony, like we can read each other's minds, he knows just how to please me. It's perfection.

"I do need to get some sleep, though," he regrettably informs me. "I'm headed out early tomorrow, and I can barely keep my eyes open. But I had to call and hear your voice. Every day we've been apart, there hasn't been a second I haven't thought about you ... about us."

"Me too," I whisper. "Go to sleep. We'll talk later."

The line is silent. A whole minute passes.

"Noah?" I ask into the receiver.

"Hmm," comes a sleepy voice.

"Noah ... you're sleeping." I giggle.

"No, I'm not ... I just ... wanted ... to hear your voice," he says, trailing off into sleep again.

"I'm here," I whisper. "I'm here, Noah."

His breathing deepens as silence fills the conversation. I don't have the heart to hang up and stay on the line, listening to him breathe a little longer. Any way I can be next to him, I want to be. At this moment, listening to him breathe calms all my nerves from the days before. I would take him any way I can, even if that means listening to him sleep over the phone.

How he has managed to turn my life upside down and make it impossible to imagine life before or after him, I will never know. I wait for that burn, that ache deep inside, and realize that I haven't felt it since that night he claimed me, body and soul, telling me that he loved me. I feel my world shifting. My usual process would be to begin wondering if that is a good thing, although I realize I don't worry if it is anymore. That's progress. I don't know where this—us is taking me, but I know I need to stick it out or I will regret it for the rest of my life.

Noah

I hadn't anticipated being gone as long as I was. The first two days were the hardest. Sleeping in the dirt, fighting a fire and taking shifts on and off for forty-eight hours was no easy task. Plus, I couldn't talk to Evelyn, and that killed me even more. When I finally did call her, I was so tired I fell asleep on the line. I woke up delirious and slightly embarrassed.

She had hung up eventually but continued to leave me beautiful text messages in her absence, making me love her even more.

The next few days we are out there are full of long, hard hours and short evening calls home to the woman I love and can't wait to get back to. I need to hold her in my arms again. For the first time ever, I'm anxious over how long I'm going to be forced to be out fighting this fire. Normally, I'm in no rush to get home, but now I'm out here wishing I had never left.

I get news the day before Christmas Eve that Rex and I would be going home the next day. Evelyn told me she was going out with Gwen that night, so I figured best to let her have her fun while I keep this little secret to myself. I want to surprise her and can't wait to see the look on her face when I return home.

I sleep like a rock, and I am relieved because I know I'll need my strength and energy for the woman I'm returning home to and all the ways I imagined making love to her since we've been apart. I'm blessed to work only half the day on Christmas Eve when the chief decides to send us home early. Rex and I head home like we have just been given one of the best Christmas presents ever.

Once home, I shower and pack a bag. I have no desire to head home anytime soon and can't wait for next week when I'll be packing up and moving to my own place and will be closer to Evelyn. I can't wait to get back to the life I left only nine days earlier. Anxious and full of excitement, I pull up to Evelyn's house and can barely contain the need rolling through my body.

I notice her car in her usual parking spot, and I'm immediately thankful she is home. I hadn't called her yet because I didn't want to give myself away and knew that she may be out once I got over here, but luckily my plan worked. Bolting from the car, I find myself running up the walk, through the door, and up the stairs to her apartment, taking the stairs two or three at a time.

Wishing I had a key, I knock on her door and hear her voice. I can tell from her tone she isn't expecting anyone. She turns the locks and with each turn, my excitement grows. I brace myself against the doorframe and wait impatiently.

When she opens the door, she's in such state of shock she gasps. She's absolutely adorable in a white tank top and pink very short pajama shorts. Her hair is down and without makeup, she couldn't have been more beautiful.

Stumbling back a few steps at first, she takes off running into my arms. I nestle my face into her hair and drink in the fragrance of her that I had been missing for far too long. A vanilla dream, I'm home! I feel myself start to become aroused instantly from her touch. It has been so damn long, and I need her now as fast as I can. I need to feel her wrapped around me for the next several hours, days even. Starting a trail of kisses, first on my cheek and then all over, she finally lands her delicious mouth on my lips. I pick her up and enter her apartment with her in my arms, kicking the door closed with my foot.

She won't stop kissing me, and I laugh when my failed attempts to stop her only make me hungrier for her.

"Uh uh! No!" she mumbles as she continues to kiss me endlessly.

"Darlin', I want to look at you," I plead. "It's been too long since I have touched you, let alone looked in your eyes."

"But I want to feel you," she begs, grabbing hold of me tighter. This is a better welcome than I had anticipated, and I let her have it. Never have I been welcomed home anywhere or by anyone like this before. She can feel me all she wants as long as I can stare in her eyes while she is doing it.

She finally calms and I find myself rocking her back and forth in my arms, our breathing slowly becoming one. Lowering her to the ground, she backs up enough to look me in the eyes. I grab her around the waist tightly. She has become even more breathtaking in the last few days we have been forced to be apart.

"God, I missed you so much," I tell her, my heart hurting from the realization. I kiss her slowly then faster, my kiss more intense the more my feelings rise up inside. Leaving her was agony, returning to her makes me complete again. It brings me home. She will always be home to me.

I need to feel her, need to be inside her, need to soothe the ache I'm feeling. I need to claim her, know she is mine in every way. That her, that this, is all we both need.

"Show me how much you missed me," she pleads through rushed breaths while I kiss her.

I back away from her, looking her in the eye. She knows just what to say and when to say it to drive me mad with need. Immediately ready to go, and knowing we have nowhere else to be but together, I grab her forcefully. She grabs back, forcing both of us up against the wall. Rushing, I try my best to extract her from what she's wearing, needing to feel her skin on mine. She does the same, kissing me everywhere she can and only breaking away to concentrate on a button or a loop on my belt.

"Gwen," I breathe out in rushed breaths.

"Gone," she answers, in between kisses. "At ... her parents' place."

Frustrated with our constraints, I scoop her up and carry her over to the couch. I have nowhere else to be anytime soon, and I'm about to take all the time I can showing Evelyn how much I've missed her. How I've longed for her, and how I never want to be without her again. I will show her as many times as she will let me and as many times as her body can handle until she's begging for me to stop and silently pleading for more. I want nothing more than to show her how she's claimed every part of me. How with every look, every touch, every breath I take with her, she is all I could ever want or ever need again.

Chapter 22

Evelyn

I need him, more than ever. More than I thought was possible. Laying me down on the couch, he peals my shorts off me slowly and I hear his intake of breath when he realizes I am bare underneath.

"God, Darlin'. How I've missed your sweet heat." His fingers trail up the inside of my thighs before his eyes lock with mine. "Take off your shirt." He demands, and I instantly rise, grab the hem and rip it over my head. Throwing it to the floor, my stare locks with his and I watch as he swallows hard and his jaw ticks as he takes in my naked body in front of him.

"You," I say rising up and grabbing ahold of his belt loop. "Are far too overdressed, Sir." I wink up at him and pull him closer. Unbuttoning his jeans, I force them down quickly and hear his sharp intake of breath above. Caressing his rock hard length through his black boxer briefs, he hisses out in approval as my fingertips feel around his tip.

"God, Ev. As much as that feels like heaven, I need you more." His stern gaze locks with mine. "Lay back." I do as he says and he groans with need when I part my legs wide in anticipation. "Touch yourself, Darlin'." He demands. Slightly shocked, but needing the sensation, I do as he says. My hands drop to my sex and I part myself, entering one finger inside. "Are you wet for me, Ev?" I hear Noah whisper. My head falls back against the couch as I pleasure myself. "Look at me!" He demands, and my head snaps forward. He ditches his boxers and my mouth salivates at his large rock hard cock in front of me. His big hands begin to stroke his dick as he watches me pleasure myself in front of him.

"Do you know, every night, I touched myself thinking of your sweet pussy," he grits out as I watch his hand pump his dick faster. "Did you touch yourself, Darlin'? Did you need me as much as I needed you."

His words make me grow wetter. I enter two fingers inside my throbbing center and run them up to my clit. He watches as I finger myself and I can see in his eyes just how hard it is for him to hold back.

"Tell me, Ev." He demands. "Did you touch your wet tight heat and make yourself cum, wanting it to be me that was pleasuring you, Darlin'?"

I did. More than once. But do I admit that?

He comes closer and I stop my movements. He grabs my wrist and forces me to stand. Taking my fingers in his mouth, he sucks my juices off them and groans as his eyes close and he savors the taste. I can feel his hard length pressed against my lower stomach and push towards it, needing to feel it inside me. His eyes open and he takes my chin in his hand.

"Turn around," he insists. I swallow over the lump in my throat and do as he says. His hands roam down the curve of my waist to my hips. He grabs my ass before releasing it and smacking it hard. I cry out from the sensation because hell, that only made me want him more. He grabs my hair back gently until his lips are placed against my ear. "Did you touch all the places I longed to be?" He asks, his hand coming around in front of me as his fingertips trail to my sex. He parts my folds and I spread my legs slightly, granting him access. "Did you cum thinking about all the ways only I could love this body." He forces me forward as his finger dips inside me deeper. "God, Darlin'. I missed this ass," he says as his hand releases my heat and comes to grab my hips and push my back up against his rock hard erection. He backs away from me and I hear the rip of foil. A few moments later, I feel his cock at my entrance.

"Noah!" I plead out between us, needing him to fill me - and fast.

"You want this?" He asks as he enters just the tip inside me. Pulling back he laughs when I groan out in disapproval. "Then tell me then, Darlin'. How much did you miss me?"

"I came to the thought of you every day," I admit, shocking both me and him from the confession. I hear his moan in approval and feel him press up against my center harder. "Sometimes twice."

"Good girl," he groans as he pushes himself fully inside me in one quick thrust. We both gasp out from the sensation. "Fuck," Noah grits out above me. "I forgot how tight you are, Darlin'." He waits so I can adjust to his length before he pulls out again and thrusts back inside me harder. He hits so deep I scream out in ecstasy. "You like it when I'm buried inside you." He says as he continues to drive into me. "Your body loves it when my cock is deep in your wet sweet heat, doesn't Ev? When I fill your pussy with my rock hard dick until it can't take anymore!"

I scream out as he dives inside my body again and again, punishing me beautifully and making up for all the days we lost. After a few minutes, he quickly pulls out and swings me around. Crushing his lips against my own, his tongue dives in my mouth with need. I match his greed with my own as we fall back against the couch. He lays me out beneath him and I spread my legs needing to feel him inside me once more.

His hands frame my face and he stares down at me with more love than I have ever felt. "God, I love you so much it hurts." He whispers between us. Slowly, he fills my body once again and tenderly starts to love my entrance. Holding my stare, I get lost in his eyes as he tells me just how much he loves me every time he pushes back deep inside me. Quickly, my orgasm approaches and it isn't long until we crash over the edge together, in a beautiful union I know I will never get with anyone else. No one will ever love me the way Noah does. He's my once in a lifetime. My only chance at one true love. And damn it if that doesn't start to scare me a little.

Chapter 23

Evelyn

"Tell me again why you have a strange and weirdly large collection of worn baseball caps and camo clothing and what I can do about it," I shout from across Noah's new small apartment. It's only been a few weeks since he returned home. We just moved our last load from his old place late last night and are now busy unpacking boxes.

"It's not strange or weird. It's a country thing baby." He smirks at me from over the boxes he's unloading in the kitchen. "I don't ask you about your collection of antiques, books, or writing notebooks, right?"

"Play nice or I might have to come across this room and make you," I tease.

"By all means, please do." He smiles mischievously, bracing himself on the counter and pushing down a few times, testing its sturdiness. "I don't believe we had a chance to break in the kitchen last night."

"I thought you were supposed to be showing me all I've been missing not being with a country boy before," I say, holding up a hat with so much dirt and sweat stains the logo is almost unrecognizable and an almost full-on camo suit that looks like it has been worn more times the most the other items in his closet. I wait to continue until I have his full attention. "This, my love, is not it!"

He flings a dish towel at me, which falls short, several feet from where I actually stand. "Watch it or I'll be forced to come over there and set you straight, woman!" he playfully says.

Smiling, I know all I have to do is continue and he'll be rounding the corner of the kitchen, making every word of his statement come true. I go back to work, unpacking and arranging his clothing. That kind of a break would be fun but there is still so much to do.

If I thought I knew Noah before, packing and unpacking all of his belongings helps me know him in ways I hadn't imagined. So many things that people don't talk about comes out in their personal belongings: clothes, movies, magazines, toiletries. I glimpse further into his world the more I continue helping him move into his own place. He's becoming more of a real person than the fantasy I fell in love with, and even through all the camo and sweaty baseball caps, I find I love him even more.

My phone rings on one of the boxes next to me. Noah looks up as inquisitively as I answer the call.

"What's up, lady?" I say into the phone.

"I'm calling to confirm that we are in fact partying our asses off for your birthday in a few weeks," she responds. "I haven't seen much of you since lover boy returned home, and now that your busy helping him move, I've barely seen you at all. You're like a ghost I used to know."

"I don't know, I hadn't really thought about it. I mean some ideas have been thrown around, but nothing is set in stone," I explain. Besides, I do not need another reminder that in a little over two and a half weeks I'll be turning another year older.

"That's not what your boyfriend's man-whore of a best friend said," Gwen angrily says.

"You're talking to Rex? Since when do you ever talk to Rex?" I ask, shocked.

"He called me this morning. I guess a party in your honor is being thrown at that damn club he owns. He left a message saying under the circumstances he had to invite me, the ass," Gwen harshly adds.

"Well, I talked to Rex about it, but I hadn't said yes to anything. I thought maybe Noah and I might just have a quiet night alone," I suggest, knowing there is bound to be a fight from Gwen. "Or maybe we could just do something small..."

"Oh hell no," she shouts back, cutting me off. "This man can have you every day of the week, practically every day of the month, but there is no way in hot Hades that he is taking you from me on your birthday! Tell him to back the hell off!"

I laugh. Noah hasn't any clue of Gwen's intentions—it was my idea to avoid the bar scene, not his. But Gwen is right. I have been secluding myself a lot lately. Maybe getting out and being around friends is a great idea. I shouldn't pass on.

"It wasn't his idea, it was mine," I explain. "But if you want me that bad, I'm all yours."

"Damn straight you are!" Gwen yells. "Can't wait! It's been way too long since we had a night out together."

"Gwen, every time I see you, it's a party," I express, half-annoyed and half-laughing.

"That's because I'm so damn fun," she asserts. "Now tell that boyfriend of yours we're staying out late. He's not taking away any more of your time from me than necessary. Looovvveee yyyooouuu!" She hangs up, leaving me giggling to myself. She is truly a great lady and an even better friend, even if her good intentions are hard to see sometimes.

"What was that about?" Noah asks, coming closer. He hands me a beer that I take willingly. I take a long drink, letting the cold bubbles start to take away the edge of moving.

"Gwen wants to go out for my birthday next month. Says Rex is throwing some party at Gatsby's for me, that we have to attend," I explain with my signature eye roll.

"I know, I'm the one that asked him to do it," Noah says, smiling.

"You? But why? I wouldn't expect that to be the way you'd want to spend my birthday with me?" I say, shocked and a little thrown back by his response.

"You come alive when you're in a group of people. Don't get me wrong, I like having you all to myself. But there is something that takes my breath away about you when we are all together. You steal the show, and damn, it's sexy as hell to watch, knowing that you are all mine." His confession is raw and genuine. I can't help but accept it beautifully for what it is—admiration for a quality I didn't even know I possessed.

"Plus, it's your birthday! I wanted to throw you a big celebration, marking the first of many we will hopefully spend together," Noah finishes explaining. He takes a long sip of beer and lets that thought resonate a little further in my brain, the whole time watching me over the top of his bottle.

"Are you already planning our life together, Mr. Stewart," I tease.

Noah's eyes shine. He looks at me like he has a secret. It's a secret I want to know, but if I'm being truthful with myself, I'm afraid to find out.

"If you'll let me ..." He smiles, never taking his eyes off mine.

CHAPTER 23

They dance with a sort of mystery and take my breath away.

I was not expecting that kind of remark to come from him, and it takes me a moment to regain my thoughts after what he halfway admitted. Feeling weak all over from his response, I hadn't even noticed the air was stolen from me until I gasp to suck in more. And then it's back, the burn.

Something deep inside feels off, but I push it away for the first time in almost a month as I stare into Noah's eyes. I hope it doesn't show on my face. I'm nervous, maybe, and I fear Noah saw me blanch at his words.

Sure, I had a few fleeting thoughts over the last two months from time to time that involved a white dress and babies, though hearing it from his mouth, so plain and blunt, makes me nervous. It's one thing to think you are alone in such thoughts, it is quite another to realize they might be reciprocated.

Shakily, I ignore the comment, giving him a smile that I hope hasn't come across as forced as it feels and turn my attention back to my work, starting to unpack another box of clothing. He gets the hint and doesn't press the discussion further. Setting his beer down and grabbing me from behind, he nestles into the side of my neck. I moan happily as his lips find my skin, and he begins kissing and nibbling the spots he knows are my most sensitive.

"We don't have to go if you really don't want to," he says, half-suggesting and half-asking.

"If you keep kissing me like that, I'll do anything you want me to," I admit.

Noah laughs as he continues his torture. It vibrates on my neck, sending shivers down my spine. I tense slightly with how much it tickles and how it makes me aroused with need at the same time.

"I'm serious, Ev. If you don't want to go, we can stay home. I can think of a million things I'd do to you here that I can't do to you there." Noah's voice grows hot with passion, and I have to brace myself against a box in front of me. "Then again, I can think of a few things I want to do to you there in a dark corner as well," he says with a low suggestive growl.

I giggle. "No." I try to gain some ground and not give into him entirely. "I want to go, it would be ... good to see everyone," I admit through rushed breaths. Noah's petting slows, and he turns me around to look him in the eye.

"Good!" he says. "Because I want to throw you the best party you have ever had."

"That might be kind of tough. My dad bought me a pony when I was six!" I tease.

Noah's mouth actually falls open, undoubtedly having no response for what I just hit him with. Dumbfounded and not knowing what to say, he just looks at me. I start laughing, the joke is obvious to me but not so much to him. He catches on and eventually and laughs too.

"Kidding," I say.

"Phew, you had me scared there. Ponies are pretty hard to beat," he says, leaving my side and making his way back towards the kitchen. He grabs an envelope and returns to me standing in the living room. Offering it over, I'm a little reluctant to take it, not knowing what it was.

I stare at Noah for a moment, having no clue what awaits me in the envelope and a bit apprehensive about even opening it to find out.

"Open it," Noah insists.

I turn it around a few times in my hands, staring at the

package, trying to make sense of it and trying to guess what it is before I open it. There is something inside I can feel it, although I have no clue what it could be.

Slowly, I open the envelope and turn it upside down in my palm, trying to extract whatever object is inside. A shiny gold key falls into my hand. I look up at Noah like I want an explanation but know I don't need one.

"Just in case you ever need to use it, I wanted to make sure you had it," he offers. Still not knowing what to say, I look at Noah then back down at the key. I had thought about giving him one to my place but never actually went through with it. Besides, he always arrived after I got home and left before I did, so what was the point?

"I don't know what to say," I finally tell him.

"Don't say anything." He kisses the top of my head and heads back to his unpacking. I stand there, kicking myself for not having a key to give in return. As I watch him unpack, I feel myself loving how much he trusts me, wants me and seems to need me. He doesn't ever think twice about giving me little gestures like this, and somehow the thought never crosses my mind to do the same. Standing in Noah's new apartment, I again wonder why that is as the burn inside starts to resurface.

Chapter 24

Evelyn

My party rapidly approaches and time flies by faster than I had anticipated. Noah has been busy the last two weeks, hard at work figuring out all the specifics that Michael and Rex want to add onto their club. He spends his days at the club, measuring and drawing up plans, making whatever progress he can while the two co-owners fight endlessly over what they actually need versus what they thought they wanted.

I fill my time working. I picked up two new freelance positions in Orange County. I haven't told Noah exactly where the new magazines were located, but I'm thrilled with excitement about writing about my hometown. Normally the magazines might have hired someone else, but when I had video-conferenced with the editors, elaborating on how much I know the town, how often I still visit, and how much family I still have living in the area, they agreed to take a chance on me. I'm over the moon excited they did.

And I would be lying if I said I didn't secretly still think of that job at the L.A. Times, making sure to follow up and stay in contact with a few people in the office from time to time, knowing that persistence usually always pays off.

CHAPTER 24

The night before my big birthday celebration, I agree to meet Gwen for drinks after work. Noah happily pushed the idea, still swamped with work trying to figure out how to cut unnecessary costs for Rex and Michael's addition. Excited and ready for some girly fun one can only have with their best friend, we both decide to hit some local pubs in downtown and walk home if need be.

Our first stop is a small bar, probably five hundred square feet. The place makes up for the lack of room inside with a small patio out back. White string lights line the fences, space heaters stand in all the walkways, making sure guests were warm enough; if that doesn't do the trick there's a large old fashioned fireplace in the far corner.

I'm surprised that on this Friday night the bar is not too crowded and the patio is used even less. Walking towards the back when we get there, I hear Gwen curse and complain over my choice in seating.

"Really," Gwen says as we reach a table by the fireplace and set down our purses. "This isn't Orange County! Hell, I wouldn't sit outside in SoCal this time of year, let alone up here in this crazy weather."

It's fifty-eight degrees outside and is supposed to get much colder before the night is over. I laugh at my friend. The good thing about being acclimated to both Northern and Southern California is that you can take most any temperature the climate throws at you.

"Where is your sense of adventure," I challenge. "A few stiff drinks and you'll forget all about the cold."

Gwen can't argue with that. It's basic knowledge she knows all too well. When a waitress comes up, we place our drink orders and wait in silence. Our relationship is never at a loss for words for long, though the absence between the two of us the last few weeks makes it hard to figure out what to say first.

"Are you excited for your party," Gwen asks abruptly.

"I guess so. If I can handle two nights of back to back drinking, that is," I respond, a little uneasy, not wanting to actually go through with it. Hangovers were one thing in my early twenties, although now nearing my early thirties, they leave me hating life for several days after.

"You're just not seasoned anymore. A night like tonight is exactly what you need to get you back in the saddle again." Gwen enthusiastically expresses.

The waitress returns and sets our drinks on the table, telling both of us to yell if we needed anything else, or better yet go inside for refills. Acknowledging the fact that we are the only ones crazy enough to sit on the patio, we nod and wait for the waitress to leave before continuing our conversation. Gwen glances at her phone briefly, and I do the same, pretending to have some important information to look at when in actuality I'm just buying time. Why is this awkward? I'm not quite sure.

"Sooooo," Gwen sighs.

"Sooooo," I repeat.

Gwen takes a long drink of beer and looks off in the distance. I have never seen her like this before and wonder what's making her at a loss for words. This woman normally doesn't care what she says or how she says it, so I have no clue what is stopping her now.

"How are things with you and Noah?" she asks with a touch of hurt in her tone.

"We're good. Real good. He gave me a key," I tell Gwen. "First time in my life that has ever happened."

Gwen doesn't say anything. She raises her eyebrows and

CHAPTER 24

takes another sip of her drink. The conversation is awkwardly funny. Neither of us have ever had issues talking before, and the fact that we do now leaves me worried. I thought Gwen liked Noah, but I'm starting to think otherwise after the start of this conversation.

"What, is that weird? Too fast?" I ask her.

"No, not at all. I mean, not if your happy ...?" It's a question that startles me. Never before has she bothered to find out if I'm happy in any of my relationships; we only jumped for joy together when giddy little experiences happened and spoke death to any man if he ever broke our hearts.

"He makes me happy," I say. "I love him."

"Do you?" Gwen asks, a sense of urgency in her question which shocks me.

I sit there for a moment, searching my friend's face. Gwen looks scared, worried, mad, and hurt. I can tell my best friend wants what's best for me. It's a complete shock to me that she's questioning if Noah is it. Gwen simply just doesn't know Noah like I do. She doesn't know the man that changed his whole world around just to be with me. That took guts, and that's something to admire.

"I do, Gwen. I could hardly breath when he left me for that fire a month or so back. Thinking of not being with him scares me. I can't even imagine it. He's an amazing man, and he gave up everything for me. He stayed and changed his whole life just to be with me," I try explaining but words don't express how I feel for Noah. "That takes guts. How could I not love a man that would give up everything just to be with me?"

I want Gwen to know just how much he means to me. Part of the reason why I love him so much is because of how much he loves me. Surely that couldn't be the only reason, but as soon as the thought finds my mind, the burning fear begins to surface inside. Although this time, there's no pushing it away.

Gwen's response is slow to come, but powerful when spoken. With one simple question, she stops time and changes everything that I've been trying to fight since Noah walked into my life and stole my heart.

"But are you willing to do the same," she asks.

The question hits me like a ton of bricks. I'm hurt that Gwen would even suggest such a comment. I'm mad that anyone would think I'm the type of woman who wouldn't give back what was given. It's as if she's accusing me of using Noah or something. And then I'm sad ... sad that for the first time I'm forced to face the little voice inside me I was trying so hard to ignore. The burning reality that maybe I'm not.

I sit there, on the back patio of a local bar with my best friend, suddenly getting the wind knocked out of me. I'm forced to possibly admit a reality I have tried so hard to cover up. The thought never entered my mind before simply because I always forced it away. Now, it sticks like a bad disease in my brain, intruding and oozing its venom on my every thought. The burn consumes my body, filling it painfully, and I feel sick having to even begin to process the answer.

"Your silence, my sweet dear friend, is, unfortunately your answer," Gwen says, breaking my train of thought. The look of sadness and pity on her face is one that I've never seen before and will probably never forget.

I don't want that to be the answer. I know if I try hard, I wouldn't feel the way I did. If I could just try harder, maybe I will forget this conversation and the idea that I ever possibly felt the way I'm feeling now, faced with a possible truth I have been trying to suppress for months. I love Noah, I know it, but

CHAPTER 24

giving up a life I had planned and hoped for long before I ever met him is not something I had ever thought I would face. My mind races as it tells me all the things I don't want to hear.

Noah gave up everything for you. Noah sacrificed anything he planned before you, just to be with you. You don't love him like he loves you. You're unworthy of his love. He's better than you, and your love will never be good enough.

My mind won't stop, and I feel compelled to fight against it. To somehow push that burn back and continue not having to face the one reality I've tried for months to ignore.

"I wouldn't say I wouldn't give up everything for him. You don't know that Gwen, you don't know what we have."

"Ahh, but I know you," Gwen says. A simple answer, but a powerful truth. She does know me. She knows all I stood for, all I dreamed for. All I've set my hopes on ever since I was a little girl. That's something I can't argue with.

"That's not fair," I whisper, my response not nearly as powerful as Gwen's. Still, it's simple and true.

"Listen, Ev," Gwen says, leaning forward. "I love you. You know that!" I nod, looking down at the table and silently sitting, waiting for my friend to continue. "But you have dreams, girl. Ambitions! You live life fuller than I have ever seen anyone live it, possibly ever! The whole reason I have never given up on life is because I had you by my side, pushing me every damn day." Gwen's voice breaks, and I find it hard to contain my own emotions as a tear slides down my face. "You set the bar high, girl, and the rest of us can only aspire to follow and obtain even half the goals you have set for yourself." Gwen pauses for a moment thinking. She takes a drink before continuing. I look up, finally ready to meet her eyes and hear what comes next as one single tear falls down my face.

"I tried to let myself die when my sister did. And God knows I'm no sort of example to look up to, but you saw through all that. You kept me going. You never gave up on me, and because of that, I never gave up on myself. I won't let you give up on your dreams. If you tell me your dreams are to marry the sexy, southern, tall, construction-working, hot volunteer firefighter from Kentucky and have a million babies, possibly being barefoot and pregnant in the kitchen the rest of your life, I'll respect that! But I won't accept it! Damn it, I know you better. I know you, Ev! Just, please ... think about what I'm saying. Sometimes you only get one chance in life. I just want to make sure you don't waste it."

Gwen trails off, and I'm stunned in silence. I can barely even think, let alone form any sort of comeback to the truth that has just hit me square in the eyes. I have just been handed more information than I know what to do with and this is going to take a while to process if I even could begin to start and wrap my mind around it all now.

Looking down at the bottle in my hand, I try to process all my past, all the present, and all the future I hoped for. My breathing quickens and I find it hard to be in any form of reality. Taking a long and very hard sip of beer, I subconsciously and involuntarily decide the best option is to get drunk. And the sooner the better.

I slam back three-quarters of a beer I have left, stand, and make my way to the bar to order two more. Tipping the bartender more than anyone ever should, I wink at him and tell him to keep them coming!

Chapter 25

Noah

"Mr. Stewart ... Oh. Mr. Stewart!" I wake up to the sound of a woman's voice singing my name, trailing in from outside my apartment. Foggy and still trying to make sense of what was going on, I sit up in bed and look at the time: 12:45. Scratching my head, I try my best to focus on the voice I just heard coming from what sounded like right outside the front door.

"Mr. Stewart, are you there? Please tell me you're there ..." the voice pleads. "Mr. Stewart, oh, Mr. Stewart," the voice continues in an almost musical nature.

Getting out of bed, I'm puzzled and swear the voice sounds like Evelyn. Although if it is her, she sounds nowhere near any sort of way I have ever heard her sound before. I flip on a light and make my way to the door. The voice has been replaced with a loud obnoxious banging noise. Curiosity beckons and I swing open the door to find Evelyn a mess and very much drunk.

"Hello, Mr. Stewart," she says smiling up at me.

The effects of alcohol make her eyes glisten. She sits on the top of the steps, her back against the stair railing that leads to my apartment. She faces my door and holds a beer bottle in one hand, no doubt the object I had heard just a few moments earlier that was banging on God only knows what ... maybe the floor in front of her.

I hurry to her side, quickly wanting to help her in, and also wanting to understand what it was that brought out this side of her. Helping her up, I look around for Gwen and curse under my breath at the fact that she's nowhere in sight. When I heard they were going out, I hadn't imagined Evelyn to be the one ending the night this way.

Stumbling, Evelyn makes her way towards the door. Dropping the empty bottle, she giggles nonstop, obviously holding in a joke that she finds hysterical. Although, I do not see any humor in the situation.

"You're too kind, sir," she says, breaking away from my hold and trying to make her way on her own. She fails and starts to fall, hitting the wall and almost taking down a picture frame with her.

I'm quick to catch her and help her to the couch. Giggling and still very enthused with the situation, she sits while I turn and close the front door. Making my way back to her side, I sit down, irritated, my mind racing with what the hell is going on.

This is something I was not expecting and something I need answers to right now! What irritates me most is why she's alone and what it is that could have brought her to such a delirious condition. Damn it, Gwen!

Trying to compose herself, Evelyn sits up straight, looking me in the eye with the straightest face she can manage. Less than a second later, she breaks, laughing so hard she has to hold on to my arm to keep from falling off my couch. I find no hilarity in how she's allowing herself to behave on her girl's night out. There has to be some reason for this. Although, for the life of me, I can't start to imagine what it is.

CHAPTER 25

"Do you want something to drink," I ask.

Her eyes light up as she struggles to meet mine. "Do you have a beer?" She giggles some more.

"I think you've had enough beer, Evelyn. I was talking about water," I state firmly.

"Oh, you're no fun," she says, pushing me playfully. However, no part of me wants to playback.

"What's wrong, Evie?" I ask, trying to sound calm, though every part of me wants to hurt whatever it is that might be hurting her, making her drink more than I have ever seen her drink before. I also wouldn't mind finding her sorry excuse of a friend and getting to the bottom of how and why she showed up at my door in the middle of the night by herself drunk as hell. I've never had an excuse before to be mad at Gwen, but right now I'm finding it hard to think any good thoughts about her and how she could leave her best friend in this kind of condition.

"I was just trying to think ..." Evelyn says, trailing off. She points at me, trying to make some sort of emphasis on what she's about to say but failing horribly.

A few moments pass. Evelyn's face softens and sadness fills every part of her expression. Whatever it is that made her decide to drink so much is making itself known in her clouded mind, and I try my best to be ready for whatever it is she might be about to say.

Slowly, in a whisper, she answers me. "Why do you want to be with me?"

I pause. Is she joking? I don't know how to respond. I thought I had shown her why every day that we'd been together. I thought I had done everything I needed so she would never, ever doubt how much I care for her. She has to know how much

I love her. She has to know why I want to be with her. Where is all of this coming from?

"How could you even ask that? Don't you already know? I've told you in a million ways," I say. "Is that what this is about? How could you even question that?"

"I'm no good for you, Noah," she blurts out, sadly dropping her gaze to the floor.

Her eyes fill with tears. Her face hardens with anger, and I began to see a side of her I have never seen before. Rage and hatred fill every ounce of this woman I love. Never in our time together have I ever experienced a moment with her where she seemed to hate herself. It's almost as if living with herself and whatever is clouding her mind is an impossible task. I can't take it. How can she think about herself that way when she is all I could ever need. All I will ever want in this life.

"No good for me? Evelyn, there was a time I thought I could only hope to be lucky enough to have someone like you …" I try soothing her, but she cuts me off.

"No … no… NO!" she shouts, interrupting me and shaking her head fiercely as if she is trying to shake away the thoughts that are living there as well. "No good. I'm no good!" She's drunk and also delirious.

She waves her hand in front of her and then grabs ahold of my leg for stability. Very shaky and very drunk, she has me wondering exactly how much she's had to drink. She's almost incapable of holding herself still and in an upright position. This is not like her at all. She always stops after a few drinks, and I have never seen her even enter a situation where she might put herself in this position.

"Baby, why would you think that? You're everything I have ever imagined. Everything I have ever hoped to find." I'm truthful and hope whatever I say will stop the battle she's having with herself. "There was a time I swore I would never allow myself to feel the way I feel for you, but damn it, I could help but fall for you, Ev!"

I hate seeing the woman I love like this. I never want to see it again and have to find some way to calm the fight that's raging in her head—but I still can't make any sense of it. Where the hell did all of this come from?

"But what about later?" Evelyn asks. "What about much later. I can't live up to perfect, Noah! You think I'm great now, but what about the first time I do something wrong? What about when I'm not perfect? If I make bad choices ... when I disappoint you, and you look at me like ... like you want nothing to do with me! I don't think I could ever take you looking at me that way." She starts to cry. At first, her tears fall slowly then uncontrollably the more her thoughts resonate with her emotions.

"I would never want nothing to do with you," I tell her sternly.

"You say that now, but who knows! What if I gain weight! Or I stop putting on makeup every day! When months turn into years and time together turns into marriage ... maybe even kids ..." I smile as she babbles incoherently. I can't help myself. Her vulnerability is bringing forth possibilities that I had thought of myself but never mentioned to her for fear she wouldn't feel the same way.

She would look so beautiful pregnant. And the mention of our child in her womb makes something stir inside me that I haven't felt before.

She slows her rambling, agony consuming her with each passing moment. "What if I can't promise you forever?" she asks, tears streaming down her face.

The pain from her last comment sends me into shock. I hadn't agreed to forever with her, but I know I want her for as many days and nights that I can have her. She's it for me. The thought of a lifetime together is a big order to fill, but in the foreseeable future, I can't imagine experiencing any of it with anyone but her.

"You can promise me now. You can promise me you will wake up with those beautiful blue eyes looking at me tomorrow morning. You can let me make love to you like tomorrow isn't promised and forever is no guarantee," I say, almost pleading for a relationship that seemed so secure just a few moments before.

I have never begged before and don't know why I was doing it now. I knew Evelyn will barely remember our conversation in the morning, but I want to offer as much comfort to her as I can tonight. I want to somehow calm whatever storm is so obviously raging inside.

Her face softens. She glances my way. Mischief lurks in her eyes. Her expression changes almost instantly. Whatever I said did the trick. Either that or the alcohol haze has made it very simple to change her train of thought. Whatever it is doesn't matter since it seems to be working in my favor.

"Mr. Stewart, you are too much! I don't deserve you," she insists. She smiles at first then grabs ahold of my leg again as I see her begin to spin. "Umm, Noah …" She clutches me harder, her face looking extremely pale.

"Yes," I ask, worried for her response but knowing already what she is about to say.

"I think I'm about to be sick," she says, holding her hand to her mouth.

CHAPTER 25

I yank her to her feet and hurry off with her to the bathroom as fast as I can. As I watch her throw up, I feel nothing but sadness; sad she felt it necessary to put herself through the pain she had tonight because she has no clue what she really means to me.

I know relationships go through ups and downs. I know everything isn't always sunshine and roses. When any two souls collide, their existence is never entirely perfect, but my life has changed since I met Evelyn. And I have never questioned the choices I've made since meeting her. Sure, I remember waiting for the uncertainty once deciding to uproot my life again just for the chance to be with her, but it never came. The decision to love her was easy. I need her to know how much she means to me, and hell, I thought she did. I want her to know how much I want her with me every moment of every day, and an hour ago I would have sworn she already knew. I can't place my finger on why things have changed, and I know I need to fight to get us back where we used to be.

Even with everything I'm able to offer, I know she is free to make her own choice. I can offer myself to her in every way possible, and she could still leave. Or in the end, she could turn on me like Becky did. It's a reality I'm still coming to terms with. It's always there in the very back of my mind, but she's worth the risk. Never once have I ever been undecided when it came to our love.

I made my choice that night we had our first date. I decided to let go and let her in. Damn the past. Although, for the first time since then, she has me worried if making that choice is putting me through what I went through before. She is worth the risk, I know that. But for the first time since making that decision, I'm worried that maybe she won't always choose me.

That maybe the indecision she is wrestling with will always be greater than the love I can show her. If she's already thinking that she might not be able to promise me forever, what kind of future could there ever be for us? A future that seemed so secure when I had gone to bed now hangs motionless in the air like a bad dream I can't shake, a nightmare from my past resurfacing and sucking the life out of me once again.

When she seems like she's feeling better, I carry her to bed. I help rid her of her clothes and grab one of my T-shirts for her to sleep in. After I manage to get her into it, I tuck her gently underneath the covers. I don't join her. Instead, I sit in a chair near the bed, staring at her. I'm trying to make sense of everything that has just happened. Our world was going so great. I never saw any signs that something like this might happen. I sit in the dark, watching her sleep, trying to find any shred of light I can shine on the situation, wondering for the first time how deep her love goes for me. And being forced to realize maybe it is not as deep as I thought.

Evelyn has to feel the way I do. She has to know what kind of chemistry we have and how lucky we are to be able to have it. If she doubts anything about us at all, I need to show her just how lucky we are and how much I fully intended to fight for her. For us. Still, in the back of my mind, I know that unless she wants it too, fighting alone might not do the trick. She might still not choose me. And in the end, I could be left once again by myself. Although, shortly after we first met, I promised myself I wasn't going to let her get away that easy. And that is one promise I entirely intend to keep.

Chapter 26

Evelyn

The world seems a very evil place when I wake up on Saturday morning. Luckily, I don't have to work and don't need to be anywhere until later this evening when the party starts at Gatsby's. Trying my best to not let the piercing light of day blind me, I sit in bed and notice I am in Noah's apartment.

Visions of the end of the night come flooding back to me. I remember drinking heavily, and Gwen and me dancing at the third bar we stumbled into, a bar that just happened to be down the street from Noah's. Soon after Gwen found a guy, she plastered herself all over him, and I sat alone with the thoughts I had been trying to run from all night.

When it most definitely looked like Gwen was going home with her new bar friend, I drunkenly started my walk of shame towards Noah's place, holding my beer in my hand. I actually remember that part only because I was so shocked to walk out of the bar with it and no one said anything.

Then Noah ... I remember him, remember the room spinning, throwing up, and him taking care of me, putting me to bed. But for the life of me, I cannot remember what we talked about. It couldn't have been bad, could it?

I move towards the end of the bed and sit for a moment, debating when I should actually attempt standing. I feel worse than I have in years, thanks to those good old IPAs I love to drink so much. I never drink more than I should, a habit I broke in my early twenties, after one too many nights like last night. I hate the fact that I was weak last night and shamefully succumbed to stupid behavior in order to deal with things I didn't want to face.

Taking a quick short glance around the apartment, I notice Noah is already gone. I remember him having to work a job in the morning and am relieved I don't have to face him just yet. For the first time in months, I'm slightly nervous about seeing him. Not remembering our conversation last night but remembering how drunk I let myself get, I'm sure it will make things awkward between the two of us.

Deciding what I need most is a hot shower, a huge breakfast, coffee, and my own bed, I slowly make my descent from Noah's. I then began slowly changing into my own clothes. Glancing at my phone, I notice Gwen has already texted me this morning. She tells me she has grabbed the car and wants to know where I am and if I need a ride, having already been by the apartment and noticing I hadn't come home.

I quickly text her back that I'm at Noah's and tell her how to find me since she has never been here before. I'm thankful that Gwen is better at this hangover situation than I am. I feel like I can't even function, and God only knows if I'm going to be able to anytime soon.

Gwen texts back that she's on her way, and I brace myself, trying to get ready to face the daylight outside. The sun, of course, has to be especially bright on today of all days. My mouth is dry, my head pounds like the overly loud bass in

CHAPTER 26

Gatsby's on a Friday night, and my body feels heavy, making me think twice before making it move. Every step feeling like a huge hurdle as I try and will my body to do what I need it to do just to make it home.

God, I hate hangovers.

Once I make it back to my place, I text Noah to let him know I'm home, trying to act as normal as possible. He doesn't text back right away, which is a little out of character. When he finally does, all he wants to know is if it would be okay if he didn't pick me up later and we could just meet at the club.

Trying my best to not feel the littlest bit upset and hurt he wouldn't pick me up, I tell him it's fine and I will ride with Gwen but can't wait to see him there. He texts me back that he's busy and going into a meeting so he won't be able to respond, ending with a quick "love u," and I respond the same. Something doesn't seem right, but I try to ignore it and tell myself I'm overreacting and overanalyzing the situation.

After a meal with enough calories to last me a week, a couple of Advil, and several glasses of water, I decide a nap is exactly what I need to help the situation. I lock myself in my room, closing the blinds and not wanting to think about last night. The worry of not knowing exactly what I said and what transpired keeps me awake awhile and makes it difficult to get the rest I thought I would.

Am I sure I didn't say anything horrible? Why can't I remember? It's strange and out of character for him not to pick me up for a party that he planned. Maybe he had something come up? Still, even with all that, I also find myself wrestling with what Gwen had asked me last night as well. Would I give up everything for him? Could I?

Eventually, I fall asleep and hope that when I wake up, things will be back to normal. I'm hopeful at best, but there is still something lingering that I can't quite put my finger on.

Noah -

Friday goes by in an angry rage. I hadn't slept much the night before and now my frustration is off the charts. I can't hide it. I can't make sense of it. Damn it!

The more I think about it, turning over every word Evelyn spoke, the more I become more irritated than I have been in years. I lose myself in my work, hitting things in place with extra force and slamming things down obnoxiously. Fuck it, I don't care. The good thing about being my own boss is that I can act any way I want to.

Evelyn texts me around lunchtime and somehow it makes my mood even shittier. I can't make sense of why but know it can't be good. The night before leaves me with so many unanswered questions and painful memories of rejection that I've only spent the last year and a half trying to forget. It hurts to think maybe she doesn't love me as much as I love her. That maybe she couldn't, or rather wouldn't, give me her world like I have so easily given up mine.

So I make up the lie that I have some meeting, try to end it sweetly, and got my ass back to work as fast as I can. What if I can't give you everything? Her statement clings to my every thought, creeping in at every moment just when I think I've finally succeeded in making my mind go silent. Hell, there it is again, torturing me. Eating me alive. I can't shake it.

Isn't that what you do? When you fall in love, isn't that supposed to be the most natural part? I want to be with her so badly, I did whatever it took to keep us that way. If she can't do the same, what the hell am I doing here? And where in the hell does this leave us?

CHAPTER 26

I thought everything was great. It hadn't felt more perfect with any other woman before in my whole damn life. Not even Becky. But damn it if I wasn't now slightly regretting it all, thinking I should have stuck to my original plans. I should not have fallen for a pair of blue eyes, long blond hair, and a body sexy as hell.

Fuck me.

So here we go again.

Then, like an even worse nightmare, reality sets in, tormenting me and not allowing any kind of escape. The one thing I know I could never run from.

I love her.

Damn straight I do. That is what got me into this mess. And I thought for sure she felt the same damn way. I didn't think I was running off headfirst into this thing like an idiot again. I thought that I could trust her.

What if I can't give you everything?

Fuck that. Fuck this. What the hell did I get myself into?

As evening approaches, I try my hardest to forget all that is still raging inside of me. I want to turn off my mind and enjoy the night. Maybe what I need is to see her again, hold her. That connection between the two of us is always so strong. Somehow maybe that might make everything all right and calm the anger and nerves I've been dealing with all day.

I'll be able to tell if things are okay between us by looking at her, spending time with her, and feeling her in my arms. I want more than anything to act like things haven't changed, that I haven't been fighting the hugest war in my mind all damn day.

I'm late getting off work, which means I'm late getting home and now late arriving at her party. I hadn't intended for it to be that way, but it's unfortunately how it happened and to hell if I could have helped it.

I should have picked her up, I know that. The last thing I want is to make her feel unwanted after last night, and damn it if I didn't think about that earlier. Maybe some light arguing followed by a round or two of make-up sex is exactly what I need. What we need. A means to an end to put whatever the hell last night was behind us. But there is no time for that, and now I'm here finally about to face whatever it is that got us to where we are, questioning the one thing that came so easy. Our love.

Stepping into Gatsby's, the place is roaring, just like you'd imagine it would be back in the twenties. It's packed and music blares from a DJ booth set up behind the very elaborate bar. Our group has reserved a special room in the back of the building. I slowly make my way through the crowd in that direction.

Entering the room, I first notice a few of Evelyn's work colleagues. Then there's Rex and Michael. Trevor has shown up as well and is busy talking to Gwen. I can't help but cringe a little when I see Gwen. The fact that she left Evelyn in the condition she did last night still bothers me.

And Trevor, well he can go to hell. The sight of him makes the thoughts I've had all day surface again. I know he'll do anything to try and make Evelyn his. I do my best to push that away when I glance around the room.

There's my girl!

She's looking absolutely ravishing in a light blue dress that hugs her body in all the right places. Her hair is long and cascades in beautiful curls down her back. She hasn't noticed me yet, and I take my time walking up behind her. Slowly, I grab her waist and notice she jumps slightly as I pull her closer to me.

CHAPTER 26

I need contact. I need to feel her, be with her. I breathe her in. Her signature vanilla scent mixes with the smell of her shampoo and all things that make her the woman I love. It calms me a little as a sliver of peace works its way into me for the first time since last night.

She doesn't turn to look at me right away. Instead, she continues the conversation she's having. Her reaction burns me a little, and I try my best to ignore the sting. I tighten my grip and nestle into the side of her neck, right where I know it drives her wild. I don't care that this room is full of people. I need that connection. That spark. I need her, and I hate the thought that any part of us might be ruined.

Instead of arching her head to the side, allowing me more access and room to do as I please like usual, she shrugs me off, looking at me annoyed and rolling her eyes slightly. That's definitely different. Evelyn never rolls her eyes at me, and I can't for the life of me understand why she's doing it now.

"Nice of you to finally show up," she says as the person she's talking to takes their leave.

"I got stuck at work," I try explaining. "I wish I hadn't. I'm sorry I couldn't be there to pick you up. Happy birthday, darlin'. How was your day?"

She backs up a little, putting more space between us. Extremely hurt and confused, I release my grip on her waist.

"It was great," she over emphasizes. She watches me for a moment, but I have no clue what to say next or how to proceed. This is new and is not exactly the welcome I expected. After a moment, her eyes meet someone else's across the room.

"Excuse me, Noah," she says angrily and pushes past me to talk to whoever caught her eye.

Ok, what the hell happened now? Who is this new woman

and what did she do with the one I love? Why is she so upset? And what the fuck is with the cold shoulder? Shouldn't I be the pissed one here?

I make my way over to the private bar, which includes its own personal bartender. Normally, I try to stick with beer at parties, but tonight I feel like bourbon.

Ordering two double shots, I pause briefly before shooting back the first. Taking a deep breath, I take the second quickly. Shooting it back with extreme force, I feel oddly better the more the liquid burns going down my throat.

Looking back at Evelyn, I notice her gaze meet mine. She looks slightly confused, a little sad, and still obviously very mad at something I can't for the life of me figure out. For the first time since we've met, I can't read her. Returning my attention back to the bar, I order another. I take it hungrily and feel the tension that had built during the last twenty-four hours slowly start to fade away.

Chapter 27

Evelyn

For whatever reason, Noah has royally succeeded in totally pissing me off. First, it was his awkward and delayed reaction to my text message earlier. Then the fact that he didn't insist on picking me up for my party that he was throwing for me making me even madder the more I thought about it. And I thought about it a lot. That, plus the conversation with Gwen the night before, is all that rolls through my mind, making me hate myself, hate him, and hate this stupid night.

Not able to hold my anger back, Gwen and I had discussed all the reasons why I felt the way I did while getting ready for the party. Our conversation didn't help the situation or my growing rage one bit.

He never called when he got off work. Just another way in which things didn't seem right either; he always calls or texts.

Then he showed up forty-five minutes late to a night that he had planned, especially for me. To top it off, he walked up to me like nothing was wrong, nothing was different and wanted my attention directed one hundred percent at him right away.

The bastard!

Even if I am slightly overreacting, I really don't give a shit.

Maybe it is time shit hit the fan so I can figure out this whole damn picture. That's just the kind of person I have always been. I need to break first in order to put it all back together again.

Ignoring something that I know had to be dealt with over the past few months is not something I normally do. Meeting things head-on has always been more like my style. It's time to meet our reality head-on and see if it's strong enough to handle the truth ... whatever that is. Time to fight like hell to figure everything out, even if that means facing a reality that life is not always sunshine and rainbows.

I glance in his general direction. To make matters worse, if that is even possible, he's now sitting around the bar with Rex and Michael, shooting back shots and continuing to ignore my existence. I mean, truth be told, I did shrug him off, but damn it he blew me off first! In fact, he blew me off all day. Not really the special birthday present I was expecting from Mr. Used To Be So Wonderful. Now I can't help but hate everything about my boyfriend.

He looks back at me once, but never even tries to look at me again. I thought maybe he might leave the bar and come find me, try and talk to me about why I was so upset now that maybe I had time to cool off. Instead, he continues drinking—and drinking a lot.

You're just fueling a fire, asshole, I think silently to myself. He should be smart enough by now to know how women tick. What a certifiable idiot. Fire lit, I'm sure as hell ready for a fight. I hope he's ready to go round for round because it is going to be a long night.

I look over to see Rex falling off his barstool and Michael barely able to stand himself. It's a good thing they own the place or they'd all be thrown out. They have people they trust

CHAPTER 27

filling in for them out front, and unless all hell breaks loose, which never really happens in a small town like this, they're actually free to do what they want at their own club for once.

Deciding to use the restroom to freshen up myself and my mind, I realize a break from the party is just what I might need to figure out the next step to take. I make my way down a small hallway to the ladies' room and am thankful it's empty. I take all the time I need, staring at my reflection in the mirror, trying to think of my best options and regain control over not only my thoughts but my life.

Still undecided after nearly twenty minutes later, I open the door and hope I can make up my mind before I return to the room. Walking back down the hallway, I look down, consumed in thought and not watching where I'm going. I bump into someone from behind and grab on to the person to stable myself in my heels.

"I'm so sorry," I began.

"You can bump into me anytime, Evie," Trevor says, turning around to look at me. He smiles big and bright as he continues, "Are you enjoying your party?"

I think for a moment about giving him a short and sweet answer and then push past him in order to return to everyone. Although I know Trevor and I have history, he will be able to see past anything I'm trying so hard to hide. It's probably wrong to lean on him with my frustrations, but I have no one else to talk to. Even Gwen got tired of my rambling earlier this evening, and although it could pose to be a bad choice, maybe talking to someone, preferably a man, is how I can work through this.

"Actually, no," I say, relief flooding me as I let my guard down and finally allow some of my emotions out.

Trevor's smile softens and a look of concern flashes in his

eyes. "Why?" he asks, taking a moment to step closer. The look in his eyes is unlike anything I have ever seen before. I don't know how to read him.

"Just not really my scene anymore," I try to explain. "Plus, I had a really bad night last night and an even worse day today."

I shake my head, remembering aspects of why I feel exactly the way I do. I want to forget it all and rewind the last twenty-four hours of my life, change what I can, and have the best night imaginable. But that's impossible.

"If you were my girl, I'd make sure and plan you a party you wanted. Not leave you alone while you were so obviously upset," Trevor says, taking another step closer.

I know I should run. I know I should push him away. But I continue to stand in one spot. Maybe it's the comment that he made, something I was totally not expecting, or maybe it's the lack of attention from Noah. Whatever it is, I know deep down inside staying any longer in this conversation is a bad choice. Still, I don't move.

"I haven't been your girl for a long time, Trevor," I tease him, a little nervous laugh escaping my lips.

I hope that he gets the hint. Our conversations have teetered on this kind of talk before. However, with a response like the one I just gave Trevor, he always backs up and doesn't press further. Something inside me, though, tells me with the way he is looking at me right now that is not about to be the outcome tonight.

Trevor's talk slows, almost becoming a low, sexual growl as he steps into me further. I back up and feel the coldness of the wall behind me. Growing more nervous, I look around him to see if anyone might be coming down the hallway.

"I still wish you were. I remember everything about you, Evie.

And I know you better than any other man. I know what you like, what you don't like, and better yet, I would never ... ever ... ignore you. Never hurt you," he says, pushing up against me.

"Trevor, please ..." I plead nervously.

I push his chest slightly, trying to add some distance. The conversation has gone exactly to the place I didn't want it to. I had hoped I would never be in a position like I am now with Trevor and almost blame myself entirely for it, having not taken leave when I knew I should have. I always trusted him not to push our limit before, and he never has. Until tonight.

Trevor grabs my hand as I place it on his chest, pulling me into him closer and keeping a strong grip on my wrist. He takes his time looking at me, examining every curve, every part of my face. I become scared. I don't know what he's thinking or what he might do. In fear, I freeze, scared to move, hoping I'm dreaming.

"I want to be with you, Evelyn. It kills me seeing you with someone else. Let me try to make you happy," Trevor persists, pulling me closer. We're face to face, both our bodies pressed up against one another. I don't know what to do. I can't think fast enough to try to defend myself. Before I can push Trevor away, he does the unthinkable.

Grabbing me hard, forcing me against the wall, he quickly captures my lips with his. It catches me off guard, and I grunt when he makes contact. He grabs me tighter, thinking the grunt means I obviously like what's happening. He begins to force himself harder on me, almost as if forcing it will make all he wants and all he desires come true.

I eventually break free from Trevor, pushing and clawing my way out of his arms. He resists me, yanking me back to him as forcefully as he can. Pulling with all his might, he persists in trying to get me back where he so obviously wants me most.

I push back harder, wiping my mouth, trying to get his taste off my lips. This trip to the bathroom to get my head straight has turned out to be the worst idea I've had in a long time—even worse than getting hammered drunk last night.

"Oh my God, Trevor," I yell. "Are you insane? What the hell are you doing? I don't even know what to tell Noah!"

"You don't have to tell me anything!"

We both turn and face the one person I hoped I wasn't going to see. The one man I couldn't face, not right now. But there he is, standing in the entrance to the hallway, fists clenched, ready for a fight.

Noah -

I don't know why, but something felt off. I saw Evelyn leave towards the restroom and noticed Trevor follow. Not only that, but a large amount of time had passed since either one of them had resurfaced. Almost twenty minutes actually, if I am reading the clock right through my cloudy brain.

A little drunk, I stand and make my way over to where they disappeared. I trust Evelyn, but Trevor is another story. Rounding the corner, the one scenario I didn't want to see comes into a full and very clear view. Trevor has his hands all over my girl, kissing her and trying to touch her in places only my hands belong.

In one split second, all the rage that had been building all day shoots through me, and I'm not able to contain it any longer. Evelyn pushes away and I hear her speak. I hear my voice respond, but don't have time to process what it is I said. I lunge forward, wanting—needing to hurt Trevor in any and every way possible.

Evelyn barely has time to move out of the way. In one clean

shot, I hit Trevor with so much force he falls to the floor. Scrambling to his feet, he flies into me, pushing me up against the wall. I hit his sides, every which way I can, trying to break free. Finally making contact with one of his ribs on his right side, I swear I feel it crack under my fist.

Evelyn's shrill yell breaks my concentration for a moment and allows Trevor to get a good punch in. There is a loud ringing in my head and ears. I duck the next time, forcing Trevor to have his fist meet with the wall behind me. Coming back to standing, I'm able to get another good hit right between his eyes, causing Trevor's nose to start bleeding.

Evelyn has run off by now, and Trevor and I continue to stand there in the hallway, throwing punch after punch at each other. All the aggression that has built between the two of us since Evelyn came into my life is now finally exposed. Hit after hit, punch after punch, we are finally having it out, fighting for the woman we both love.

About damn time! I've had enough of Trevor's shit. A hit to his stomach and he topples over in pain. Straightening himself back up, he takes a swing at me, but I dodge it, stepping out of the way. Another hit to the side of his head and he staggers backward a bit before regaining his stance.

Come on, Trevor! Fucking show up for this fight already before I knock you the hell out like I should have done months ago!

He swings at my left side, and when I step to the right to get out of the way, his other fist comes up, making contact with the right side of my head. I stagger backward slightly and feel another punch in the middle of my stomach.

Fuck. That one hurt. Although it only seems to fuel me, making me want to end this little fucker faster. He stepped over the line. You do not touch what is mine. And she is mine. Fuck whatever she said last night. Fuck the "What if I can't give you everything?"

Adrenaline always brings about instant sobriety, and I'm so over this shit. I'm done. Time to put the pieces of my life back together and stop playing this damn game. She's mine, not his. And this damn act she's pulling over last night is bullshit.

With each swing, I make contact: one to the right then one to the left of his head. He falls back slightly. One more and his eyes close as he almost falls to the ground. Coming back at me, I make contact with his stomach then one more to the head. His eyes are swollen. Blood is everywhere—his face, my fists—and still the rage inside only continues to fuel me.

DING DING DING! Times up, Trev. It's time I put you in your place like I should have done that first night at Evelyn's parents' house.

I don't know who got there first, but soon two people are breaking us apart. Rex is pulling me back, and Michael stands in front of us, trying to control Trevor.

"She doesn't belong with you! You don't deserve a woman like her. She's upper class, and you're low as shit," Trevor screams at me. Just as things seem to be calming down, both of us are now being pulled into separate corners.

I lunge forward, not caring who I hurt but needing to break something, hopefully Trevor. My fist collides with Michael's nose and it immediately squirts blood everywhere, right at the exact moment Evelyn comes barreling around the corner with Gwen behind her.

"What is wrong with you?" she screams, rushing to her brother's side. "Are you ok, Michael?"

Gwen stands nearby, watching the scene unfold, a look of

CHAPTER 27

accomplishment shining bright in her eyes. She accesses the situation, taking in every detail of what just played out and loving every second of it.

"I'm sorry, I didn't mean to," I say, trying to step forward but Rex blocks my way.

"Move, man," I yell at my friend. But he won't. He stays put and gives me a look that tells me to calm the fuck down and back the hell up.

"Fuck!" I grit out between clenched teeth. I pull at my hair and continue to pace back and forth in the small space I'm confined to. I look at Evelyn, silently pleading for her to look back.

"See what he's done, Ev? Why are you even with this piece of shit," Trevor seethes, looking at me when she starts to walk over to him to assess his wounds.

"Shut the fuck up," I yell, lunging for his ass again only to fall short as Rex pushes me forcefully up against the wall and back into my corner.

Evelyn continues assessing the damage. What the fuck! Why is she touching him? Stop placing your hands on that piece of shit, baby. I might not look any worse for wear, barely having a scratch on me, but to hell if I can stand the sight of her hands on him right now.

The fact that I'm not her first priority turns my blood to fire. It speaks volumes about the many things that have been going through my mind all day, the nightmare that I've been trying to avoid. Even though I had been fueled by the events of the day and one too many shots of Woodford Reserve, I know I'm not totally in the wrong for what just happened.

It's the look she gives me, though ... Sadness. Hurt. Hate. It has me questioning why I wanted to fight for her in the first place. What the hell is going on here?

Those things should not be questioned! Not when a man comes across what I just did! That's a damn certifiable fact any red-blooded man would argue. Being forced to question myself now makes me think twice about ever fighting for her again.

She doesn't say a word. She stands in the middle of all our friends and gives me that look. That look that reaches deep into my soul and scares the hell out of me. My heart breaks seeing that look. Why is she so cold? What the hell has changed between us?

This is not over. We're not over.

"I want to go home," she says, beginning to cry.

"I'll take you," I began.

"NO," she yells so loud everyone in the group flinches.

Evelyn turns to Gwen. Gwen nods and hooks her arm through her best friend's. Quickly, both girls start to make their way towards the exit. At first, I stand there, shocked, as the realization that she doesn't want me hits and slowly sinks in.

"Evelyn," I yell after her. "Evelyn!" When that doesn't work, I take a different approach. "Darlin'! Baby! Where are you going? Come back!"

But she's gone. I watch her walk out the door and know I have to let her go. Whatever it is that she's fighting, I can't help her. Hell, I can't even help myself right now. I just hope wherever she's headed I won't lose her.

Chapter 28

Evelyn

Neither Gwen nor I say one word when we leave Gatsby's. The car ride home is silent. We don't even bother turning on the radio.

When we arrive back at the apartment, we still choose not to speak. I take straight to the bathroom, stripping my clothes and makeup, hoping to strip the night away as well. I hop in the shower and turn the hot water up as high as I can. I want to feel it burn.

Steam encircles me and with it agony, misery and pain. I feel my tears fall before I even notice I'm crying. And after the realization hits, I lose it. Curled up in a little ball on the floor of my shower, I sob harder than I have in my whole life.

I pull at my hair, crying painfully. I want to make sense of everything that has suddenly happened in my life but feel like I can't even begin to process it all.

Why did Trevor do that? What was Noah thinking? Did he think I was asking for it? Did he think I was enjoying Trevor's hands and lips on me?

Why am I so irritated at Noah anyway? So he worked late. So he didn't call. I was already at the party anyway. He had told me to catch a ride with Gwen. Maybe he knew he would be working late. He did try when he first got there, and I was the one to brush him off.

What did I say to him last night? Maybe it was something really stupid and fucked-up. God, why for the life of me, can't I remember?

And damn what Gwen said to me the night before! Would I really not give up everything just for the chance to be with him?

Just when I've sat on the bottom of the shower floor long enough to have myself convinced that I just maybe could give up everything to be with him, the fear rises. That burn. Damn it that burn that makes me feel like I can't. I just can't.

Can I?

Eventually, I make my way out of the shower, find my pajamas, and curl up on my bed. A knock sounds at my door, and Gwen slowly pushes it open. She looks at me and I think she might say something. I wait but sometimes there are no words.

Gwen sits down on the bed next to me. The look she gives me matches the way I feel inside. As much as she had questioned me and Noah the night before and wanted me to be sure, I know she wants me to be happy first. We sit there in silence the rest of the night, not saying a word and yet saying so much at the same time. She watches as I cry and then regain strength to only break down again. She never judges, just sits with me and silently hopes right alongside me that everything will be ok.

Sunday, I stay in bed. I can't face the world and don't want to try. I get up only use the restroom and crawl right back to bed afterward. I still haven't heard from Noah, and the longer I go without word from him, the more I honestly don't care.

CHAPTER 28

Around noon the text messages start rolling in, first from Rex then from Michael. There is even one in there from Trevor, apologizing and wanting to talk. I have nothing to say to him and swear I most likely never will again.

Finally, there's one from Noah. At first, they're sweet, then pleading asking me to talk to him. When he gets the clue that I'm not responding, he asks me what's wrong. Then they turn heartbreaking and defensive saying how he doesn't understand me.

I'm not even sure I understand myself.

Turning my phone off, I find more peace in not knowing they're coming in than having to read any more messages he may have sent.

When Monday comes, I still haven't turned on my phone or responded to any of them. I find relief being able to lose myself in work. I'm on deadline with seven stories I have to wrap up before we go to print tomorrow, and throwing myself into work proves to be my only solace and exactly what I need.

I feel somewhat refreshed, having stayed in bed all weekend, not having talked to anyone or even checked my email or social media. I feel ready to face the week with a new outlook. I only hope it will be better to me than the events of last weekend, and maybe soon I'll start to wrap my brain around what happened and what I just might want to do about it.

I know I have to talk to Noah, so I make a plan to go over to his place after deadline. With work behind me, maybe I can think clearer and we can make some sense of everything that happened over the last few days.

Finally turning on my phone around lunchtime, I start off by checking voicemails and leaving the numerous text messages flooding in until later. There are a few voicemails from people

I had contacted late last week about stories I needed to write. Then are a few from Noah that I skip past, not ready to hear them yet and needing to stay in work mode, but the one that stands out to me the most is the one I never expected.

At first, I don't believe it, trying to let it sink in and wrap my brain around it. I press repeat. Excited and extremely nervous, I wait to hear the voicemail again:

"This message is for Evelyn Monroe. This is Carol with human resources here at the L.A. Times. We received your application, resume, and writing samples and would like to schedule an interview for the open reporter position. Please give us a call at your earliest convenience, if you are still interested in the position. We look forward to hearing from you."

This is it! My dream! Someone pinch me because this can't actually be happening.

I sit there and replay the message again, scribbling down the phone number she left at the end of the message. My eyes are as big as saucers, and my heart beats out of my chest. My smile is wider than it has ever been before.

If I land this job, I can move home. If I get this position, I can make the dream I've carried with me my whole life a reality. In one instant I have just been handed the possibility to not only launch an amazing career working for one of the top newspapers in the country, but I'm able to move back to where I always felt like I belonged.

I stand, a little shaky, and head outside to my car before making the call. I want privacy that the office does not provide. I climb into the driver's seat, shaking and extremely giddy. I wait for the person to pick up the phone as my future hangs in the air with each ring.

CHAPTER 28

"LA Times, this is Carol."

"Hi, Carol. My name is Evelyn Monroe, and I received a call to set up an in-person interview," I respond, trying not to sound as eager as I feel inside.

"Evelyn Monroe, good to finally talk to you. The office is all abuzz since they opened your portfolio. The editors are very excited to speak with you, young lady."

Learning my writing has made such an impression, I smile wider. I can't believe that they like me as much as they are saying they do. I'm so thankful for the opportunity, I don't even know what to say in response.

"Well, I hope I can live up to your expectations," I manage.

"What does your schedule look like? When will you be available for a meeting?" Carol asks.

"Well, I can be available anytime you need me," I say, trying not to sound too desperate and forward. "I actually have an appointment in Orange County this weekend for a freelance article I am writing."

"How about Thursday? We've had a cancellation, and I know I can squeeze you in."

"Thursday?" I echo, trying to pull myself together even though my excitement is almost uncontainable. "Thursday's perfect! I'll be there!"

"Great! We have your email here and will send you the specifics. We look forward to sitting down with you, Mrs. Monroe," Carol says, concluding our call.

"I look forward to it too," I say.

I hang up, feeling like I'm on cloud nine. I never thought something like this would await me this Monday morning. After a weekend like I had, this is just what I needed to start feeling alive again. For the first time in days, I feel the joy come back into my body and love every ounce of it.

I have so much to plan before leaving. It will be a few long days in the office to be able to take off the rest of the week, but it's worth it. I can drive down Wednesday night and stay with family

My mind races with all the possibilities this job could offer. I'm finally within reach of being able to obtain all I've ever wanted. All I've ever hoped and dreamed of. I can't wait to tell someone.

Noah! I need to tell Noah!

He might not understand at first, but maybe he will after we talk. He'll be happy for me, won't he? Because he loves me, doesn't he? I would be happy for him if the tables were reversed.

There is no time like the present. I put the car in drive and want nothing more than to speed like hell through town, down to Auburn. It's Monday and I know he'll be at the club. I drive as fast as my car and traffic will allow, anxious to share my good news with the one person I love most in the world and hopefully make right whatever exploded between us over the weekend.

Chapter 29

Noah

After Evelyn hadn't responded to any of my attempts, my decision is simple. I fought all I could and can't fight anymore. I poured my heart out for reason's even I don't understand. She has dissed me repeatedly, and yet like a sick glutton for punishment, I still come back for more.

When Monday rolls around, I drive to work, feeling worse than I could have imagined. Having drunk myself to hell all weekend, I'm forced to face that our love is gone. No one has ever treated me with such disrespect, except for one person—and I made sure to erase her from my life. Throwing myself into work, a sick feeling comes over me when I realize I'm going to have to do the same with the only woman I have never wanted to live without.

I don't know if I'm coming or going or what to make of my life. This is absolute bullshit. I know one thing: deciding to stay and move closer to be with Evelyn is turning out to be the biggest joke of my life.

I busy myself with work, and it isn't long before I thankfully lose my train of thought, preoccupied with all I have to get done that day. Rex and Michael are there, and after some very awkward moments, we seem good, silently forgetting what happened and moving on. So here I am, in the back of Gatsby's, trying to focus on work and decide how best to approach the rest of my life now. Without her.

"Excuse me, do you come here often?" comes a playful voice from behind me.

I don't have to turn and look to know who it is. My heart already breaks hearing her voice. I pause for a moment but then quickly continue the task I'm working on before she renders me speechless yet again with that damn pull she always seems to have on me.

She walks up to my side and leans against the table I have my plans spread across—plans I was trying so hard to fix and make sense of before she walked in, smelling of my past and tearing me apart. It's a past that's going to take all my strength to walk away from ... if I know what's good for me.

God, I'll miss her smell, the way it lingered around me, the way it turns me on and makes me want to do things to her I know I'll never want to do with any other woman. Fuck, this is going to be harder than I thought.

"What, you're not talking to me now?" she asks.

I sense the sadness in her voice and hate myself for not breaking like I want to and forgetting everything I've felt up to this moment. I want to grab her and kiss her, long and hard, until we both can't think or feel anything but the way things should be between us. Until carnal need takes over and we have to restrain ourselves from taking it further on the workbench in front of me. Just like we used to. In the past.

How did she already become my past when just last week she was the only future I would ever need?

But I don't. And something in the back of mind, something

that sounds a little like regret, plagues me. I push it away quickly and instead continue to focus on the task in front of me.

"I don't think we have very much to say to one another," I tell her, still not looking up.

"Come on, Noah, you know that is not true," Evelyn stiffens then softens her stance as she slides closer. It makes my breath catch, and I hope like hell she doesn't see.

"I want to talk to you about something ... something I hope you'll be happy about," she says, searching for any way she can to get me to open me up.

"Oh, so now you want to talk? Seems to me like Friday night all I could get out of you was a cold shoulder," I snap, moving to the other side of the table to try and put some distance between us.

"That's not fair and you know it," she snaps back.

I push back from the table and look her in the eyes. God, she's gorgeous, makeup fresh and perfect, her hair slipped back in a low ponytail. She's dressed in a black blouse and a pinstripe pencil skirt that hugs her waist and ass perfectly. High heels top it off, and I almost lose all control. Regaining my thoughts, I decide I'm not going to let her have the last word.

No matter how good she looks, how good she smells, or how much I know no other woman will ever compare to her—to this, I have to stand my ground. She has to hear me out. I might need to make her my past, but if there is even the smallest hope for a future, she needs to listen. She needs to understand.

"Really, Evelyn? I'm sorry. Yes, please tell me how I can help you? What is so urgent that now you find the need to want to speak to me even though my endless attempts for your attention over the last few days repeatedly were ignored," I yell, watching her flinch. I can't help it. She drives me mad. You don't treat people you love like this.

Evelyn backs up! I've hurt her, I know it. But she's hurt me too, and I need her to know that. No more fucking games. I want her to feel the pain and the sting that still lingers around my heart and every thought in my mind since she showed up drunk at my door last Friday night.

"I wasn't trying to ignore you! I was just trying to figure some things out," she explains, sounding a little shaky.

"Well ..." I snorted. "I'm glad you figured out whatever it was. Now excuse me, I'm trying to work."

I look back down at the plans and hope like mad she gets the hint and leaves me alone. I want to leave it the way it is. I can't say goodbye to her, not like this. Whatever she figured out, good! But I'm extracting myself from the situation like I should have months ago. I can't let myself get hurt any further than I already have. I guess there really is no future for us after all.

"I came to tell you that it looks like I might have a job offer," Evelyn says harshly. "In LA. They want to meet with me on Thursday!"

I look up at her shocked and extremely pissed. What did she just say? I can't believe what I'm hearing. She's leaving? How long has she known about this? Is this what her drunken night was about on Friday? Is this why she continued giving me the cold shoulder at the party and all the days that followed? Is this what her lame "What if I can't give you everything?" was all about?

"It's with the LA Times, baby," she continues, and I cringe when she calls me baby. The sting lingers far too long. I have to close my eyes, hoping the hurt will ease quickly. Still, she continues, "This is a really great opportunity for me. And I wanted to share it with the man I ..."

"With the man you what, Evelyn? With the man you love? Don't bullshit me! You're just as bad as the rest of the people in this damn state. Always thinking only of yourself!" I yell at her.

"I'd hoped you'd be happy for me." She starts to cry. Tears stream down her face as she stands there watching me. Neither one of us says anything more. The tears increase their speed, faster and faster, and she cries, "Why are you being like this?"

"Happy for you? Happy for you, Evelyn!" I shout louder. "You have to be fucking kidding me! I changed my whole life around just to be with you! Just to be able to hold you, to love you. To wake up next to you every damn fucking day! And for what? So you could leave me!" I step towards her with each word I scream. She backs up, fearing me and my wrath. I admit I'm losing it. For once she's going to listen to what I have to say.

Her tears are replaced with a fiery defense. "I didn't ask you to change your life for me!"

"Yeah, well I never guessed you'd want to leave. So the joke's on both of us ... baby!" I take my time with the last word. I want it to sting as bad as it did when she tried using it on me a few minutes earlier.

Evelyn's tears turn into full out sobs. Her body convulses in front of me, and it takes all my strength not to break and hold her in my arms. Hold her the way I want to.

She's leaving. She didn't choose me. She chose herself, something I never imagined she would do. Something I hadn't even considered when I made plans to stay with her. It hurts deeper inside than anything I have felt before.

In all we shared, as short as it was, I never imagined it ending this way. I thought we were special, what we had was special. Not everyone gets lucky enough to experience that kind of love. I could be strong and count myself lucky for being able to have had the opportunity. Although right now I just want to forget her. Forget everything about her and hope that one day I can learn to live without her.

She chose her.

"I hate you," she whispers as her tears fall more and more. She takes a few steps backward, still not taking her eyes off mine. I can feel the hatred build more and more between the two of us. "I hate you!!!" she screams.

"Yeah, well, I'm not too happy with you or your damn choices right now either," I spit back at her. "So looks like that makes the two of us, darlin'."

She glares at me, and I know if there was ever a moment where I might be able to reach out and grab her back to me, it would be right here, right now.

I have a choice: I could break and follow her wherever I can and wherever she'll go just to be near her.

But I can't.

I let the moment pass. I let it slip right through my fingers, feeling like I have fought all I can for her and for us.

I'm done.

I don't know how to fight anymore.

She runs faster than I have ever seen any girl run in my life, straight out of Gatsby's and out of my life. She bumps into Rex on her way out the door, and he tries to grab for her to find out what's going on. Evelyn is running too fast to be caught, and Rex turns his attention to me instead.

Walking up to me, he has the look only a protective brother

can give. It isn't often that I feel small in Rex's presence, being several inches taller than him, though the look he gives me makes me feel only a few inches tall. Right now, I swear if Rex wanted to, he would beat the shit out of me. A part of me doesn't blame him one bit.

I debate kicking my own ass for the mistake I know I just made. He slows a few feet away and looks at me like I'm the worst man to ever walk the face of the earth. Time stretches over a few awkward minutes before he speaks.

"Now what the hell was that about," Rex begins. "You going to explain to me why Ev just ran out of here crying worse than I have ever seen? You're lucky Michael didn't see that shit or your ass would be thrown the hell out of here."

"I don't know." I sigh, running my fingers through my hair in desperation and exhaling a deep breath.

"It's over, Rex." Those three words ring out through the space between us like the end of the world, registering with my brain and then my stomach, making me feel sick and weak.

"I'm not going to sit around and play any stupid games," I continue. "She knew how I felt about her, and she wants something else. If she wants to go, I can't stop her. I can't change her."

Rex pauses for a moment, examining the situation and taking in what I've just told him. His face hardens as he begins to yell, "You have to be the stupidest bastard on the face of the planet to let that walk out of your life!"

"I told you she doesn't want me anymore. I tried, man!" I start to walk away. I don't want to hear anymore. I want to be left alone, and for the first time in months, I'm ready to leave. I'm ready to go home. To get out of here and put as much distance between me and the West Coast as humanly possible.

"Please! You're so full of shit you can't see through it anymore!" Rex yells.

He's standing right in front of me now, challenging me. He wants to hurt me as much as I just hurt Evelyn. I can feel the tension. Rex wants to damage me like he thinks I just damaged her, one of his oldest and dearest friends. The sister he never had and will always protect.

"What am I supposed to do?" I ask. "Beg. Plead. Follow her everywhere like a little damn puppy! I'm not a pussy, Rex! I have standards! She wants to go, she can go! Like I said, I can't stop her!" I shout. I shove him and I'm surprised when he doesn't charge back.

A silence falls upon us as Rex stands in front of me, sizing up the situation. Time draws on slowly as I wonder what in the hell he's thinking. He stands there processing everything that I've just said. He dissects me and my words carefully before responding. Eyeing me up and down, his callous face softens, almost sad for me over what I know I've just lost.

"Don't look at me that way," I say. "Fuck your pity. This is all on her."

Taking another minute, he finally responds, "Evelyn is the type of girl you never stop fighting for and never stop trying to make happy! Most men go their whole lives just wishing they could have someone, anyone, anywhere close to the kind of woman she is. And if you think you're above that, you're not the kind of man I thought you were!"

I let out a sigh of defeat, wondering how I even got into this mess in the first place. Looking at my friend, I beg for his help, not knowing where to go from here. Fuck if he didn't just hit me with the damn truth. The truth I have been fighting for days.

"What am I supposed to do?" I ask.

"Well, for starters, you can let go of your fucking pride," Rex yells. I laugh. He's right. Evelyn deserves better than this, and damn it I have just gone and screwed it up royally.

"No," I say, shaking my head. "No, that's not it. She made her choice. She is going to LA." I look off in the distance, trying to wrap my thoughts around what just happened.

This amazing once-in-a-lifetime kind of woman is southern California bound and most likely never looking back after the way I just treated her. There is really only one thing to do and for the first time in days, I don't have to think twice about it.

I grab my phone from the table where the plans are scattered all over and feel my pockets for my keys.

"How long of a head start do you think she has on me," I ask Rex, breaking out in a run for the exit.

"The way she was running, and how she drives when she's mad, there is no telling. She could already be in Fresno by now," Rex hollers back at me. "Be careful, though, it looks like we are getting rain for the first time in years. Watch yourself."

I look outside and notice rain has begun to fall. The storm they said would finally roll hasn't failed. The roads will be extra slippery now with this being the first rain in months. Looking back at Rex, I nod.

"Yeah, I know, slippery roads!"

"NO!" Rex yells. "Because if you hurt her again, I'll kill you." I laugh, knowing he will.

Reaching outside, I run across the parking lot. When I get to my truck, I'm dripping wet. Damn, it really is coming down, reminding me of the strong thunder systems that come through the south.

I back out of the parking spot but get stuck waiting for another car to back out behind me. Damn it. I felt anxiety rising up like vomit inside of me.

I have to get to her.

I have to fight like mad to hold her until she won't leave me. She couldn't! Not now.

I stop in a line of cars exiting the parking lot. What the hell! There's never this amount of people around Gatsby's in the afternoon. The rain makes people drive stupid, especially in a state that doesn't normally see it, almost making them forget how to function behind the wheel.

Finally making it out of the parking lot, I try my best to speed around some of the cars that are driving slower than molasses. Where would she run off to? I could try her office? Maybe her apartment?

I should have grabbed her, made her listen. I should have tried harder and not let my stupid insecurities get to me. If she wanted to move, then I would move too—If she would have me.

She might have dreams she needs to fulfill from before we met, but she is my dream, and I'm not going to let that go.

The cars in the road suddenly come to a complete stop. What the hell! I punch the steering wheel. I do not need this right now. I look around the cars for a way that I might be able to forge ahead, but there's nothing.

A few minutes pass and an ambulance drives up the side of the traffic. Well, that can't be good. Maybe they'll get it cleared fast, and I can be on my way.

I try calling her but there's no answer. It goes straight to voicemail. I try again, but I get the same thing. It doesn't matter, though. I'll find her and make her listen.

CHAPTER 29

I won't let her get away.

I can't.

Almost twenty agonizing minutes later, traffic slowly starts to move. The rain still pounds down outside and it makes it hard to make out any sort of the wreck as I pass. The ambulance is gone, not having far to go as the only hospital in town is just a little ways back down the road by Gatsby's. With so many people standing around, police and construction work on the road, I can't make out the car in the wreck. Whatever happened doesn't look good.

When I finally pass, I speed up. The rain has slowed some, and I need to get to her as fast as I can.

I stop by her office first. It's about fifteen minutes down the road. They haven't seen her since lunch. Great! I thank them and get back to my truck. I pull my phone out of my pocket, unsure if I should try her again or maybe Michael or Gwen.

Damn it, darlin', where are you?

I jump in the cab of the truck and make it a few minutes down the road towards her apartment when the phone I'm still holding, trying to figure out who to contact next, starts ringing in my hand.

I glanced at it. Gwen. Well, damn if this isn't perfect timing. She has to know where she is, and even if I have to endure her screaming at me for letting her run off in tears, which she undoubtedly knows by now, then so be it. I just have to know where she is.

"Gwen!" I answer quickly. "I know what you're going to say, and I don't blame you but ..."

Her sobs cut me off. I wait for her to control herself. Did she call me by accident? Why is she crying?

"Noah?" she begins in a shaky voice.

"Yeah?" I question, my voice just as shaky. She doesn't answer me. "Gwen, what's going on? You're scaring me? Is everything ok?"

"Noah ... it's Evelyn," she says in a whisper.

My breath stills. My heart skips a beat, slamming straight into the bottom of my stomach. My hands turn clammy as I clench the steering wheel harder. A haunting silence flows through my brain as I put it all together and my world shifts, stops, halts, and is forever changed.

What in the hell did I just do?

Devotion

Chapter 1
Evelyn

The smell of gardenia's fill the room as the Santa Ana winds pick up and blow through the open window above the sink in the kitchen. Calming me for a brief second, the smell is followed by the sound of wind chimes beautifully making a musical song only they know and can carry on the large breeze blowing through Huntington Beach today.

When the sounds and the smells mix together I can almost let go, almost forget everything that has happened in the last few days and finally find a sense of stability that has seemed lost for so long.

The Santa Ana's are blowing in full force, and with them, the smell of the ocean can slightly be made out as the warm and dry gusts blow around outside drifting in through the open window above the kitchen sink. The smell of sand and the salty beach just a few short miles away helps me grab ahold of my life's anchor, and makes me feel rooted. Maybe now I can finally figure out what I want in life. What I need, because Lord knows

I've made a royal mess of things.

The coffee finishes brewing in the pot under the window sill, and when all three smells collide - the coffee, gardenias and the ocean mixing with the beautiful melody of the wind chimes - there is only one place I can be. The only place that has ever felt like home and made me feel whole.

But now, a piece is missing.

My grandmother comes into the kitchen through the sliding door which leads to the backyard. Shooing one of her cats inside, she proceeds to fill its dish nearby from the pantry. Her short hair is windblown from the gusts of wind and she slowly kneels low to fill the dish for the furry friend which is more like family. She doesn't say a word, but stands up tall and then proceeds to take two coffee cups from a close cabinet filling them to their brim.

Walking over to me, she sits my cup down on the small kitchenette table and tugs on a few strands of my hair a couple of times. A habit she has whenever I am sulking and quiet too long, and a trait I have missed since she has been gone.

My grandmother sits across the table from me and doesn't speak at first. She looks at me, reading me. Examining me. Knowing everything that needs to be said and just the way it needs to be spoken. Shaking her head a few times, she looks away out across the backyard at the winds blowing the trees furiously and takes a sip of her coffee.

"You don't look too happy for someone who just landed themselves a job at the L.A. Times, Evelyn." She says to me, obviously annoyed at my silence.

My grandmother's perfectly manicured nails begin to rapidly tap against her cup. I always loved her nails. They were the perfect shade of coral with a gold palm tree exquisitely displayed on her ring finger's nail bed. Something I have always tried to emulate since her passing, but I am never able to find that perfect gold palm tree, no matter how hard I try. Still silent, I look out across the kitchen and through the window into the yard. Fighting the urge to cry, I fight with finding a way to put into words exactly what I am feeling. Why after being handed everything I ever wanted, it still isn't enough.

"I'm happy." I finally manage. "Honestly I am."

My grandmother turns and glares at me. Looking deep inside me, its obvious she knows me better than I could ever know myself. I have missed her so much in the last few years since she was no longer with us. I often find I struggle to try and understand myself as well as she obviously knew me.

"I swear, this was my dream." I start out saying, as I search my grandmother's eyes for a truth so evident that I still can not grasp it. "I worked hard for this. I finally landed myself a great position. I will be making enough money to afford to move back home, live here and be able to be around family. You know how bad I've always wanted to be back here with everyone. These are my roots. This is my family."

I'm searching, I know it. The look in her eyes tells me to dig deeper. But I can't seem to make sense of all the emotions piling on top of each other inside. I find myself searching for an answer that had felt secure my whole life, and now only feels like a stranger. But my grandmother isn't buying it. The winds pick up again and knock over something in the backyard. Slamming against each other, the wind chimes make more of a crashing sound than the beautiful melody heard just a few minutes earlier. The cat jumps at her dish as the gate nearby beats against its locks and then runs and hides in another room.

And then, it is peaceful. Clear. Calm and absolutely obvious.

"Evelyn," my grandmother sternly says. I glance up to meet her eyes. Stability, strength and years of lessons hang in them as I sit ready to hear the advice she is about to give. Connecting my thoughts with the truth, as heart-wrenching as it might be, is what I know I need to move forward.

"Dreams change," she says. "People change, and there is nothing wrong with that. Life is full of ups and downs. Lessons and victories both big and small. We can't always predict what is going to happen to us, and that is ok."

A small tear rolls down my face as I come to terms with the fact that I could never have prepared for this. For him. For us.

A curveball of massive proportions that forever changed my world. Although I know in my heart everything that has changed is for the better, letting go is always the scariest part. Especially when you have always believed your happiness could only come from one dream. One hope that you hold every other dream's credibility up against.

"Life is a road," she continues. "And sometimes it changes directions. Life can often hand you detours, and sometimes the road less traveled is full of greater stops along the way and breathtaking scenery you would never be able to see otherwise. Do you get what I am trying to say?"

I nod. My head hangs low as tears began to fall out of my eyes and splash against the top of the kitchen table. With every tear that falls, I feel myself silently starting to let go. I know I have to and even though the choice comes instinctively, even though a weight begins to lift - it still hurts inside.

"Life is a road to be filled with laughter and happiness." My grandmother says softly. "A road to be shared and enjoyed to the fullest, no matter what you have to give up along the way. A road never to be traveled alone, and never to be taken for granted. The ones you love may not always be there, and you have to take your chances."

My eyes shoot up. His words, *I will take my chances* rings through my brain. As I grasp to get back to that moment, to that time - I hear it.

Beep. Beep. Beep.

I can't shake it, and as I try to understand what it is, I feel this moment begin to slip away. My grandmother slowly seems more distant. Faded, and not entirely clear. An understanding look graces her face, and then it's back.

Beep. Beep. Beep.

"Honey," she whispers gently with a smile. "Your road doesn't lead here anymore."

The realization hits as the final thread of a dream I forever had drifts away. I grab out to try and grasp her hand. To try and hold onto this moment, and the truth she just gave me.

Beep. Beep. Beep.

She smiles slowly as she begins to disappear. I don't want her to go. I need her. Need her strength. Although, I somehow know the weight that has suddenly started to lift off my heart is enough. She gave me what I need to find new strength, and I will always remember her words and finally be able to accept my road which is forever changed.

The smell of gardenias, coffee and ocean fade. In its place, sterile, cold and unfamiliar fill my senses.

Beep. Beep. Beep.

There is that noise again. The sound of machines and hushed tones of people talking fill my ears. Heavy. My eyes are so heavy.

Beep. Beep. Beep.

"I think she's coming around now." I hear a man say. It's a voice I don't recognize as I try and will my eyes to open.

Who? Who is coming around? My body stiff and motionless feels heavier than I have ever felt before. Pain. Excruciating pain fills my body as my brain struggles to understand what has happened and what the man is talking about. My eyes slowly start to open as a bright light fills my vision only making me close them quickly once again.

Pain. So much pain.

My right side stings with a fire I have never felt before. My mouth is dry, and the ringing in my ears fills my head worse than any migraine I knew was humanly possible. As I struggle to try and make sense of it all, flashes come back to me. I close my eyes tighter as memories flood my senses.

Beep. Beep. Beep.

"David!" I hear my mother's trembling voice. "David! Hurry, come quick! She's opening her eyes. Evelyn. Evelyn, darling, please wake up. Honey, open your eyes for me."

Why are my parent's here? I try to rotate to the side and stop immediately as a stabbing feeling fills my body. I can't scream. I can't make a noise. My breathing, which always seemed effortless, is now slow and agonizing as I struggle to fill my lungs with air.

"Slowly now." Commands the man's voice at my side once again. "Take it slow, Ms. Monroe."

I open my eyes slightly and look at him. In his white coat,

he stands at my right holding a clipboard as he examines the length of my entire body before going back to writing on his pad of paper. Slightly glancing to the left, I notice my mother sitting at my side as she grabs my hand and squeezes lightly. My father looms over her, a look of concern filling his eyes that I have never seen before.

"You gave us quite a scare." The man at my right says. I watch as my mother's eyes fill with tears. My father puts his hand on her shoulder for comfort as she tries to keep strong. I turn back to look at the man I don't know next to me. Finally meeting my eyes he smiles. Reaching up he checks the bag attached to the IV I only then notice is strung to my right hand.

"I will give you three a moment while I go order you some more fluids," he says. "It could've been way worse young lady. You must have a major guardian angel up above looking out for you."

I close my eyes as my grandmother's words fill my head. Your road doesn't lead here anymore. I feel a lonely tear roll down my cheek before I hear the man speak again.

"I will just be a minute," he says. "You're one lucky girl, Evelyn. Do me a favor and slow down and enjoy the ride next time, ok? There are only a few things in life worth risking it all for."

Keep in touch

Want to stay in the know for future releases, promotions, sales, book signings and more? Make sure you follow along by clicking on one of the links below:

FB Page: https://www.facebook.com/evelyn.montgomery.372019

FB Group: https://www.facebook.com/groups/451248859032018/

Twitter: https://twitter.com/Author_EvelynM

IG: https://www.instagram.com/evelyn__montgomery/

Goodreads: https://www.goodreads.com/auth…/…/18183163.Evelyn_Montgomery

BookBub: https://www.bookbub.com/authors/evelyn-montgomery

Newsletter: https://mailchimp/f85a44acc860/evelynmontgomery

Want More?

If you want more from The Kismet Series, look no further!

Devotion - The Kismet Series Book 2: Evelyn & Noah's Conclusion

WANT MORE?

THE KISMET SERIES | BOOK 2

DEVOTION
EVELYN MONTGOMERY

Buy Here!

No word, no call, no backwards glance. I am left with just the memories of what Noah gave me. After recovering from my accident, I'd give anything to change the way we ended, including giving up my dream at the L.A. Times.

After a letter arrives shattering what little hope there is left, I know what I have to do, and don't waste time doing it. Jumping a plane to the South, I am determined to make him listen. But when a ghost from his past makes an unexpected appearance, will what we have be enough to bring us back together? Or will I loose him forever to a secret I never knew he held?

After being put in my place with an overheard confession, I figure to hell with love and the West Coast. Hitting the road, I only have one place to go. Home to Kentucky. But hell if I knew what awaited me when I stepped foot back on Southern soil.

Trying to forget the girl I left behind, I am forced to face another ghost from my past. One I thought I escaped long ago. She brings with her a secret, a secret that steals any chance of a future with Evelyn away just when we're finally starting to put our pieces back together. But will what we have be enough to weather this storm? Or will it finally break us?

Here is what people are saying about Devotion:

"I finished this one in less than a day! I couldn't put it down. I just love Noah and Evelyn! Their story was so heartbreakingly good. They have a love that could withstand all the ups and downs that get thrown at them.
I recommend everyone needs to go out and read both of these

books! Yes there were times I was yelling at my kindle but you know that means, it was written very good!"

Reckless - The Kismet Series Book 3: Rex & Gwen's story

INDECISION

THE KISMET SERIES | BOOK 3

RECKLESS

EVELYN MONTGOMERY

Buy Here!

WANT MORE?

He's rough, arrogant, sexy and irresistible as hell. The stereotypical ladies man that I swore I'd never fall for. He stole my heart once before when we were kids, and I promised myself I would never give it to him again.
One night, a few drinks and memories neither one of us could escape lands me right back to where it all started, or should I say ended. But when push comes to shove, will he be ready to hear the truth about our past and face the secret I've been holding in for over 10 years? Or will he run like I always knew he would? The one reason why I never let myself get too close to him again. As they say, tigers can't change their stripes, and I won't let him make a fool out of me trying.

She's stubborn, hot-headed and has a temper worse than any woman I have ever met before - but damn it if that doesn't just make me want her more. Like an idiot I let her walk away from me before, but hell if I will let myself make that mistake again. She's mine, and I won't stop until she knows it.
But moving forward means facing the demons in my past. The secrets I've never told her about that one night 10 years ago I planned to promise her forever and never showed up. A secret that has eaten me alive and kept me away from her all these years when all I have ever wanted was to hold her again. This time though, I won't let go, and she has another thing coming if she thinks she is getting away from me that easy. As reckless as our love has been, I will never stop fighting for her. After all... her, me - that is all I know that is right in this world.

Here is what people are saying about Reckless:

"Oh man have I been waiting for this book since ending Noah

and Evelyn's story!

I have been dying to find out all the secrets between Rex and Gwen, and Evelyn Montgomery did NOT disappoint!

I loved how fierce and sassy Gwen has always been, but to see how much the past and her relationship with Rex can make her so vulnerable about broke my little heart. The past with her sister and how she just wanted to her the man she loved as a teen say he loved her back.

Rex, that cocky man! I knew deep down there was a soft side to him. I am so happy we got to read about it. He equally broke my heart multiple times. Dealing with his past and the family he grew up with. All he wanted was love but didn't know what to do with it when he finally had it.

The angsty relationship they have is perfect and I loved every minute of this book!"

Like what you read?

Don't leave without writing a review. In today's world, books only do as good as the reviews they receive. Just a few sentences can help make all the difference to these characters and their world. Leave a review today and let others know what you think.

Review Here!